The Secret

The Secret

Eva Hoffman

W F HOWES LTD

This large print edition published in 2002 by
W F Howes Ltd
Units 6/7, Victoria Mills, Fowke Street
Rothley, Leicester LE7 7PJ

1 3 5 7 9 10 8 6 4 2

First published in 2001 by Secker & Warburg
a division of Random House

ISBN 1 84197 518 4

Typeset by Palimpsest Book Production Limited,
Polmont, Stirlingshire
Printed and bound in Great Britain
by Antony Rowe Ltd, Chippenham, Wilts.

To Cleo and Anna, two unique young women

Acknowledgements

My warmest thanks go to Frederika Randall, Marta Petrusewicz, Alina Wydra and Johanna Roeber, for their discerning readings and much needed encouragement; to Martin Rosendall, for casting a scientific eye over the manuscript and for his invaluable comments; to Gill Coleridge, agent *non pareil*, for her support and good judgment at every juncture; and to Geoff Mulligan, for his faith in this book and his always wise editorial guidance.

Of course, I've always had a secret. Have I always known it? I suppose I have in a way – in the way that children know such things. That is to say, I knew and didn't know. But could I have been called a child, was I a real, an authentic child?

I had no doubt I was, of course. Which perhaps proves the point. You are what you think you are, aren't you? Especially in the most essential matters, who on earth is to judge the nature of your nature, of your character, of your innermost self, expect you, the subject, yourself? And yet. And yet.

Indeed, I felt I had an almost ordinary childhood. Blessedly ordinary, it might have been, given that I was growing up at a time when ordinariness was becoming the most exceptional condition, achieved only by the unusually lucky, or the unusually sane few.

Does that mean she was unusually sane, my mother? The possibility is unpalatable, but entirely plausible. She certainly gave the impression of being perfectly normal – and, after all, how do we judge others except through impressions, through appearances, largely or minutely observed? Even if we don't judge ourselves in such ways at all. But then my mother had an exceptional talent for simulation.

We lived in a small college town not far from Chicago, in a rambling wooden house with two porches, a leafy yard and pleasant, eclectic clutter inside, spanning in styles from Victoriana to virtual *trompe l'oeil*. From the outside it was the kind of place you hardly see in the movies any more, on the grounds that it's unrealistic. Which I suppose it is. Midwestern towns like the one we lived in have been on their way to extinction for a long time now.

Still, my mother wasn't exactly a provincial pastoralist. She had lived in New York before I was born, but after ten years of working hard and riding high she became sick and tired of its aggressions, greed, false sophistication and filth. She found the ever muggier, pollution-spewed summers wearying. She'd been a highly paid investment consultant, but by the time she left Manhattan she was more than ready to give it all up. At least, that is how she told it to me, much later, when I was old enough to understand such things. As long as she was striving and testing herself, she thrived on the no-holds-barred competitiveness of New York's financial world, on its adrenalin-driven energies and high stakes. But once she reached a certain point on the career ladder – it was not the glass ceiling, she had broken through that – her work went utterly flat on her. The meaning had gone out of it as if by evil magic, turning to dross and dust. That's what she said, I remember. She needed something else – a new purpose, a more primal, deeper connection to life. And my mother wasn't someone who was easily prevented from getting what she wanted. Or at least from going after it. Like so many of her generation, she was wilful and proud of being so. She thought the world belonged to her and that she could only improve it. She had the right ideas, the right values and the right strategies. It followed that she should have what she wanted.

She had me. I became her new project, her great enterprise. She came to the Midwest, she told me, partly because she thought it would be a good place for a child to grow up. There were still the elements here, there was still nature. She thought that was terribly important, no matter how uncomfortable or excessive the elements got sometimes, what with the deadly cold and the deadly hot temperatures, which drove people into subterranean corridors and into their own, carefully controlled environments. She'd been involved in some kind of political movement in her twenties, to do with saving the earth and going back to nature, and she spoke about it with a nostalgia and a vehemence which baffled me. I didn't understand how anyone could be so passionate about politics. But anyway, in moving to the Midwest, she was among other things following her principles.

And so our little town became her refuge, our hideaway. Not that she stopped working altogether. She was very good at what she did and once in a while her former clients still sought her expensive advice. I knew when this was happening, even when I was little, because my mother would suddenly become distracted and absorbed by something other than me, pulling interminable sheets of paper out of the printer, and studying insect-like columns of figures even as they emerged from its aperture and fell into the tray. Then she'd sit down at the computer and type out a response to what she'd read without pause or hesitation. There was always a small hurt on such occasions at being ignored by her for a few minutes; but there was also fascination in watching her, for even as a small child I was impressed by the assurance of her gestures, the glint of concentrated thought in her eye.

But such derailments of attention were rare. Mostly she devoted herself to me. In New York she had hustled in an antheap of collective activity, the press of a thousand bodies. I was to be an individual, a creative work. Paradoxically. Ironically. Anyway, we kept very much to ourselves when I was little. Aside from the minimal social contacts required by a small town – a hello to the recharge-station attendant, a what-do-you-recommend to the visual entertainment vendor – we hardly talked to anyone for days. It was easy to be a hermit in a Midwestern college town and I don't think I really

4

knew another child until I was five or so. Later she started going to occasional parties, not to bring attention to herself, but to deflect it. Occasionally, I was allowed to visit other children, or play with them in the park; but for some reason none of my fledgling friendships lasted more than a few weeks. Something would always happen and I would be told not to play with Lucy or Ronnie any more. Sometimes I felt a pang of disappointment, but it soon went away. My mother was sufficient for me; when I was with her I felt no other needs.

Neither did she, apparently. I was a late child, by her generation's standards. She had waited until her forties to have me because she had wanted some unencumbered adulthood. As always, she got what she wanted. She seemed to have had a halcyon youth – at least in her recounting of things. College, success, boyfriends, working on the cutting edge of the global economy. When she was in her mid-thirties she met my father. Or so she told me when I asked what happened to my daddy. But she wouldn't tell me much else. She said such things happen all the time, you meet someone and then they disappear. Especially daddies. She promised to tell me more when I grew up, when I was ready. I think I felt dissatisfied by this even when I was a child, but I nodded my head and didn't enquire further. Anyway, there was plenty of evidence that she was right. So many other kids I knew had no daddies, or had daddies who were not real daddies, although the children tried to treat them as if they were, and to believe they were as good as the real ones would ever have been. Good-enough daddies. Almost real daddies. The nuclear family – the nuke – was dead as the dodo by the time I came along. It had exploded, or imploded, or done both at the same time. I had seen films about mom-dad-kids kinds of units on some of the classic two-dimensional videos, and I knew that such families were either hilariously happy in their togetherness, or lived in sheer torment and hell. I also knew one or two children whose biological parents were actually married, but it's not as if anyone expected this condition to be permanent. So I didn't think there was anything abnormal about the absence of a daddy. Once, when somebody's real uncle or unreal daddy lifted me up and put me on his shoulders, I felt a shadowy longing. So this was what male shoulders were like, straight and steady, this was the feel of masculine energy. Daddy energy . . . But mostly, I didn't think about my father, didn't speculate or fantasize. Mostly, the daddy-space was a blank. My mother was enough for me; she supplied all my needs. She focused on me and coddled me and loved me half to death.

'Do you realize how significant that phrase is?' my Adviser has asked me.

Oh yes. I do.

But when I was little, I only knew that she was my mummy, mine, for me. She was quickness, animation, a flash of a beautiful smile, neat deft movements as she combed my hair, or flicked through the pages of some financial report. She was the source of play and pleasure and every gratification. She gave me just about everything I wanted and probably much more than I needed. I had robodolls, cuddly and talkative, of all races and colours, all the virtual videos I could watch and ingenious mind-advancing games in every material and medium. Perhaps too many. My mother thought she had obligations to my mental potential, and she had no doubt as to what that potential might be.

But Mummy was also an enfolding, warm, comfy place I could run to whenever I inflicted some small injury on myself, or felt in the slightest sad or upset. Then she would lift me up and fold me to her till the heat and softness of her body enveloped me and absorbed whatever small unhappiness was inside me into herself, until I felt dozy and fluid, like those amoebae under a microscope that maintain their amorphous shape for a moment and then merge with the organic surround. Or else she would gaze at me intently to see what was the matter, her eyes widening and then narrowing to a pinpoint as they travelled into me and then funnelled me up, into herself. I looked very much like her, even as a child. I was blonde and blue-eyed, with the same broadly spaced eyebrows and high slant of chin; and I felt, as I raised my face to hers, that I was looking at the very image of beauty, but also at an enlarging looking-glass, into which I entered through her eyes and in which I dissolved, becoming indistinguishable from her, becoming her. My unformed, liquid sounds blended with her responding voice, which cooed and put into words everything I couldn't say. Then I had a languid sense of fullness, of safety. This was love, sweet love. There were times, it is true, when her gaze probed too intently, as if I held some secret she was trying to unriddle, as if I were the mirror which could tell her things. Then her gaze lengthened even more and became abstracted, as if I were inanimate, or a precious object she needed to study. When that happened, I'd turn my head away or try to wriggle out of her arms. Then she'd raise my chin with her finger and say, 'Look at me . . . look at me,' and I'd face her directly as if under a spell, and re-enter her eyes, and we'd be together again.

So, although I find it hard to convince people of this, I had a happy childhood in that big rambling house. Or at least a perfect simulacrum of one. But was it? Was it an imitation or the real thing? After all, I had no reason to suspect anything. But yet: although I didn't suspect, somewhere – I would be tempted to say in my soul, if that word weren't such a travesty in my case – I knew. I knew there was something wrong and strange without ever being able to put a name to it, to form anything as coherent as a suspicion. Did I know intrinsically, from the beginning, through a sort of infant precognition, or did I deduce something subliminally, from minute and scattered clues? The clues were there, in disconnected, small incidents, sudden insertions of oddity into the smooth fabric of my days, like tiny incisions which pierce the skin and are then covered over.

There was the time when my mother picked up the telephone and said, in response to the voice on the other end, 'Mom?' and then looked at me and put her hand up to her mouth. She shooed me away, but I kept standing there, listening. I was about three years old, and I didn't understand the import of what I had heard; but the word 'Mom' was extremely interesting. It was in fact arresting; it fixed me in place. 'No, you can't see her,' my mother was saying. 'It's a little late, after the things you said to me. Anyway, I don't see why you should want to. You didn't want her to come into the world in the first place.'

'Who was that? In there?' I asked, when my mother came off the phone. She was very agitated.

'Never mind, poppet,' she said, 'it doesn't matter.' She lifted me and kissed me and I sort of forgot what I'd heard or stored it in some out-of-the-way place, out of consciousness, I suppose.

There was another time when I came upon her unexpectedly in the study and saw that she was looking at a large, leather-bound photo album. When she noticed me, she snapped it shut. 'Show me!' I said, with a predictable reflex of curiosity about what is forbidden. 'No,' she said severely. 'This is not for you to see.'

'Are these photographs of you when you were a little girl?' I asked hopefully. I had seen a photo album once, at a birthday party for a neighbourhood girl. After we'd had our cake, she brought it out proudly, and we all leafed through its pages with great excitement, pointing to the photos of her parents, her relatives, herself. Of course, the parents were divorced, but that made it even more interesting. There was the girl's father, made fascinating by absence . . . And when we came upon a photo of her mother when she herself was a child, we paused in wonder. Was it possible that her mother had once been little? But my mother had never shown me any pictures of herself, though I sometimes asked her whether she had any and even nagged her about it. I wanted to know what she'd been like when she was young, when she was, unbelievably enough, a child. But then my curiosity evaporated in the fullness of her presence, which replaced the need for any images.

'This has nothing to do with you,' she said in answer to my question. 'You shouldn't pry so much, it isn't nice.' She put the album away and locked the drawer with a decisive turn. My mother was so rarely annoyed with me that I felt the click of that key as a slap, a punishment. It made me panicky to feel her pulling away from me, even by a millimetre. But what had I done?

'You were curious, that was what made her uncomfortable,' my Adviser interpreted. 'Gifted children often are. And after all, you were exceptionally clever and sensitive. And alert. Your mother might even have been a little envious of you. It happens, you know.'

But how could my mother be envious of me, given what she knew – given the nature of our bond? On the other hand . . . I remember her reading *Snow White* to me when I was little. 'Mirror, mirror on the wall, who is the fairest of them all?' she intoned, and glowered at me whimsically, pretending to be a bad stepmother. 'Well?' she asked. 'Who do you think is the fairest? You or me?'

'You!' I said delightedly, pointing a finger at her. She smiled and kissed the finger; but suddenly her eyes became both focused and remote. It was that look I remembered even from my infancy, as if she were interrogating my features to discover something, trying to look through me and past me, as if my face were the face of fate.

'You'll be so beautiful when you grow up,' she said finally and ran her fingers through my hair.

'Why?' I asked. 'How do you know?'

'Well, you have a beautiful mother, don't you?' she said, trying to sound light. But her eyes weren't playful at all. 'And you still have everything before you,' she added. 'You'll always be so much younger than me.'

As she scrutinized me, her expression became even more detached, more coldly contemplative, until something else entered her eyes, something that scared me: stoniness is the best word I can come up with for it, a kind of matte lifelessness, as if in that moment I ceased to be her daughter, the child she knew so intimately. As if I, or she, were far, far away. The Strange Look. I recognized it, but could do nothing about it. I tried to turn away from her gaze, but found myself unable to do so, as if I were turning into fixity, into stone myself.

Then, when I was about six, my mother's sister came to visit. I'd been prepared for it and I was very excited. We had never had house-guests before, and I hadn't even known we had any relatives. So I felt delight as soon as my aunt – the intrigue of that word! – came though the door. She was shorter than my mother and less beautiful. Her hair was darker. And yet, she was unmistakably my mother's sister, and I ran up to her before she could take off her long fur-lined coat. I jumped into her arms and she lifted me up with a 'Whoa, there!' She was smiling delightedly too. But when she perused my face, her expression changed to something else: surprise, unease, and something more indefinable – something like fear. 'She looks just like you did, doesn't she,' she said over my shoulder to my mother.

'Do I look like my mother?' I asked in some perplexity. I wanted to know whether that was good or bad.

'Yes, you do,' my aunt said in a subdued voice. 'You do.' She set me down carefully, as if I might be breakable, and I saw her facing my mother, with that peculiar expression on her face. My mother looked back unblinkingly and said, in an oddly harsh voice, 'Are you envious? Is that it? Is that your problem?' Then her mouth sort of contorted and she said, 'I'm sorry, I really am.'

I'd never seen her like that, had never heard her apologize. I was terribly confused.

The visit wasn't what I had hoped for. My aunt was called Janey, a name that suggested to me a world of friendliness. I had hoped for a sort of older friend, someone to whom I could confide my childish thoughts even more deliciously than to my mother – since my mother already knew everything. And Janey tried. She tried to be very nice to me, but it was clear she thought there was something – well, not quite right about me. She bought me gifts and played games with me; but her demeanour when she was with me was peculiar, veering between compassion and repulsion. The way you might act with someone who's not quite right in the head, perhaps, or who's severely damaged. Sometimes, when I made an overfriendly gesture, like climbing into her lap or kissing her, a look of panic would come into her face. Then instantly she would look stricken and I could see the effort of restraint, as she tried to smile and kiss me back and be affectionate towards me. I kept approaching her eagerly, skipping up to her, climbing into her lap, hoping each time that things would be different. But they weren't; and after a while, I stopped hoping and became mopey and muted.

Sometime during the visit I overheard my aunt and my mother quarrelling in the study. Their voices rose and fell. 'How could you?' Janey was emitting angrily. 'How could you do something so . . . monstrous?' I remember the word 'monstrous' in particular because I was interested in monsters just then, and wondered what kind of monstrousness my aunt meant, and how my mother could have possibly done anything a monster might.

'Who are you to tell me what I can and cannot do?' my mother responded in a steely voice. 'Who are you even to ask such questions?'

'I happen to be your sister,' Janey shot back, 'but not even God on high could ever tell you anything. That's your problem. You think you're above all judgement. You think the rules don't apply to you. Fine, do what you want. I couldn't care less what you do with your own life. But what about her? Did you ever think of that? What it would be like for her?' Now I was very frightened. I knew she was referring to me.

'Don't you worry about her – or me,' my mother said. 'We'll be fine. We are fine.'

There was a pause. 'It was wrong,' my aunt said. 'It was just plain wrong, to do it like this.'

'Nothing is ever as plain as it seems in your little world,' my mother said. 'The rules change all the time, that's what you've never understood. That's your problem, for your information.'

I may not be able to vouch for the verbatim accuracy of this memory; but what I do remember with a physical certainty is the tone and texture of that awful moment, the sensations aroused by the sisterly exchange. That is, after all, why I remember the episode at all. I know that as I stood there, riveted by the voices coming out of my mother's study, I felt a dense darkness come over the hallway, as if the sun had been there and had gone; and I sensed a cold, scary emptiness opening within me, where a cosy warmth and safety had been. There was something monstrously out of kilter connected with my birth. It was wrong of my mother to have had me; therefore I was wrong, a mistake, a result of bad judgement. I might have not lived, and it might not have mattered . . . Perhaps it would have been better, less bad, if I had not been born. But there was something even beyond that, beyond this opening into childish existential doubt – the normal doubt experienced by creatures who have just emerged from non-existence and are aware that Being is a tenuous circumstance. As I stood there and listened, I felt, beyond the scary gaping space, an intuition of another kind of Being, inorganic, non-biological, non-human entirely. The Weirdness. The Thing. The black matter lurking in the back of myself, into which I could vanish or metamorphose, within which I existed only by some grace or whim.

When my mother and aunt came out of the study, I was playing with my robodolls on the carpet, trying to restore myself to my familiar world, to myself. My aunt stooped down and picked up one of my toys. I didn't look up. She patted my hair affectionately and then I did raise my eyes, some hope returning. But I must have done something bad again, for as I smiled up at her, I saw her mouth twisting as if she were going to cry, with sorrow but also with something like dread. Her eyes became distant. I receded to a vanishing point. It was like my mother's gaze when she penetrated me too piercingly, and went beyond me, as if I were a thing. The Strange Look. My aunt saw. She saw the Weirdness, and it turned into the strangeness in her eyes.

But what was it I knew and how – what kind of thing, what kind of knowledge? Was I nursing an obscure sense of rejection, of injury? A childish sense that I didn't fit in, wasn't accepted? That I wasn't loved? Would that it were so simple.

'All children feel they're different sometimes,' the Adviser advised me. 'It's part of the family romance, or rather anti-romance – the fantasy that you've been left on your family's doorstep by mistake, and that your parents are not the humble and ordinary mortals you know, but some grand or royal personage. Then, when you discover they're just themselves and that you're bound to grow up ordinary too – well, that can

16

cause great disappointment. A kind of narcissistic wound. Such feelings are not unique to you, you know.'

No. But my condition isn't exactly standard, either. Anyway, my mother did not seem ordinary or humble to me. She seemed imperious enough, though I did not imagine a king for a father. Quaint old notions, I think they may have drained from our imaginations through sheer disuse. But then I continued not to imagine much, along fatherly lines. Does that show anything in itself, the utter blankness where at least a fantasy of a father might have been? Does it prove what I am most afraid of? I keep looking for proofs, irrefutable demonstrations, one way or another . . .

But whatever it was I knew, however I knew it, it was neither a feeling nor a fantasy. It was a knowledge embedded so deeply and inarticulately within me that it might have been part of my cellular structure. A knowledge in the body, the material self.

I think the Weirdness and the Strange Look became all ravelled up in my mind till I didn't know which came first. Perhaps the Weirdness provoked the Strange Look. But I think I also took the Strange Look in and turned it on myself like a dark laser beam, until I came upon my own absolute strangeness, my mineral self. A stranger in myself is the familiar old trope. But no. What I encountered was nothing so anthropomorphic. There was somewhere in my small body something

17

I could only call IT, something that was in me, but was not-me. When I was about seven, I started looking at myself in mirrors like an addict. I had a secret and I wanted to divine it. I thought perhaps I could discover it in the mirror, by surveying my own face – the image in which my mother discerned something I could not know or see. But as I kept staring at myself, the opposite happened. Instead of giving me a key to what was inside me, my face began to break up into separate features, which seemed to have nothing to do with me, with being Iris. A small nose, well-delineated chin, pink cheek, cute childish lip . . . Were they really mine, I wondered? And then, frighteningly, the features themselves splintered into even more abstract bits of surface, curve, colour and glint. Each time I looked in the mirror, I was at first pleased with what I saw; but as I kept peering insistently, relentlessly, it was the IT that gazed back instead of myself.

'I think you're talking about the unconscious,' my Adviser offered. 'After all, "It" was the name Freud gave to the Id, the early, pre-verbal part of ourselves which becomes increasingly inaccessible to us as we leave infancy behind.'

Freud. The grand anatomist of the individual self, the diagnostician of its late civilized ailments, the herald of its disintegration and demise. I wonder what he would have made of my dawning twenty-first-century condition. As it is, and much as I might wish it otherwise, he is no more relevant to me than those kings and queens of yore.

I wonder when I first began to suspect as well as to know. Did it happen gradually, through an accumulation of oddities, or through a dimly growing intuition that my secret was held within my mother, that she knew fully what I sensed through a glass darkly, that she was the very knowledge I was seeking?

My mother. She was not quite a mother and more than one: home, sibling, the larger part of myself, as much me as my limbs or bloodstream. Most of the time we seemed to move in an idyll of seamless attunement, in which our desires echoed in each other as in a watery reverberating chamber. We read and listened to music together and visited virtual cities hand in hand. We walked the streets of London and Stockholm and Paris for hours on end, and she showed me her favourite spots and important landmarks. I often dressed in miniature versions of the clothes she wore: light, rustly, shiny suits in the winter, with a heating chip implanted in them; summer dresses of exquisite Venus silk and Mars cotton, cultivated for delicacy and lightness. She had good taste, my mother, and she could afford almost anything she wanted. We took long drives through the countryside, which were even better than the virtual rides because there were smells, breezes, sudden rains. We could turn down a country road which beckoned invitingly, and even feel disappointment if it was uninteresting. I loved being both excited and disappointed, and the unpredictability of sudden showers, and the buzz of insects among the grass and trees. But most of all, I loved just driving along with her and looking at her beautiful, unmarred face.

Often, we didn't talk for hours at a time. We didn't need to. We coasted in the car, submitting to its smooth motion and simply imbibing each other's presence. At home we spent long intervals not speaking. We moved in our own special atmosphere, as in a semi-liquid surround, an amniotic fluid that incorporated us both and within which there was a connecting passage or cord, along which silent sounds and messages and electrical pulses travelled back and forth. We seemed to move in tandem, always knowing when the other was happy or sad, hungry or impatient. Sometimes, as we looked at each other silently, I felt as if I'd entered her and was looking at myself from inside her eyes. She sponged me up and I felt some of her own substance passing into me along the connecting corridor, like nourishment, like juice.

It was the inevitable insertion of the outside world into our happy home that first stirred the breezes of unease. If we had been able to remain as hermetically insulated as we were in my first few years, I might have grown up innocent – or at least unsuspecting. My mother tried to keep the lid on the bell jar; but even she could not control all the elements affecting our lives.

When I was seven, a big thing happened. A lady came to talk to my mother from the town school, wanting to know when I was going to enrol in the first grade. The law on this wasn't clear, but it was the normal thing to do. My mother baulked. She said I was an exceptionally gifted child and she was going to educate me herself. The lady persisted. She said that no matter how gifted I was, I would be better off going to school, where I could play and socialize with children of my own age. She quoted studies which showed that children growing up in excessive isolation developed severe psychological problems in adulthood. She cited other research which showed that children taught by their own parents often could not make good use of their education later on because they rebelled against the instruction along with the instructors. At this my mother became alert. My education mattered to her above all. This was not the result she wanted. The lady, sensing she'd found a weak spot, turned to me and asked how I felt about it. Did I want to go to school with other children? Wouldn't that be fun? I felt a faint stirring of my very own wishes . . . But how could that be? I was confused. I had never had wishes of this seriousness that were separate from my mother's, and I had certainly never been asked to speak them out loud. I never needed to . . . I looked at my mother helplessly. I wanted her to give me a signal, to indicate what I should say.

21

But she must have been confused herself, for there were no clear clues, no signals pulsing along the passage. I looked up at the lady, who was smiling encouragingly.

'Yes,' I said in a small voice, 'I would like to be with other children.'

My mother gave me a sharp look – a look such as I had never experienced before. It was a look which declared that I had done something unexpected, something that didn't entirely please her.

'But I don't want to leave my mummy,' I put in quickly. Anything not to have her look at me like that.

Still, the lady persisted. She talked about how excellent our local school was, how up to date both on the classical curriculum and the latest technology. It had virtuals for practically every historical epoch, 'patient' computers for children with learning difficulties, person-taught classes in handwriting and basic maths, and something called Human Education, which dealt with the fundamental building blocks and components of human nature. 'In our school, we care about the whole person,' the lady said. 'We believe in enabling the development of all of our students' abilities – biological, moral, technological.'

I don't remember what finally swayed my mother; but the upshot was that I started attending elementary school soon after that conversation. Second grade, not first. Before I was admitted I was tested for the level of my intelligence and basic skills; the first of a raft of tests I was to undergo later . . . Anyway, it was concluded that my mother had indeed done an excellent job on me and that I was ready to leap right ahead into grade two. This was no consolation at first. I had never been away from my mother for so many hours at a time and I was miserable. I walked around the school corridors in a haze, feeling I didn't know how to look without her looking along with me, how to hear without her hearing the same sounds . . . What meaning could sounds and sights have if they didn't undergo the passage from me to her and then back, if they didn't reverberate in us both simultaneously? It was an amputation. My perceptual apparatus had been extracted from me; or else I had left it behind at home. I became vague and lethargic. My teachers kept getting annoyed with me, thinking me sulky and uncooperative. The children approached me, skipping and shouting, inviting me to join them in their games; but there was something about me that made them go away quietly. I didn't respond properly. I was the odd one out. Strange girl, strange child.

And yet for a while, briefly and amazingly, everything changed. For one thing, I discovered that reunions after partings can be sweet. My mother came to pick me up after school, and although she tried to act like any other mom when I ran up to her – taking me by the hand casually while she chatted with other adults, then walking bouncily to the car – I knew this was only façade, camouflage for others' benefit. How did I know that – and what did I think we were doing wrong? What did I think she was trying to hide? I can't say. But I know that as soon as we got into the car and out of the others' sight, we hugged urgently and looked at each other silently, as if we needed to plug back into our common wiring, our life-juices. Once reconnected, we drove home slowly, while I told her about my day and its miseries. I knew I could talk randomly and that she would fill in the gaps.

I suppose that after a few weeks the ritual of return became reassuring enough for me to become less worried, less distracted, at school. I started to join in with the other kids. They were wary of me after their first experiences, but as I cheered up they took me in gladly enough. I'd met some of them in the neighbourhood, after all, had even been to some of their homes. So now I giggled along with everyone else when we stumbled through our multiplication tables, or lurched in tandem on the *Mayflower* as it made its pilgrims' progress over stormy waters to America. During recess, I skipped rope with the other kids and joined in their circle games. Why do adults invariably keep away from those games? Why do they never try to break in? Maybe they sense that children enclosed in a circle become a tribe, with their own laws and powers. I seemed to know those laws just as the others did, although I'd spent so little time among children until then.

24

Does that prove anything at all? I got the rhythmic hand-clappings every time and the next line in the collaborative jingles. But how did any of us know the rules of these games, anyway? Nobody seemed to teach them to us; nobody needed to learn. They arose out of us like the low-wire buzz out of a busy beehive, or like the incessant movement of a high-octane, stinging antheap.

But oh, the pleasures of participation! I lost myself in those games – though in a different way than I lost myself in my mother. I whirled like a dervish, my voice getting stronger and higher pitched with every round of verse, and I emerged briskly invigorated, filled with sharp, ruthless child-energy. When the bell finally rang, we all ran into the brick building in a horde, screaming and laughing in a show of our collective force.

For a while, in the fifth grade, it even looked as though I was going to have a real friend. Daphne. Daphne Salter. She was my opposite in many ways, dark-haired and small, talkative and forthright in declaring her preferences and opinions. Someone told me that her ancestors were hippies, but I didn't know what that meant. Neither did anyone else, apparently. I asked my mother about it and she said hippies were a short-lived tribe who thrived mostly in California. Anyway, I think Daphne picked me out because I presented a challenge to her, because she couldn't figure me out. I was sometimes so smart and sometimes so vague. I had no close friends. Nobody knew my mother. And then we were the two best pupils in the class. We came first in practically every exam and figured out how to get out of the Minotaur's labyrinth more quickly than anyone else. Without any threads. So one day, when we were giggling together at one of our little triumphs, Daphne asked me if I wanted to come home with her after school.

'I don't know,' I said, suddenly deflated. It was a wonderfully tempting offer, but I knew that if I accepted it would make my mother very unhappy.

'Why not?' Daphne asked. 'Don't you like me?'

'No, that's not why,' I stumbled. 'It's just that . . . my mother . . . she doesn't like me to . . .'

'I'll ask my mother to ask your mother,' Daphne declared decisively. I nodded, knowing that if I said any more, it would seem odd.

A few days later, as we were walking out to the parking lot after school, Daphne's mother came up to mine and started chattering a mile a minute. Daphne and I looked at each other at our height, while holding our mothers' hands. 'If she came with us now, we could bring her back before supper,' Mrs Salter was saying. I felt my mother's hand tighten on mine. 'Oh please, please!' Daphne shouted, tugging at her mother. I tried not to make any movement at all, knowing, I suppose, that this could not turn out well for me whatever I did.

'I don't know . . .' my mother said. 'She has so much homework to do . . .'

'Oh, they could do it together,' Daphne's mother assured her. 'They would enjoy that.'

There was a long pause in which, I'm sure, my mother was weighing the tactical advantages of accepting and refusing. She also knew that refusal would look mighty peculiar.

'I suppose that's all right then,' she said finally. 'As long as she's home by suppertime.'

'Yeeeah!' Daphne shouted.

'Thank you,' I said in a small voice, trying not to give vent to my pleasure too overtly.

'You'll behave yourself at Daphne's, won't you?' my mother said, bending down in order to convey some extra message. Don't say too much, was what the message said . . . I nodded.

I relaxed once I was at Daphne's. Her household couldn't have been more different from mine. Daphne's parents were among those rarities left over from the late twentieth century who'd met before Daphne was born and had never divorced. So there was a real daddy, perhaps the first I'd ever met, who seemed to dote on Daphne and take a shine to me. They were traditional in other ways, too, Daphne's parents, maybe even a little sentimental. They had kept all kinds of things left over from their childhood. There was an ancient machine in their house called a record player, which Daphne's dad had inherited from his own parents and on which he played large unwieldy music discs. He had a whole collection of them, with funny names like Jefferson Airplane

27

and Oasis. They were classics, he said, and very hard to find. I had to get used to their pounding, pulsing sounds, so unlike the transparent, serene songs I was used to; but once I learnt how to listen I really liked them. Daphne also had lots of virtuals called Just for Real, very different from the ones we had at home. My mother favoured a label called Plato's Caves, which specialized in the smooth, glistening, formal look. Just for Reals were more gritty and messy, with bumpy roads and people walking around with scraggly hair and porous skin.

So I had a good time that afternoon and was asked back several times. I let down my guard enough to ask Daphne personal questions: where her parents came from, whether she loved them, who else she knew. The problem was, of course, that she asked questions back and that I could tell her so little. No, I didn't know who my father was; I'd never met him. No, my mom didn't tell me anything about him. No, I had no relatives except for an aunt, but I only met her once. No, she didn't send me e-mails, I never heard from her again. Daphne embraced me impulsively. 'We can be your relatives!' she said and I suddenly felt very sorry for myself, but also shyly hopeful. Maybe Daphne's family would become a little bit mine.

They didn't. After a while, Daphne's parents began to ask me questions as well. Where did my mother live before coming to the Midwest?

She seemed to be a big-city person, they said, so elegant and sophisticated. Why did she choose to move to this small, out-of-the-way town? Was it because she had some relatives here? I fidgeted and looked at the floor. And what about my father, Daphne's mom continued, was it really true that I didn't know anything about him? Wasn't I curious? Didn't I want to know?

'I do,' I began impulsively and then got confused. 'But my mother . . . I guess she doesn't want to . . .' And then I stopped.

Mrs Salter threw me a sharp look. 'Is there anything you . . . want to tell me?' she said softly. 'Sometimes it's good to have a special friend to whom you can tell everything, even your deepest secrets.'

This was about child abuse, I knew. I'd seen scary virtuals about it in our Human Education class, in which the 'special friend' always played an important role. I shook my head energetically. 'No!' I declared. 'It isn't anything like that!'

'Hmmm . . .' Mrs Salter said, examining my face, 'but something is troubling you, isn't it?' she asked kindly. I stood there helplessly. I hadn't realized anything was troubling me, but something was.

'Can you tell me what it is?' she asked. 'Do you know?'

'No,' I said in a small voice. 'I mean, I don't really know . . . I can't explain.'

Daphne's mom scrutinized me again, trying to

figure out what I was hiding, or at least the sort of thing I was keeping from her. But as she peered at me, something other than concerned curiosity entered her eyes: she was looking at me as one looks at someone pathetic or damaged. She didn't ask me anything more.

My mother, of course, knew something had happened as soon as Mrs Salter deposited me at the door.

'What is it?' she asked the moment Daphne's mother left.

'I want to know about my daddy,' I said. This was dangerous defiance, as I well knew. Her face darkened; I quailed.

'What were they carrying on about?' she asked. 'What did they want to know?'

'About my father,' I said stubbornly. 'Where he is.'

'I told you you aren't ready to hear about him!' she said furiously. 'Those stupid, prying meddlers, how dare they interfere!'

'But, but . . .' I was spluttering with confusion. 'They're nice, they were only asking . . . Daphne's daddy is so nice, that's why.'

There was an arrow of anger between my mother's eyes. 'Just don't forget they're strangers,' she said. 'Our affairs are none of their business. In fact, I think you shouldn't be spending so much time over there.'

I started to cry. 'But I like them,' I said. 'They're nice to me.'

Her tone changed instantly. 'Oh, my poor pop-pet,' she said and bent down to cuddle me. 'It's all right, it'll be all right. You have me. You'll always have me, even if you drop some nasty silly people along the way. And I have you. Aren't we happy together?'

I looked into her face, and one of those familiar, strange sensations passed between us, through our interconnecting feedback loop. Our umbilical cord. She was part of me, my feeding source, my necessary mirror . . . We held each other's gaze until we both understood that I was back in the system, that I submitted.

The other thing that happened was more radical and disturbing to our peace. When I was twelve a man came into my mother's life. Into our lives. Steven Lontano. Taking up with him was surely the most incautious, irrational, ill-advised thing she'd ever done and I don't understand how she could have allowed herself to make such a large mis-step. But I suppose she had her urges and they weren't always entirely within her control. We'd learned about Uncontrollable Urges in Human Education. They were classified under Emotions, and they posed a problem for evolutionary theory because they were almost invariably self-destructive. They also seemed very resistant to genetic tinkering. However, Uncontrollable Urges seemed to be a trait peculiar to humans, we were told, and therefore it was assumed that they must serve some positive evolutionary purpose, even though so far nobody was getting even close to discovering what that might be.

I don't know what purpose Steven Lontano served in my mother's life, but I know that I adored him. Once I met him, that is. For I sensed him long before that – long before I suspected his existence. I sensed him in the changed atmosphere of our house, the subtle alteration in her personal climate. I couldn't have defined it, or known what was going on. It was just that, suddenly, she'd become distracted; distracted from herself, distracted from me. Sometimes, she'd go into a state of fey merriment and pick me up and twirl me in the air. But most of the time she was less sure in her movements, less alert. She'd stop in the middle of a task – working at her computer, chopping vegetables – as if she'd forgotten what she was supposed to be doing; or she'd get up from reading and walk through the house aimlessly, and then come back, looking still uncertain of what she'd been up to. Sometimes she'd look at me and smile with a special sort of tenderness . . . But she wasn't smiling at me. This was different from when she'd enter my eyes till she penetrated all the way through to the Weirdness. No, now she was seeing something, someone, else as she smiled at me and it filled her eyes with a dreamy distant pleasure.

'Are you ill?' I once asked her shyly, after she'd looked at me like that. I have no idea why that was the question, how I'd hit on that old, old trope. Love sickness.

'No, of course I'm not,' she said, coming to herself. 'What a funny child you are. No, there's nothing wrong at all.'

But there was something very wrong, as far as I was concerned, when she went out one evening and didn't come back till the middle of the night. She'd left me before, with babysitters, but it was always clear that she was only going out because she had to and that she would be back after an hour or two. This time, though, her expression became more dreamy with every exquisite garment she put on, with every stroke of powder puff and hairbrush . . . I stood beside her at her make-up mirror, and gazed with her and into her as she gazed at herself. Two pairs of eyes gazing, at something just beyond the mirror, which I couldn't see. Which was not me.

I followed the line of her gaze, her longing, for a while after she left; but by the time she came back I was lying in the dark, not asleep, but comatose with absence. Rigid with her disappearance, which was also my own. Then I heard the front door open and her steps, running up the stairs quickly and straight into my room. 'Oh, my poor baby,' she said. 'Alone all this time?'

So the next time she got ready to go out like that, she took me along. She said we were going to have dinner with a very nice man, a very special friend.

I liked Steven as soon as I saw him. He was

tall and grey-haired and incredibly old-fashioned. Hardly anybody had grey hair any more, it was so easily avoided. His gestures were casual and sort of funny, as if every bone in his body were permeated by a mild, observant amusement.

He looked at me with a downward, slightly sceptical turn of the head, and asked me about my favourite subjects at school and cine-virtuals. He forgot me only once that evening, when he spoke to my mother in a low voice without any irony in it, and put his hand on hers. She was sitting between us, and without changing her position, or her concentration on him, she put her hand on mine. I felt the passage of their contact through her and knew he was a gift for me too.

Steven worked as an archaeologist at the local university, teaching, occasionally going on digs in the Middle East and submitting shards of ancient bone and ceramic to sub-molecular analysis. After he moved into our house, just a few weeks after that dinner, I started spending a lot of time in the room downstairs, which he used as his study. I'd sit curled up in a wine-red velvet armchair, while he stayed at his big desk, the light glimmering into the dim room through the thick foliage of the elm trees outside. Between reading my books or playing my games, I watched him as he put a fragment of antique ceramic under a special microscope, or examined some part of an ancient skeleton – a shin bone, a thigh bone – running his finger over it and leaning back in his chair pensively.

'What is that?' I'd ask. 'Where does it come from?'

'It comes from once upon a time, from a very long, long time ago,' he'd say and smile. Sometimes he explained where a piece of urn had been discovered or what catastrophe a skeleton had died in, or what sort of person a bone might have belonged to and what kind of life they might have led. He'd tell me these things in a pensive, slow way, filling in the odd detail, and summoning, through his few dry facts, steppes and early cities, rocky deserts and savannahs. I loved his stories of tribes moving inexorably over stretches of land, of wars and conquests and natural catastrophes, against which early humans had no protection or shelter. Steven's tales glided over thousands of years and gave me a scary shiver, a tingle of steep, dark, descending time. Real time, more real even than on the Epoch Virtuals. Real past, of which I had none and knew nothing, and which I longed for, without knowing it. I wanted to know where I came from, and I consoled myself with tales of those far-removed ancestors who were so little like us they might as well be another species, but who somehow ended up being us.

Steven never objected to my presence in the study while he worked. Perhaps I provided an incongruous, cheering counter-point to his trans-actions with those crumbling, bleached objects, with such a long history of death. Anyway, I felt very close to him as I sat there, and several weeks

35

after he moved in with us, he said I could call him Uncle Steve, and for a while, I almost came to believe he was a real relative. Almost . . .

My mother was besotted with him. We both were. The three of us started doing things together that the two of us had never done by ourselves: going to restaurants, to the nearby lake beaches, to the mountains for whole weekends. On long drives, we played games or composed limericks for which we made up alternate lines:

> There once was a man from the moon,
> Who came down to earth at high noon.
> As round him he looked,
> He got quite spooked,
> And went back a regular loon.

Steven gave me guided tours of Pompeii and the Pyramids, and took me to a space museum not far from our town. I loved the place, with its sleek, shiny rockets which you could steer to practically anywhere in the galaxy, and the fluorescent, padded suits you put on to enter the gravity-less environments. There were models for projects which never got off the ground, like space-station restaurants from which you could see the earth revolving as you ate your dinner. One of the models had been turned into a real restaurant, from which you could watch the earth on the screen, and rockets gliding past each other like graceful, vertical whales.

36

For a while – a blessed, long while – we were a threesome. In the evenings we often sat cosily around the living-room fireplace and watched something on the Data Dispenser, or just talked. My eyes would move between Steven and my mother, as he put his arm affectionately round her shoulders, or as she followed the movements of his hands fiddling with some graphics, an expression of almost sleepy contentment on her face. I'd look up at her, into her, and sense the line of connection between them, a line which extended through my mother to me, and I'd start feeling sleepily contented myself. She for him, and I for him in her . . .

So it was only natural that I wanted to sleep with them sometimes, to partake of the warmth which coursed between them and which, I felt, also belonged to me. I was twelve; before Steven moved in I often slept with my mother. Sometimes I made my way to her bed instinctively, in my sleep, in the middle of the night. She'd put her arm around me without waking, and our breathing immediately co-ordinated into a common rhythm. There was nothing to occasion notice in this; we blended as naturally as two streamlets of water, as mother and kittens in a newborn litter.

Natural. Instinctive. I shouldn't be allowed to use such words, perhaps no one should, any more. I am the thing that interrogates their very meanings. Still, that's how I felt, and who knows, who knows what that shows?

Anyway, I continued to come into my mother's bed after she started sharing it with Steven. I'd half wake up in the night, and somnabulistically transport myself to their bedroom, my blue blanket trailing behind me . . . The first time this happened he woke up and asked in a whisper, 'What's the matter? Did you have a bad dream?' I shook my head and got into the bed. I didn't want to be woken up fully. My mother stirred, but didn't wake up at all.

'Don't you want to go back to your own bed?' he whispered. 'I'll read to you, from that book you really like.' But I must have been falling asleep already because I don't remember anything else.

The next time this happened, though, he was more decisive. He lifted me up before I could get into their bed and started carrying me back to my bedroom. I struggled and cried out. My mother woke up. 'What are you doing?' she said sharply. She was addressing the question to Steven, not to me.

'I'm just taking her back to her bed,' he said, sounding surprised at her protest. 'She'll sleep better there.'

'Let her sleep here,' my mother said and it was a command. 'She's used to it.' He complied, but I felt his body stiffen as he placed me on the bed, between them. He lay down next to me rigidly, not sleeping, and preventing me from falling asleep for a long time.

'You have to take some responsibility for this,'

the Adviser told me. 'Even retroactively. It was your desires which were driving the situation. Your impulses. Of course, your mother could have – should have – intervened. After all, you were trying to take Steven away from her. You wanted him for yourself. There's nothing unnatural about this, especially in a young girl with no father. It must have been very confusing to have Steven in the house. But your mother should have made you understand. She should have set some limits.'

But it wasn't like that. It was natural in a different way. I didn't want to take Steven away from my mother; I wanted to share him with her. Or her with him. Or rather, I did share her – and him. We had everything in common, my mother and I, and the constant, silent passage of substance between her and me meant that he passed between us too, that her sensations about him were my sensations and that she passed from me to him, or I did, in her person . . . Oedipal rivalry? That was the phrase the Adviser was pleased to use; but no, that would have been much too simple, too clear for our case . . .

But Steven's unease about the situation did not abate. When I turned thirteen he decided to have a serious talk with me. He summoned me to his study for the occasion and sat across from me in the high-backed velvet chair.

'Iris,' he said formally, 'I want to talk to you about something.' I looked at him expectantly. I thought maybe he was preparing a trip for us, or a treat. 'It's about your . . . sleeping habits.' I must have given him a glum look.

'I know you don't want to talk about this,' he said, 'but we have to.' I waited. He tried to start up again.

'Iris,' he said, 'you grew up without a father and I realize that can be hard on a young girl.' I waited, stubbornly silent.

'I can imagine that sometimes you've really wished you had a father.' He paused. 'But maybe you don't quite know what having one means.'

Despite myself, I was roused to interest. This was a subject close to my heart. 'What do you mean?' I asked.

'I mean . . . a relationship with your father is not like that with any other man. He's . . . well, he is your father and not a friend. I mean . . . he's a friend, of course, but not a friend you could turn into . . . What I mean, Iris, is that you don't sleep with your father.'

'You mean because of the incest taboo?' I asked. I'd learnt about that in Human Education.

He looked rather startled. 'Yes,' he said. 'But the incest taboo isn't just some silly rule that people follow because somebody told them to. It's something that people actually feel.'

'But what if I don't?' I asked.

'Well, yes,' he said thoughtfully. 'That's where not having a father comes in. But then you have to learn, that's all.'

'What do I have to learn?' I asked.

An expression of exasperation crept into his face. 'Iris,' he said, 'I hope we're good friends?' I nodded. 'And that you feel about me a little as you might about . . . well, an uncle, or perhaps even a father?' I nodded again, suddenly suffused with warmth. He'd never said anything like that. No one had ever said anything like that. 'Well then,' he said, as if he were arriving at a QED, 'you have to stop sleeping in our – in your parents' – bed.'

To me, this was not a QED. 'But you're not my real father,' I said. 'And I was here first.'

He was taken aback. 'First,' he repeated. 'Where on earth do you get such ideas?' I shrugged. I didn't know. I was just stating the obvious. 'But actually,' he said carefully, as if trying to impress something on me, 'you weren't. First, there was your father. And now, I'm the first in your mother's . . . affections. Those kinds of affections, anyway. I know this may be difficult for you to accept, that it may take time before you really understand. But she chose me to be there for her, you see.'

'No,' I said stubbornly. 'She chose you for both of us.'

I think this was perhaps the moment when he realized that he was out of his depth, that there was something about me – about us – he hadn't taken into account. The ghost of a suspicion, a recognition, passed over his brow, but it was as if he couldn't catch it. He made a gesture as if he was shaking something off.

'Look, Iris,' he said, more firmly, 'I don't want

to be unkind. I know that my presence here must be hard on you sometimes.' I made a gesture of disagreement. That wasn't it at all, I loved having him there.

'Well, whatever the problem may be,' he continued, 'I simply will not tolerate your coming into our bed again. That's the rule from now on. Think of me as a cruel stepfather if you want, some ogre patriarch from the olden days. Maybe we can make it a game of a kind. But anyway, from now on, it is the law. Steven's law. Stepfather's law.'

He was as good as his word. When I next came towards their bed, in my half-sleepwalking state, he stopped me right at the pass, lifted me up and carried me to my room in a way that brooked no protest. I lay awake, feeling cruelly frustrated, my whole being concentrated in a need – no, just a plain necessity – to be with my mother and him, in their bed. Even though my bedroom was too far from theirs for me to hear anything, I thought I sensed my mother stirring. A few moments later she came into my room and without either of us saying anything, she got into my bed and put her arms around me. I saw her eyes giving off a light that reflected mine; then I fell asleep.

But the mood in our household began to shift after that. I was growing into adolescence; I was becoming more and more like my mother. My predilections turned out to be her predilections. I was good at maths and computer calculations, just as she'd been. I seemed to like the same foods.

I was prone to the same illnesses, slight bronchial infections and earaches. I spoke with the same intonations; and, most of all, I looked more and more like her. It wasn't a resemblance – it was, for all the difference of age, an almost peculiar repetition, as if in me she was being herself once more. Our features were the same. So were our flesh tone, hair colour and our gestures. We echoed each other in everything: the spread-fingered way we pushed our hair back out of our faces, the stance we took, slightly favouring the right hip when standing still, the exact pout of lip when we put on lipstick. Like all women of her class, she looked much younger than she was; by the time I was in my teens, we looked like sisters who, by rights, should have been twins. Or like identical twins who by some fluke were ageing at different speeds.

At the peak of our love for each other – our unity – we took pleasure in the doubling. We caught each other sometimes in the midst of a reiterated gesture, and gave each other a look of amused complicity. My gesture meant more for thus being mirrored. My pout, grimace, shoulder-shrug was no longer just an unthinking reflex, but a reflection of her, who was the source of all significance. I think she must have felt the same when this happened – no longer just herself, but a model, a prototype whose meaning was assured by its re-embodiment. We never talked about it, but we knew we shared a delectable, frightening, powerful secret – though what it was, I still could not have said, or maybe, could not allow myself to say.

Sometimes I caught Steven looking at us in a puzzled, restive way, as we giggled together or came out with almost the same words at the same time. When we talked intimately, it was difficult to figure out who was speaking, whose voice was saying the words we both thought. I once saw a documentary film on an almost extinct Eskimo tribe, in which two small women with long black plaits played an ancient game. They stood facing each other, very close, and made low, reverberant, almost underground sounds, as of cattle lowing, or those unearthly, under-earthly Tibetan horns. The women seemed to blow these sounds – which were of a song, or story – into each other's mouths; but after a while the voice emanated inter-changeably from the throats of either woman, or sometimes from inside the one who wasn't singing, who wasn't moving her lips. It was as if they shared a voice box between them, or an echo chamber where the sounds bounced back and forth between origin and receptacle. This was how it was between me and my mother as we talked over the day's events face to face.

And there was between us such a unison of thought, of response and preference, that it amounted to a kind of telepathy. One semester, in our art class, the teacher asked us to do hand-painting instead of computer graphics. She had the idea that this was good for you, that it boosted your creativity because the handmade object was somehow more authentic. Actually, I must admit I enjoyed it. I spent a lot of time in the class painting a landscape, vaguely of a moor, in louche mauves and gloamy greens. Not that I have ever seen a moor, though my mother may have told me about one. But for some reason, my images were clear, even if my depiction was not. When it was finally finished and I brought it home, my mother glanced at my handiwork, and then looked at it more carefully, a small frown gradually giving way to a small, impish smile. She held her finger up, as if to say, 'Wait! I have a surprise!' and ran down to the basement, where she kept various documents and memorabilia under lock and key. She came back with a little framed painting in her hand, which she handed to me wordlessly. It showed a landscape, not a moor, but a meadow; but the colours, the basic design, the morphic forms of the plants and the sky, were all the same. Her signature, executed in girlish, obedient lettering, was in the bottom right corner. The handwriting might well have been mine.

'The moor used to be my favourite landscape,' she said a bit wistfully. 'I once spent a summer on Dartmoor in England; I wonder if it still exists, if there are still real ponies running about on it.'

Then there was the time when I came home early from school because I sensed that something had happened to her. When I ran up to her room, she didn't even ask why I was back early. She was looking white and damp, droplets of moisture forming on her upper lip, her hair uncombed and limp. 'What's wrong?' I asked. 'What happened?' 'Hepatitis A,' she said. 'It's harmless if caught early. But you'll have to watch out for it when you get to be my age. You'll undoubtedly get it too.'

Steven came out of his study. 'Why are you back so early?' he asked. I shrugged. 'I knew she was sick,' I said. He looked at me rather sternly. 'How did you know?' I shrugged again.

'Did you call her at school?' he asked my mother. She shook her head. 'But I'm glad she's here,' she said, 'I had a feeling she was coming.'

The look which came over his face then was the Strange Look, and this time it hovered over my mother and me, over both of us. We looked back at him from the bed; two pairs of eyes, identical and identically unmoved. He left the room without saying a word.

I suppose I understood obscurely why we unnerved people, my mother and I. I suppose I should have been unnerved myself; but I wasn't. It was natural to me, after all, the shared mother-me medium, the matrix, the symbiotic soup. I moved in its languid, liquid, milky atmosphere as if it were normal air.

'You're describing a pathological version of the mother–daughter bond,' the Adviser declared. 'A relationship in which there isn't enough separation, so that the daughter gets submerged and lost.'

As if mother–daughter love weren't always

pathological – if you want to see it that way. And as if pathology were an adequate word to describe the nature of my link with my mother. Of our inevitable inextricability. Of our luxurious, terrible sameness. Our identity.

Still. Even while I moved in the matrix without self-consciousness – almost without consciousness – I was becoming aware that those outside our dyad thought we were distinctly odd. When my mother waited for me in the parking lot after school now, or when we walked down the street together or through the supermarket, people turned and stared at us, and I could follow the progress of their reactions, predictable after a while, from a kind of warm bemusement – look at the lovely mummy/daughter pair! – to a vague discomfort and averted eyes. Once we ran into Daphne and her mother at the supermarket. I hadn't seen them together for a long time and I felt a twinge of envy at their sheer . . . normality. Daphne was already taller than her mother and darker-toned; they were chatting companionably as they picked groceries off the shelves. 'Hello!' we all said as our carts collided and Daphne's mother launched into her line of quick patter. It's been so long, she was saying, it's such a pity, we don't see enough of Iris these days, I hear she's doing so well at school. My mother and I smiled politely from our identical height. I think our eyes were not suffused with warmth. Daphne's mother paused momentarily and took in our expressions. 'How much you look like your mother, Iris,' she said in an awed voice. 'Well, it was nice to see you,' she added and put her arm around her daughter protectively. 'I hope . . . I hope you're both well.' Daphne and I waved at each other uncertainly, for old times' sake, but I could tell she found me baffling too.

At school I was again the odd one out; not only marginalized, but actively ostracized. There was a mean little clique of cool kids in the ninth grade who picked on me as their designated scapegoat. It started with the arrival of Agnes, a pale, small girl who came to our town from Los Angeles and who wanted to make friends with me, perhaps sensing I was a fellow outcast. I didn't reciprocate; I had had enough adventures in making friends, and besides, I didn't relish her reasons for favouring me. Pale, frail Agnes had a reputation as a goody-two-shoes; but she turned out to have rich reserves of malice stored in her prepubescent heart. After I rebuffed her advances several times, she unleashed her venom on me with full vengeance. She managed to inveigle herself into the cool clique and proceeded to recruit its bored members into her campaign against me. She must have orchestrated it well, for suddenly nasty tales about me started circulating in the school. What were they, these tales? I never found out exactly, but when I dared I could just about imagine: incest, murder, felony; they all would have fitted my case, would have provided a plausible explanation for the puzzle, the curious fact of me and my mother. And, of course, no one loves melodrama like adolescents, for whom it corresponds to their garish emotional world. So when I dared, I tried to imagine what they whispered among themselves as I passed them in the hall: that I was the fruit of an incestuous union between my mother and her twin brother; that my mother had murdered my father – because he was also her father; that my mother snatched me away from her twin sister or had to come to the Midwest because of some big financial scam . . . When I dared – though this was not often – I wondered if I should give credence to the rumours I imagined; I wondered if they weren't rumours in my own head. In the meantime, my classmates continued to treat me with the uninhibited cruelty of which fourteen-year-olds are so singularly capable. In class I was shunned and left out of shared projects; in the cafeteria there were titters and cold, condescending glances as I walked past to sit at an empty table. I tried to brush it all off, not to look at the clustered teenagers as they turned their hard eyes on me, not to mind; but with each act of meanness I felt weaker and more ashamed. Each attack somehow confirmed my sense that I was being punished because I was guilty, that the hatred I drew was provoked by something in me – my essential, ineluctable wrongness.

It all ended with someone tripping me on the stairs of the school building; I saw Agnes's pale face behind the offender, cold-eyed and tight-lipped, as I fell and tumbled down. I was badly bruised by the time I reached the bottom; it was a few moments before I could pick myself up and walk away. But Agnes's ferret face pierced and hurt the most. I knew that, obscurely, it was related to the Weirdness – the undefined, inarticulable Weirdness, which never really let me go.

My mother was already waiting when I straggled to the parking lot; for some reason she'd come to pick me up early that day. She looked at me wordlessly and brought out a Kleenex to wipe the smudges off my face. She went to my school the next day, to confront the principal; I think the culprits were brought to justice. My mother would have accomplished that much. Certainly, when I went back to school everything had changed; no one dared bully me in the same, brazen way. But in the meantime I stayed at home for several days and cried, going over each slight and insult in my mind, and injuring myself with them all over again.

I feel, I felt, I have a feeling . . . But can a creature like me actually have feelings? I believed I did, of course, right up to the moment of discovery. I believed it as I cried in my bed, and as I felt – felt! – a nauseating amalgam of anger and shame. Afterwards I could never be sure. Could never be sure what I felt; could never be sure that what I felt were feelings. Which meant, in effect, that I didn't have them. A feeling is a feeling only if it's incontrovertible, imperious, whole; if it comes over you uncoaxed and unforced. If you cannot help it, if it's outside your control, if it announces itself like some pure message from a source within. But me – did I ever have my very own feelings, natural, unbidden, original? Springing from a deep well of myself? Or were they all replicated feelings, received in the body, programmed in the brain?

'I think you're idealizing the idea of feeling,' the Adviser declared, 'or fetishizing it. It's a common enough mistake, to think that our emotions are entirely subjective. Entirely spontaneous.'

But what if it's a mistake necessary to life? To remaining who we are? Who you are? And what if it's a mistake we can no longer make?

'Actually, we have always known how to control feelings,' the Adviser continued. 'It's called self-discipline. Self-management. And of course, we now know how to alter them, though I myself don't favour that kind of thing. But anyway, we've had lots of time to learn that our subjective states aren't that mysterious. Or that unique.'

Well, yes. I've been coming a long time. And you've been preparing for me, step by step.

'On the other hand, to believe that we are entirely managed by some kind of program or outside force is also irrational. Paranoid, you might say. In fact, it is mad.'

But I am not mad, and I am the most managed of them all.

I think it was the incident of the fall which spilled the cup of Steven's disquiet. Shortly afterwards I overheard him and my mother arguing in his study, their voices tense with held-in anger and somehow loud despite their willed restraint.

'I must know what's going on here,' Steven was saying stiffly, insistently. 'Why doesn't she have any friends? Why doesn't she bring anyone home? This isn't normal and I don't see why you think it is!'

'I don't care about normal,' my mother said. 'Normal usually isn't very interesting. I have my reasons for doing things as I do.'

'Which you won't tell me,' he said in a strangled voice. 'I can't stand all this . . . mystification. I'm in the business of solving mysteries, not wallowing in them.'

'Don't you trust me?' my mother said. 'Can't you leave well enough alone? I mean, we're getting along, aren't we?' Her tone was not conciliatory.

'I want to trust you, I need to trust you, that's why I'm talking about this,' Steven said, his foot stamping out the rhythm of his phrases. 'But how can I, if you don't even tell me about . . . about your daughter!'

'I have a past,' my mother said. 'My past is my own business. I'm sure you don't tell me everything about your life before either.'

'For God's sake . . .' Steven began. 'I'm the man you're living with. I'm the man who loves you. Whom you supposedly love. I mean, I love you, Elizabeth! I feel . . . oh God, you know how I feel about you. But how can I keep on feeling like this, if . . . I mean, what's the point of love if you won't let me know you? What on earth is the point?'

'Love me, love what's mine,' my mother said.

'Mine?' he repeated. 'What a strange phrase to use.'

There was a silence.

'Of course I love Iris,' Steven resumed, trying to control his exasperation, trying again. 'I care about her. But I have to know what's going on here, in this house. I can't live with you and be in the dark about . . . about who you are.'

I felt as anxious, as afraid, as when I overheard the conversation between my mother and my aunt all those years ago. And why, it now came to me with a poignancy: why was it that I never saw my aunt again?

'Whatever it is,' Steven said more calmly, 'I wish you'd just come out and tell me. I think I can accept almost anything about you by now, except this . . . this utter withholding. I don't understand what you could possibly be so afraid of. Or ashamed of.'

'I'm not ashamed of anything,' my mother said in a steely voice.

'Then why . . .' Steven began and then, as if he realized something, as if a penny finally dropped, he stopped in his tracks. 'There's something really peculiar between you and Iris, isn't there?' he finally said, stating it more as a fact than as a question. There was a further silence and then he came out of the study. I was standing right outside the door, wide-eyed and still; I didn't bother to pretend I hadn't been there. He put his hand on my shoulder and looked right into my face, my eyes. 'Poor Iris,' he said. 'Poor child.'

A few days later, Steven once again summoned me to his study. We'd hardly talked in the intervening time and it was a new kind of tension I felt as I came into the room. He was holding a delicate white bone between his long fingers and he looked serious and sad.

'I'm afraid this will be difficult,' he said, after I curled into my chair and he drew his near me.

But of course I already knew. 'You're leaving us, aren't you?' I said matter-of-factly.

He nodded.

'But why?' I asked. 'Why?' As usual, there was a strange slippage in my mind. I knew, but I didn't understand.

'It isn't easy to explain,' he said, 'but I want you to know that it doesn't have anything to do with you. I don't want you to feel that you did anything to bring this about.'

I didn't feel that. I felt what my mother must have felt, what I knew she felt: pain, rejection, hurt.

'You don't love us any more,' I said flatly.

'That isn't quite true,' he said. 'I still . . . well, I'm still in love with your mother. I don't know if you can understand this. I don't even know whether I should be talking to you like this. But

54

I didn't want to leave without saying something to you. Although I'm sure your mother will talk to you as well. She's a compelling woman, your mother,' he added inconsequentially, 'as you will be. You're becoming very . . . attractive already.'

'Then why?' I insisted. 'Why are you leaving us?'

'Oh Iris,' he said, 'things change. All that ever happens in the world is that things change. You see this bone?' He ran his finger up and down the fragile object almost caressingly. 'This once belonged to a human creature with flesh and eyes, with hopes, desires and disappointments. And do you know how many such humans have lived on this earth already? Lived and died and had their fates? How many generations upon generations? Things come and go. People come and go. Feelings come and go. Everything changes, except the fact of change. It doesn't matter as much as we think it does. We don't matter so much, maybe.'

'But what has changed?' I insisted dumbly, stubbornly. 'We still love you, we want you to stay here.'

'I wish you wouldn't speak in the plural all the time,' he said, his voice suddenly brusque. 'To be frank, I find it a bit . . . distasteful. This is about me and your mother. As I have so often told you. We have our differences and we find that we can't resolve them satisfactorily. That's all.'

'Are you afraid of us?' I asked, speaking out of some intuition, or hunch.

He was taken aback. 'Why on earth do you ask such a question?'

'I don't know,' I said, suddenly feeling very small and desolate. 'I just think sometimes we make people uncomfortable.'

'Why do you think that is?' His tone was again protective, kindly.

'I don't know,' I said helplessly. 'There's something weird about me . . . about us. Isn't there?'

He didn't answer for quite a while. 'There may be something, Iris,' he said. 'Something not quite . . . regular. But I don't know what it is either. I guess that's really why I'm leaving.'

I nodded. 'We'll miss you,' I said in my small voice.

He didn't say anything for a while. 'I'll miss you too,' he finally brought out. 'Both of you.'

He raised my chin so that I would look at him and tried to smile at me encouragingly. But, despite himself, the line of his mouth faltered and formed itself into something worried, troubled. He gave me a peck on the cheek and embraced me briefly; I did not respond.

On the day of his departure my mother and I left him quite alone. We heard him rattling about in the study, putting his artefacts and instruments into boxes. We saw him carry the boxes out into a van he'd hired. We watched him as he stood outside, trying to compose himself before coming back into the house to say goodbye.

We were sitting at the kitchen table and we

looked at him indifferently as he came in. He gave us one of his raffish, charming smiles. It was a brave gesture. 'Well, ladies,' he said, 'I wish this weren't happening. Really, I do.'

'But it is,' my mother said.

'Don't go tough on me, Elizabeth,' he said, his bitterness returning. 'It's you who's throwing me out, really.'

My mother's brow raised itself in an ironic flicker. 'What convenient logic,' she said.

'You know you could have made it possible for me to stay,' Steven said, 'so you must have wished to make it impossible.'

My mother raised an ironical eyebrow again, as if this reasoning proved her point, not his. In the silence that followed, Steven looked at her, and at me beside her, in a way which acknowledged defeat. We returned his gaze steadily; we were not giving an inch. For the moment I was on her side, receiving her anger and hurt into my body, so that it stiffened into an upright spine. I am sure our two pairs of eyes, following him in tandem as he gave us a wan wave and moved towards the door, must have seemed to Steven quite uncanny.

It was after Steven's departure, though, that I started changing sides. We were both made desolate, my mother and I, by his absence. But I think somewhere in the unspoken reaches of myself, I started blaming her for what happened; I felt she had taken Steven away from me, had let him go through her negligence, or her stubbornness.

And then there was the secret. Steven had confirmed that there was one, had unwittingly roiled and rankled that place where I knew and didn't know. Over the next two years we chafed at our common grudge, our grievance. Not that we talked about it – we didn't need to; but the atmosphere in the echo chamber, the bell jar in which we lived, was becoming denser, dirtier; something was polluting the air. It was in an effort to swim out of it, to catch a cleaner breath, that I began a series of wilful, risky confrontations with my mother.

'I want to know,' I said one evening after dinner, 'I want to know about my father.'

'I told you. When you are eighteen.' There was no need for niceties, for preparations of the main topic. We understood each other all too well. Except she knew something I didn't, something crucial to me, to my life, to my continuing to breathe. I was determined to wrest it out of her, wrench it out.

'I can't wait that long,' I said. 'If you don't tell me, I'm going to run away.'

'Don't be silly,' she said coldly. 'You can't do that and you know it.'

'I will if I have to. I'm going to look for him. I bet there are records somewhere.'

'Don't threaten me,' she said and then, amazingly, something like fear crept into her eyes, her voice.

58

'You can't fight me,' she almost whispered. 'It's impossible. You can't fight me without fighting yourself, and I won't allow that. I must stop us both.'

I was terrified by her fear and I felt its force: she was right, fighting her was like fighting a Siamese twin. But I tried.

'You can stop it by just telling me about my father,' I pleaded. 'I mean, how bad could it be? Was he a horrible man?'

'No,' she said quickly. 'No, you mustn't think that. It's nothing so . . . banal.' I waited, but there was nothing more.

'Then what was he like?' I wailed. 'At least tell me that, tell me what he looked like! I mean, I feel like he never existed, like I've never had a father . . . Except for Steven, and you threw him out!'

She started to say something angry and then looked at me and our eyes got ravelled up and confused. I was looking from within her, she from inside me . . . We were suddenly suffering together, she the container and completion of my feelings, I an extension, an emanation of her gaze.

But still she knew something I didn't. I tried again, although it was almost unbearable. 'Did you do something really, really awful?' I asked, without looking at her. 'Something criminal? Is that why you can't tell me?'

She sighed. 'Let's stop this, please,' she said. 'Please. I wish your imagination weren't so trite. There are just certain things you aren't ready to know. That's all.' Then she added pensively, this time only to herself, 'I never thought it would be as complicated as this.'

'What? What?' I asked quickly, hoping to trap her into saying something unguarded. 'What's so complicated?'

But she wouldn't say anything more.

'You were, of course, engaging in a massive projection,' is how the Adviser diagnosed this phase of things. 'You had always attributed your own feelings to your mother and now you were transferring to her your fears about who your father might have been. Maybe you were symbolizing your own awakening sexual feelings that way, by imagining a sort of violent sexuality between your parents.'

Projection? Please! Why would I need anything so kinky, so convoluted, to imagine my mother's feelings? No, my access to them was more direct than that. Except the access, along one crucial route, was breaking down.

My mother had a different explanation. 'You're an adolescent and adolescents fight,' was how she put it. 'It's just that you've chosen to pick your fights in this . . . unreasonable way. But I suppose I should have expected it. I had every evidence . . .'

'Of what?' I leapt in. 'What evidence?' I thought perhaps it had something to do with my father, his temperament, his tendency to fight – I would have given much for any hint of a father.

'I mean everyone knows that daughters want to distance themselves from their mothers at a certain age. Though I'd have thought you might have avoided such a silly impulse.'

'Why?' I said. 'Why?'

'I mean, it isn't as if I haven't given you everything you've wanted . . .'

I suppose that was a kind of standard, motherly thing to say. But I wasn't convinced. This wasn't about the normal difficulties of motherhood and adolescent rebellion. There was something wrong with her phrasing. There was something wrong with the way I was torn if I wasn't mingled with her, and the way our doubling was beginning to make me feel. Now, when I raised my hand to my hair in a movement identical to hers, the gesture was no longer elevated to significance, but reduced to ghostly automatism. I was her pale imitation, I could only do what she could do, be what she could be . . . I felt the Weirdness returning, as each day we went through the paces of our mirroring minuet. And still there was nothing else, nothing to add to the two of us. The dense matter behind my mind threatened to suck me into its bitumen vacuum when I met the silent blankness where my father should have been. No, this was not about adolescent development, but about beginnings. There was something wrong at the origin, at the very root.

I was seventeen. I had to know. But this was the one

thing, apparently, which I couldn't know through her, with her. There was something that divided us, some place where she was inaccessible to me, where our unspoken pact and premise of unity was broken. I couldn't penetrate her on this subject, she refused me entry. This was not only painful in the extreme, it baffled belief. How was it possible for my mother to withhold something from me, she who was intertwined with me in the very fibre of her – of our – being? How could it be that she had within her thoughts, desires, tactics from which I was excluded? Still, it seemed she did. She had secrets. Secrets which were the key to my secret. But she hid them within her and I couldn't prise them out of her by my – our – usual methods. I was going to have to find them out myself. In the following few months I turned into a domestic, an internal spy. I ransacked the drawers of her desk when she went to buy groceries; it was easy to force them open once I had decided to. I found files of financial documents, records of intricate transactions, bank statements which showed me that we were very well off. I combed through the basement and the attic, all in brief, furtive panicked forays, when she went out to do her errands. It made me feel dirty and it didn't yield much; but I kept on going. It became a kind of compulsion – my secret life revenging itself on hers.

Then, finally, there was pay-off: an old, metal filing cabinet at the back of the unused basement space. This was the treasure chest. The upper drawer contained neatly tied, dark green folders, which I perused quickly, hungrily, dirtily. One was clearly the boyfriend file. It was filled with old e-mail printouts from boys or men who were flirting with her, or who were already her lovers. I read them closely, not so much for content as for tone. I tried to discern whether any of them sounded like letters from a potentially serious partner, a potential husband, a potential father of her child. But there seemed to be nothing like that. The communications were variously insouciant, clumsy, risqué, challenging; none of them struck the deeper, calmer note.

Behind the boyfriend folder there was another one, containing letters quaintly handwritten, on stationery with patterned borders or with bunches of flowers in the corner. These were dated mostly from the 1980s and they were signed 'Mom' or 'Mom and Dad'. My mother's parents. I felt faint and nauseous when I realized what I was holding in my hand. These were her parents – therefore they had to be my grandparents. It made sense, didn't it? But even if it did, it was utterly implausible. I had grandparents who might still be alive. But in that case – who was I? A girl with grandparents? And who, who on earth was my mother, this daughter of parents who wrote letters by hand and whom she never, never mentioned? This was a revolution and it dimmed my eyes and made my chest heave. It was a while before I could focus on the letters themselves.

'Dear Elizabeth,' went the first one I picked up, 'I know we've just hardly left you, and here I am writing to you, probably before you've had time to settle in. The truth is that I'm indulging myself, by which I mean that I'm writing to you because I miss you terribly. I know this is probably an excessive and inappropriate reaction – after all, we're supposed to be happy when our children embark on their own lives, and of course I am happy, really happy for you. And proud too. It's quite something for me to think of you as a freshwoman at Princeton, the former bastion of male privilege . . . But then, thank heavens, there are fewer and fewer bastions left, and I thrill to think what opportunities are open to you, what vistas and options. It really is better to be a young woman now than when I was growing up, crimped in girdles, and worrying about whether to go to "first base" or not. But maybe I shouldn't be telling you such things, I guess they're always embarrassing when they have to do with your own mother, liberated young woman though you are. I guess I'm indulging myself in every way. But I feel we're friends, Elizabeth, real friends. And I do miss our conversations and just having you around. Well, I won't go on, in case you think I'm playing the *femme pathétique*. I know how you hate that. And right you are to dislike it, too; it's a terrible feminine tendency, this *femme pathétique* stuff. Anyway, it's not all that long till semester break, is it? When you come home. But you

64

must write in the meantime. No, let me rephrase that: I wish you'd write. How is that for being a well-behaved mom?

'Nothing much to report from here. Dad is working on an industrial espionage case whose ins and outs I can't follow, although he's all het up about it, and I'm trying to write a snappy ad for a new soft drink, and feeling a bit ashamed of myself for giving in to the worst of American commercialism. Though the drink is harmless enough, I guess. At least, so I try to console myself. Well, I'd better go and try to cope with the empty-nest syndrome. It might turn out to be a full-time job. (Joke.) Take care of yourself, and enjoy yourself too. Lots of love, Mom (Dad sends his love too).'

I was close to tears when I finished. This was so . . . nice. So warm and funny-tender and full of ordinary feeling. Family feeling. I'd never come across anything like it and I was confounded and moved and upset. Who, where, were these people, these grandparents who cared about their daughter like that, the grandma who wrote these letters, so touching, so vulnerable, so – so *handwritten*?

The folder contained lots more letters and now I ran down to the basement whenever she was out of the house and read them, rocking back and forth and feeling sorry for myself. They were chronologically arranged and they traced my mother's trajectory through college and business school. My mother did very well in both, of course, and her parents were as proud and excited as if nobody had done well in college or had been brilliant before. The letters detailed visits back and forth, my mother's friendships with interesting people (just about everyone she met seemed to be fascinating or important or a genius of some kind), her first fast steps on the career ladder. For a while a friend of my mother's named 'Stan' figured prominently in the letters, and I pored over every sentence that had his name in it. But then he disappeared, without any explanation, and much too early for me. For my advent in my mother's life.

But as my trips to the basement continued and the narrative of the letters unfolded, the tone of these parental communications began subtly, slowly, to change. My grandparents – I had to keep reminding myself that this was who they were – began to disapprove of certain things their daughter did, though they never said so overtly. They clearly weren't crazy about some of her boyfriends. ('He seems like a nice enough young man, though I must say nose-rings aren't my favourite kind of accessory. There's something that bothers me about them. I mean, I can't imagine . . . well, I can't imagine kissing somebody with a nose-ring, to be perfectly frank. But maybe I don't have very much imagination. Or maybe it isn't my business to imagine. And then, not to be too nosy (!), what does the choice of this accessory say about him? I know these things are supposed to carry messages, but I can't read the symbolism. Or is the symbolism to shock old fuddy-duddies like me?

Though it seems like a lot of trouble to go to, just to annoy the older generation. Maybe there is another purpose to it that I can't discern. I wish you would explain, though you seem to be less willing to do so all the time. And I hoped the generation gap would never come between us. Anyway, enough about the nose-ring. But, if you must know, I also worry about the fact that this young man of yours is a drop-out and doesn't have any plans for the future, etc. How's that for being old-fashioned? Anyhow, I know you're not about to marry him, and this is not intended as interference – I know how much you don't like me interfering. But I hope we're still friends and can be candid with each other and I thought I'd bring these things up in case you wanted to talk about them – you know, to leave the door open to disclosure.')

As the correspondence progressed, it was clear that the daughter – my mother – saw her parents less and less and that they were very unhappy about it. ('I don't meant to guilt-trip you, you know I don't like to do that – my mother did it to me, and it didn't help – but still, still, Elizabeth. Is a visit once a month too much to expect, when you live only a short distance away? I appreciate that you're busy. I appreciate that your career is glamorous and important. I appreciate that you need your fix of fun and social life. I'm not so old as to have forgotten my own youth entirely. But we don't want to lose touch. We want to continue to know you. Dad would never say it, but he gets upset when you don't visit for a year at a stretch. He feels rejected. He feels hurt. Does it matter to you? I hope it does. You know how he is, such a softie, really.')

In the meantime, there was news of their own friends, second divorces, third marriages, professional awards, horrible unidentified illnesses and one case of attempted murder, by a woman they knew, of her own husband. ('Can you believe that Maureen would have been capable of such a thing? Submissive Maureen?' my grandmother wrote to my mother. 'But perhaps we shouldn't be all that astonished. It's often the quiet types, as they say on TV. Perhaps we shouldn't be astonished at anything any more. I don't want to go on about basic values, but people are becoming so . . . well, not how they used to be.')

Gradually, something else entered into the letters, a chillier reserve. My mother started working at a high-powered investment firm specializing in non-friendly takeovers and she was involved with some jet-setting software mogul. She was hardly seeing her parents any more. From an angry letter, it appeared that she didn't show up at her sister's wedding. ('I frankly don't understand the nature of your decision,' my grandmother wrote. 'I can't follow what's happening to you any more. Are you perhaps jealous of Janey? If so, I think that's frankly very unkind of you. After all, you always got what you wanted and there's been no shortage of men in your life. But I worry that the problem is even worse, that you're forgetting how to love your family. Or is it to love anyone at all? I would be deeply unhappy to think that this were true, and yet, I worry about you, Elizabeth. I worry about you in fundamental ways. Anyhow, the plain fact is that you've hurt Janey a lot. Hurt us all. And that counts. That still counts.')

After that the letters slowed down to a trickle – two, three a year – and then stopped. I couldn't figure out what transpired exactly, whether there had been a final breach or only a growing disappointment and a gradual cooling off; but as the letters fizzled out my resentment rose. It was her fault, my mother's. That much was clear. She had managed to alienate these lovely people and to deprive me of them – just as she had deprived me of Steven. Maybe – but I stifled the thought before it could rise to consciousness – she was a horrible person. Whoever she was – for, all of a sudden, she had become utterly unfamiliar – I felt cheated, betrayed, robbed. I wanted more letters, more story, more prehistory. I wanted a past, my very own family past. I wanted to know my grandparents.

But until I got to the bottom of this, until I knew more, I had to keep the search for my secret secret. I had to keep my discoveries inside, deeply wrapped and hidden, because otherwise she would sense that something between us had altered. It made me feel both powerful and foul, as if I were making my way heroically through a slimy bog.

★   ★   ★

It was only after I finished the grandparent file that I moved on to the lower drawer of the filing cabinet. I had to be disciplined about this underground activity; it was explosive enough. The lower drawer contained memorabilia, mostly from my mother's school and college years. Innocent objects – ribbons for winning hundred-metre races, a dried orchid, report cards neatly arranged from grades one through twelve. I glanced at them quickly and ascertained what I already knew: my mother had been good at exactly the same subjects as I, weaker where I was weak. There was, startlingly, a condom, which I recognized from Sex Education, and a small metal ring. At the back of the drawer there was a photo album and, as I pulled it out, I realized I had seen it before – that this was the album she had once snapped shut when I was a child and came upon her unexpectedly. I opened it – then shut it quickly. This time it was I who was almost too nervous to look. But I had to. I opened it again. And there was the photographic record of my mother's childhood and growth. Elizabeth, in tiny bell-bottom trousers, stroking a kitten in a suburban garden; Elizabeth and her sister, in the cutest little blue dresses, at some children's party; Elizabeth at about twelve, in a skimpy shirt and top, her breasts just beginning to bud, holding a boy's hand not very shyly; Elizabeth in a satiny long gown, holding a diploma in her hand, apparently at her high-school graduation. Etc., etc. Perfectly standard, not very imaginative photos. Except

70

for one thing: the child, the girl, the sensuous adolescent in those snaps was me. Not like me, not resembling me. The styles of dress were different and the backgrounds were not ones I recognized. And yet there was no doubt. I was looking at myself and I was queasy with a confusion that bordered on terror. I was her, I was her, I was her . . . Then who was I, who was she, what had she done? Did she steal my soul, my very self, or did she give me her own, by an unspeakable act of black magic? Was I a spectre, a creature of her fantasy, or was I the dreamer, inventing both myself and her? My mind kept reeling till I almost blacked out. Then I dragged myself upstairs to wait for her return.

She knew something had happened this time. 'What?' she asked. 'What is it?' My look must have conveyed something new, some depth of dread and determination, for she didn't even try to fob me off with some enticement, or divert me by asking about my homework.

'I see,' she said instead. 'Do you think you could at least give me a clue?'

'You don't give me any clues,' I said sullenly. 'Not about anything that counts.'

She sized me up sharply. 'Is that what this is about?' she asked. 'The same old problem? Or is there something else?'

'No,' I said. 'There's nothing else. I want to know about my father.'

She got up and looked at me from above. 'You know what our agreement is,' she said.

'Why do you think I'm going to change my mind?'

'Because you must!' I cried. 'Because I can't stand it any more! You have no right to keep this from me – I bet you don't even have a legal right!'

'Ah,' she said coldly. 'I don't think you should bring legal rights into this. I know a bit more about them than you do, I'm afraid.'

I tried another tack. 'Why won't you tell me?' I pleaded. 'At least tell me that much, the reason why you can't tell me.'

'Because I don't think you're ready for it,' she said. 'Because I think you wouldn't understand. Because I made a decision and I'm going to stick to it. I'm going to tell you when I am ready.'

I studied her face. She didn't seem to be lying. Did she perhaps not know herself?

'It's being in the dark I can't bear,' I said. 'I can take almost anything else, I promise you. I don't care if I'm illegitimate . . .'

She was shaking her head with exasperation. 'Please,' she said, 'don't probe. You're not illegitimate, I can tell you that much. But you're not going to get anything out of me by this prodding and prying.'

'This is cruel!' I shouted. 'This secret isn't only yours – it's mine too!'

She looked thoughtful. 'Yes,' she said. 'I can see how you might feel that. But it isn't like that. In a way, it's none of your business. Nobody has any choice about . . . about who their parents are.' Her voice was becoming icy.

'I know I have no choice, but I have to have knowledge,' I said. 'How can I go on living without knowing where I came from – who I am? How am I supposed to know who I'm supposed to be in the world?'

'You've lived quite happily without knowing till now,' she said, reasonably enough. 'Can't you wait just a little longer?'

'No,' I said stubbornly. 'I can't.' I looked at her directly and she held my gaze, till the harshness in our eyes began to flow between us and intermingle until it was a shared harshness. My anger at her was anger at myself; her refusal of me a refusal of herself. Her reflecting face held mine and looked miserable. We were a joined creature and this pain was its awful logic.

And yet, in the next few days, I felt horribly alone. As did she. The aloneness enveloped us in a vaporous heaviness, a shared weather. I escaped only when I slept – I think. The next time she had to go out I went straight to the basement. I did not expect to find anything else of great interest, but at the very back of the lower drawer there was a stiff grey folder which held some basic documents: passports, vaccination records, my mother's employment contracts. There was also, in a transparent plastic covering, her birth certificate; behind it, there was another one like it, which I knew would be mine. I turned it face down, and took a deep breath. I was about to learn the secret of my birth, the name for my strangeness, for that no-name space beyond the line and outline of my familiar self.

I turned the certificate over. It said:

Iris Surrey, born at St Clare's Hospital, Manhattan, on September 30, 2005.

Weight: Seven and a half pounds.

Condition: Excellent.

Colour of Eyes: Blue

Distinguishing Marks: None.

Mother's Name: Elizabeth Surrey.

Father's Name: None.

Method of Birth: Cloning.

Laboratory: Rosen, McPherson & Park.

It was about an hour, I think, before I walked upstairs and into an altered universe. During that interval I sat in the basement, in a stupor that was nearly cataleptic. In an instant my suspicions were replaced by the Knowledge and the Knowledge was too terrible for thought. So I didn't do anything as coherent as think during that stunned hour, when I crouched there without changing position, my birth certificate grasped in my immobile hand. But I was permeated by a nearly unspeakable recognition: I was a replica, an artificial mechanism, a manufactured thing. I was unnatural. My sense of myself as a young girl with her very own, unique self – an illusion. My feelings, my precious feelings – an illusion. A sleight of hand. I was nothing more than a Xerox of her cellular matter, an offprint of her genetic code. A microchip off the old motherboard. That was what my half-knowledge had been about, the Weirdness beyond the line of my familiar being, the It in the deep cavity of my mind. Now I knew and the knowledge nullified me. I was not Iris. I was not anyone.

Still, I staggered back to my room after an hour or so. What else could I do? I was a thing, but a living one. The illusion somehow persisted. Gradually, I came out of my stupor and dragged myself upstairs. I looked around my still childish room – the robodolls decoratively arranged on various shelves, the stuffed animals plumped up against my pillow, the gently moving images of my favourite weave'n'wave group shimmering on the wall – and I experienced something like vertigo, a reeling of vision. The meaning of everything in the room was suddenly transformed, as if by the wave of an evil magic wand. I had gathered these things as symbols of my safety, of my passing childhood, in this cosy, snug nest. Every object had its silly, trivial, warm associations. But there was no safety. The cosy nest had been inhabited by a shadow, a sham. The objects were a farce. The room buzzed with anxiety, with molecular movement, with merely material existence. It might as well have been a place in outer space.

Still, I threw myself on the bed, face down. What else was I to do? I knew no other movements, no other gestures. I couldn't turn into a pillar of salt or a monument of stone just like that. Unless I died or went mad right there, my consciousness – oh, so cruelly – continued to feel itself as . . . mine.

But it suddenly felt itself as utterly, fantastically, galactically alone. No greater degree of aloneness was possible than that which came to me with the revelation that I was my mother's exact double.

76

The person who was my closest kindred, to whom I most wanted to turn to in this cruel dilemma, was the source of the horror I'd turned into. She was – this was my awful realization – the true face of the Weirdness. If I looked at her with my new knowledge – but how could I, how could self collide with itself without an implosion, a splitting of the molecules, a nuclear fusion and fission?

I threw myself on the bed and couldn't cry. A handmade creature has no right to tears, unless it's turned on by a switch. Cranked up with a handle. Then it can shed them like those automata of old, one by one, big, round and nauseatingly moving. Hideously, meretriciously affecting tears of an automaton crying for its own non-human condition . . .

I couldn't cry like that. Besides, no one could help me in my new state, and you cry only if there's hope of help. Instead, as I came to, as the sheer shock of my discovery wore off, I tried to grasp what had happened in its upheaval, its overturning earthquake. I tried to sense who this new person was who was inhabiting my replicant body. I couldn't. I had suddenly become an alien to myself, a creature so strange I hardly dared to think what it was. I could only sense some horrifying paradox, like a fault line, or a seam of acute pain running straight through my being.

I heard the turning of a key in the door. The paradox bit more deeply into my flesh. I didn't know how I was going to face her, face my other, uncanny visage.

'Iris?' she called. I didn't answer. I could sense her standing still in the hallway, listening to the atmosphere of the house. I could hear an intake of breath, as she paused in perplexity or anxiety, could hear her walking up to my room slowly, evenly. I didn't turn when she came in. 'Iris?' she said, the anxiety in her voice rising. 'What is it, for God's sake? What has happened?' She came over to the bed and turned me over. I stood up because I couldn't stand her hovering over me, from above. There we were, looking directly at each other. The paradox tightened like a pincer. Her symmetrical face, with its large blue eyes and full curved lips, was suddenly terrifying, alien with unacceptable familiarity. I turned away in repulsion, in cold fear.

'You found out, didn't you?' she said. As usual, not many words were needed between us. I said nothing at all.

'How?' she asked grimly. 'Who told you?'

I wielded the birth certificate in her face.

She ascertained what it was and her mouth set itself into a straighter line. 'You went through my private things,' she said. 'You spied.'

'It's no use,' I brought out. It was difficult to speak. 'You are . . . you're the one who's done something terrible.'

'This doesn't change anything,' she said quickly. She tried to take the birth certificate from my hand, but I pulled it away angrily. 'I was going to tell you sometime . . .' She stopped, to take in my state. She must have thought about this scene before. The discovery scene. But undoubtedly she had imagined it differently. This was happening too soon and outside her control.

'It changes everything,' I said dully.

'No,' she said, infusing her voice with authority. 'It changes nothing. You're still my daughter. I'm still your mother.'

'My twin,' I said, and I was shocked to hear the word come out. 'That's what you are. My fucking identical twin.' I wanted to hide from what I was saying; but there was nowhere to hide.

Now she looked frantic, scared. 'Iris,' she said, almost pleadingly, 'you're my child, whom I love. My daughter, my little one. Get this meaningless piece of paper out of your mind. Forget you ever saw it.'

I was almost undone by that 'child', heart-torn, sick with longing for my mother, craving her comfort even as I loathed her, as I wanted to negate her. And yet nothing could be negated or reversed, the Knowledge couldn't be undone. I looked at her and the vertigo returned. My mother, my twin, my mother, my matter, *materia materna*, from which I was made. My mother, my self. My mother, my monstrousness.

'How could you?' I whispered. 'How could you create yourself all over again? How could you just . . . make something that's another you?'

She put her hands on my shoulders and shook me, the way she did sometimes when I was small, and when I lost myself in some depthless, dimensionless reverie. 'Stop this right now,' she ordered. 'Calm down!'

But this was not about reverie. This was about a new, awful wakefulness. I had emerged from my trance, my intimations and suspicions, into the darkness of this full knowledge, and no matter how much I wanted to return, revert to my entranced state, I couldn't.

'I feel like some . . . alien,' I said, to myself as much as to her. I was still trying to fathom, to define, my new condition. 'A cyborg.'

'I wish you'd stop this,' she said urgently. 'You're saying silly things. You haven't changed, you're still my daughter, my daughter, my daughter! You're Iris, the same Iris as always. Would you undo that? Do you regret being brought into the world?'

I was caught, caught in the vice. For of course, I couldn't want not to be. I couldn't cancel the fact that I was, couldn't unwind time back into the time of my non-being. Except that as I looked at her, I knew that in me, in my body, time repeated itself in some ghastly glitch, a hiccup, a mechanical snag. I looked at her face, which was going to become mine, and I knew that I had already been. There was no necessity, no need or reason for me to be all over again. I was a superfluity, a technical non-being.

'It doesn't matter what I want, does it?' I said. 'How can a copy have desires of its own? A clone.'

She looked frantic, then composed herself. 'That's just a word,' she said and tried to take my hands in hers. I stepped back angrily.

'Why did you do this?' I hurled at her. 'Who are you, anyway?' For now I realized that I didn't know this either.

Her mouth set itself into stubbornness. 'I'll try to explain sometime,' she said, 'but not when you're in this mood.' She looked at me and relented. 'I wanted a child,' she said, 'and I couldn't have one . . . naturally. That's all. But anyway, it's not important why. You're here, with me. My Iris. That's what counts. And I'm not going to let you go.'

I peered into her and was sucked into her eyes, and saw something from within them, saw her desire for my birth, for another her/me . . . Did that mean I'd given birth to myself? But the thought was unsustainable. I was being sucked back into our oneness, the amniotic fluid. The paradox dissolved into eddying, swirling confusion. 'Help,' I whispered, not knowing suddenly where I was, from which point, which one of us my voice originated. From which point I originated. 'Help me, please.'

She put her arms around me, and I clung to her, as I did when I was little; but this time, I felt, yet again, the dizzying contradiction. I pulled back.

81

'Nothing, nothing is ever going to be the same,' I said helplessly.

'That's enough,' she said sternly and pushed my hair back from my face in a half-tender, half-disapproving gesture. 'We'll talk about it some more in the morning. After you've had some sleep.'

I thought there'd be no sleep, but that night I slept. I sleep. I dream. What does that prove? What does it even show?

My dreams that night were of division and subdivision, of doubling and splintering. There was She. Her face, her large body, standing majestically on a podium, or maybe an altar. She was holding two identical dolls in her hands, letting them dangle carelessly, till they fell and cracked. Each of the dolls opened and split into more dolls, till there were two rows of them, identical dolls facing each other with sightless eyes, perfect in their plastic pallor. She. Her face, her body. She cracked, as if split by lightning, and suddenly there were two of her facing each other. Her and me, me and her. Her face was marble-smooth, flawless, with the eyes blank, as in ancient sculptures. She was a perfect sculpture, with the deathliness, the deadliness of perfection. She picked up one of the dolls and dandled it maternally, and then put it up to her mouth, as if to swallow it . . . But this was too horrible even to dream.

I woke up screaming. She was there, sitting on my bed, her hands on my shoulders.

'You were having a nightmare,' she said. I felt enormous relief, the sense of rescue I'd always experienced when she came to retrieve me from my bad dreams. Then I remembered and turned my head away, trying to bury my consciousness in the pillow, trying to regain my unconsciousness, even if it meant a return to those terrifying images. At least they were only images, while her presence had all the solidity of a nightmare that could not be dispelled.

'What were you dreaming about?' she asked.

I shook my head wordlessly. She looked displeased. I'd always told her my dreams readily, as if recounting small tales from faraway lands.

'Try to go back to sleep then, she said, 'and try not to have any more bad dreams.'

'It's always a shock when we discover we're the product of nothing more than human matter,' the Adviser said. 'You're not so exceptional in this respect. We all feel chagrined when we first realize we're of man and woman born. So to speak.'

So to speak. Exactly. For I was not born like that. I was fabricated, manufactured, produced in a lab somewhere, by men or women in white coats. I made the point yet again, bitterly.

'Well, of course, we'd all prefer more divine origins,' the Adviser fudged neatly. 'We'd all like to come into the world trailing clouds of glory, wouldn't we. Maybe that's the origin of religion, in fact. No so much the desire for an afterlife, as for a pre-life which would confer on us some sublime, or at least magical, significance.'

He looked pleased with himself, as if this were a nice little new thought. Well, at least I stimulated new thoughts; I forced them on people.

'So our first response to the discovery that we come from our parents,' he continued, 'is to want to attack them. Not only, perhaps, because we want to possess our father or mother, but to revenge ourselves for the insult. To destroy the evidence of the mundane, petty, fleshly means by which we came into the world. No child likes to discover what really went on between its parents to result in its birth.' He smiled again, with considerable satisfaction. He was having a good day.

I shouldn't be mean about him. He tried his best to help me and he tried hard to assimilate me into his world, to make me feel that I wasn't so different from everyone else. From the Others. Still, he kept slipping into the old vocabulary. The old concepts. Our parents. Fleshly means. How could he help it? These were the fundamental laws, the elementary table of the human condition. But I'd just discovered I was the violation of the laws, the most basic givens. I was born of my mother, who was my identical twin . . . What words have we for that? No, I was beyond the pale, beyond the borders of known vocabulary. The only proof that I could exist was that I did exist. It's the proof we have of all aberrations. It seemed hardly enough.

And yet he was right too, my Adviser: the desire

to destroy – to destroy something – had sprung almost as soon as I saw my birth certificate. All through the next day I felt rage rising. I couldn't look at her and she didn't force me to. I guess she was biding her time. But there was no time, I didn't give it to her. That afternoon there was a phone call from a girl I knew at school. My mother picked up the phone, and even as she was exchanging some pleasantries, I saw a look of dour determination enter her eyes.

'No, I'm so sorry,' she said, 'Iris is not feeling well today. No, I'm sorry, she can't come to the phone, she's asleep.'

She looked at me soberly, warningly. I didn't protest.

But as I realized what she was doing, what she was planning, I knew with a certainty that I had to escape as soon as I found my chance. To leave the home which had all of a sudden become a special kind of hell.

I sneaked out a few days later, in the small hours of the night when I knew she'd be most deeply asleep. I behaved as well as I could during the preceding days, so as to mollify her, throw her off the track. We talked little and circled round each other uneasily. I practised holding my thoughts in, keeping them out of her purview, out of her sight. That night I packed a few things into my lightest aerobag, and made sure I had my special trust fund cheques. Then I walked out of the house in which I'd grown up and into the grey, misty dawn. I think I was surprised that the world hadn't completely disappeared as a result of my discovery, that the streets of our suburban neighbourhood hadn't melted or contorted themselves into some volcanic shapes. But they hadn't, they were as straight and gridded as ever, as if nothing bad had ever happened in the world. I walked through our neighbourhood and into what passed in our town for a centre accompanied only by the occasional barking of an early-waking dog. There was a lone cab at the taxi stand and I asked the driver to take me to O'Hare Airport. I wasn't sure what I was going to do once I got there; but the ride was long and, by the time we arrived, a thought had crystallized: I was going to find my grandparents. That was the purpose of my escape, my necessary mission. I was going to reclaim my lost grandparents who – I realized this in a sudden, jolting flash – were also my parents. For if my mother was my twin, if my flesh was identical with her flesh, then my real origins lay with them – the ones who had created the really new life, had given real birth. Of man and woman born . . . Maybe this was true even of me. Maybe there was some hope in travelling back in time to rediscover my human, my natural origins . . . Tumbling back to my true parents, so that I could be sure, once and for all.

At O'Hare I studied the big schedule board and picked out the next flight to New York. At this time of night there were plenty of seats left. And so I sat stiffly next to a window, trying not to sink into sleep and the nightmares which awaited me. I'd left on an impulse so incontrovertible that it amounted to necessity; and I'd discovered the purpose of a quest so necessary that it could not be gainsaid. But in the meantime, I was on my own as I hadn't ever been before, severed from Her as I'd never imagined being severed. Severed, and yet connected as I could no longer bear to be connected. She'd be awake by now, sensing my absence, my entirely unimaginable absence. I imagined – no, I saw – her pacing up and down the living room, looking out of the window, peering into the darkness. She looked angry and pale. I saw her pick up the telephone and hesitate, and then, humiliation written on her face, dial a number. My school? The police? I looked into the plane's window, and saw a vague, blurred outline of her face. I wanted to cry, to scream, and saw my features contort themselves as hers did in my mind. I felt, as the plane cut its way through the upper atmosphere, that the bond, the cord along which nourishment passed between us, the substance which allowed us to live, was stretching and thinning till I nearly doubled up from pain. I seemed to have very little breath; the deep air depended on her. How could I have done what I was doing? But, somehow, it had to be done.

The flight took care of a part of it. It took me to New York, a passive cargo, and deposited me at Kennedy Airport. The air outside was so muggy it seemed to be made of dirty broth. I got into a taxi and realized I didn't know where I wanted to go.

'Where to?' the driver asked.

'A hotel,' I said.

He looked at me suspiciously. 'Whaddaya mean, a hotel? You know where you're going?'

'The Sheraton, that's where,' I said quickly. There had to be a Sheraton somewhere.

'The one on Seventh Avenue?'

'Yeah, that's the one,' I said, relieved.

Plato's Caves hadn't taken us as far as the airport, but I started recognizing things as soon as we got into Manhattan. The sweep of the East River as we descended down East Side Highway, the canyon effects as we went down 57th, the boxy buildings on Sixth Avenue; I'd been there before and I wasn't sure which kind of being there was more satisfying. The virtuals gave the city to you head-on and well-framed; this way, urban scapes veered past at odd angles, as the taxi lurched stupidly and came to a grinding halt in front of red lights. The driver never said another word. I guess he was concentrating on his driving, though the nonchalance with which he performed his manoeuvres didn't serve to reassure.

The lobby of the Sheraton was packed tight with a group of South American tourists, dressed in brightly coloured tracksuits and tinkling jewellery. They were pressing forward in a relentless mass, shouting to each other across the lobby and breaking out in bursts of riotous laughter. I

88

squeezed in at the back and kept jostling against soft or hard-edged bodies as they surged towards the reception desk. The clerk – he had a large safety pin stuck through his ear – looked vaguely surprised when I got there. Blonde girl, and so young too.

'You with them?' he asked, none too graciously.

'No,' I said. 'I'm on my own.'

'You old enough to be here?'

I nodded and he enquired no further. He proceeded to find me a room and said I'd find my luggage at the chute outlet. Live bellboy twenty dollars extra. I said I could carry my own luggage, I didn't have much. He looked at me rudely and handed me the key.

My room was on the twenty-seventh floor. It was square and beige, with shabby light-effects meandering depressingly across the ceiling; but it looked out on a glittering cityscape. Now that I was standing still, the view from the window was even more impressive than the virtuals, and more majestically static; it didn't zoom between remote and close up. I surveyed the panorama of spires and towers, the procession of glass and stone slabs standing in their ranks like giant guardians of a mystery religion. I tried to pretend to be excited, the way a young girl should be when she's in the Big City for the first time on her own. But how well can you pretend to yourself? If you try too hard, you turn as gimcrack as a badly made marionette. As I stared, the scene outside the window turned into an unconvincing stage set

– a cheap simulacrum of a city I'd seen dozens of times before. I turned back into the room and stood there, not knowing how to move, what to do. My body felt like a large, heavy object I had to carry around with me; its movements were the weighted, burdensome movements of a beast being dragged around against its will. Inadvertently, I caught sight of my face in a mirror and was fixed by its strangeness. It was mine and yet not mine at all. As I peered into the familiar, the remote image, Her face emerged within mine and I saw her, pacing up and down the living room, waiting for the police to report back to her; waiting for some information to come through. Pretty soon she'd know I bought an airline ticket to New York. Pretty soon she'd try tracing my payments and purchases. But she wouldn't be able to do it, I was pretty sure. She had set up the trust fund in my name as a locked tax shelter; I was the only one who had access to it. Of course, she'd never thought this would be a problem . . . Was it possible that she could outwit even herself? But anyway, for a while, she'd have a hard time finding me – if I didn't want to be found.

I didn't. And yet her twin face hovered over me when I lay down on the bed, looking at me sombrely, sternly, sadly. When I finally fell asleep, my dreams were of reflections and watery mirrorings. I was in a graceful sailboat, its shape doubled in the water, elongated and shimmery, gliding effortlessly forwards. The inverted mast beckoned me under and I started to climb down, following its curve. But it was only an image, glimmering and insubstantial, and it slipped out of my hands. I began to run out of breath, to suffocate, and tried to make my way back up through the water, to put my hands round the pole, but it was only shadow, a liquid nothing; and I thrashed desperately underwater, trying to catch hold of something solid, and realized I was holding on to flickering light. There was a sound of a boat siren, grave and gritty, and it pulled me out of sleep, and into the wail of a receding police siren and the buzzing, loud and insistent, in my own head.

For a few moments after waking up, I submitted to the pull of the dream images, their beckoning, dangerous beauty. Then I remembered where I was and why. Remembered, and felt the kind of shock that people who'd been badly maimed probably used to feel before every part of the body could be fixed and replaced. I'd read about it somewhere, the phenomenon of phantom pain, and how its sufferers could forget what had happened, what they'd lost, while they slept. During the night they were perfect and whole, dancing or speaking eloquently or slaloming on skis down a snowy slope; then came the rude awakening, the return to consciousness, the awareness that they could no longer move their limbs, or speak without slurring words, or that they no longer had an eye or a leg. I woke up to the shock of the Knowledge: except my condition could not be cured by the addition of anything at all. I would have to extract myself from myself, subtract from the human store what had been so carelessly added, in order to cure myself of this.

In my half-awake state, I felt waves of longing pulling me towards her siren image as towards deep-water rest, and then counter tides of repulsion and nausea, throwing me back to shore before I could reach her and drown. Then I sat up in my bed as if pushed by an impelling hand. There was something I had to do: I must start on my searches, my researches, right away.

All I knew of my family, 'my' family past, came from those grandmotherly missives penned on the cream-coloured stationery. The address on the letterhead – 1125 Park Avenue – was firmly registered in my memory. The letters were written about twenty-five years ago, of course, but a Park Avenue apartment isn't something one gives up easily. That much I knew. If they were alive, they might still be there; I decided my best bet was to follow the physical trail. After a soggy Sheraton breakfast, I set off for the address which, in the past months, had acquired such misty, such mystical resonances in my mind.

It was still early morning when I started walking uptown. There were not many people around and the pavement, after a night of rain, gave off a not unpleasant smell of water on dusty stone. I began to feel a kind of excitement after all – the excitement of walking for the first time through a place I knew so well. As in the countryside, there were elements of surprise in the actual. Or maybe just of actuality. The bumpiness of the sidewalks, the sweetish odours emanating from makeshift cafés, the screeching noise of metal shutters rolling up as the bodegas opened up for business, the calls of the synergetic juice vendors summoning people for a quick boost on their way to work. And then the gathering crowds, filling the streets as I approached 65th Street, slowing my progress till I finally ducked into a smelly subway entrance and took the uptown train. I emerged on Lexington and 86th and realized I was within a few blocks of the address. I walked towards it slowly. Now that I was this close, I felt a new apprehension. I had no idea what I'd say to my grandparents. I had no idea what they'd say to me.

I wanted to turn back; but I knew I mustn't. All too quickly, 1125 Park Avenue came into view. I contemplated the behemoth structure from across the street. It was just like the others lining the broad avenue, impenetrably monotonous and almost stupidly grandiose. Such an enormous expanse of thick stone and squarish symmetries, such opaque solidity. Or so it felt to me. Was that because I was on the outside, longing to be in? Longing for something warmer, less stony than myself? Almost humanly longing, almost humanly fearing . . . There was no postponing the moment

93

any longer. I crossed the street and walked into the marble-floored lobby.

'Yes ma'am?' the doorman said. 'How can I help you?'

I'd forgotten about this part, though I shouldn't have. The liveried doorman looked a spitting image of the ones I'd seen on Plato's Caves. He was short and sturdy, with a big paunch under his uniform. He barred my way, emitting a beep from his automatic metal detector.

'I . . . I'm looking for Mr and Mrs Surrey,' I blurted out. I think I was hoping he would say he'd never heard of them.

But instead he looked at me more carefully. 'The old ones?' he asked. 'Is that who you lookin' for?'

'Yes,' I said uncertainly. 'Yes.'

'You remind me of somthin'' he said, peering at me again. 'You a relative or somthin'?'

'Yes,' I said. 'A relative.'

'So how come you didn't know old Mr and Mrs Surrey gone?'

'I . . . I've been away a long time,' My stomach lurched, though I didn't know whether it was from disappointment or relief. Or just from hearing their names uttered so casually. My mythic grandparents. It confirmed their existence as actual people, and I didn't seem to be ready for that.

'When did they move?' I finally asked.

'Oh, about five years ago or so,' he said. 'Yeah, five years.' He looked at me appraisingly. 'But Miss Janey still here, she took the apartment after them.

94

She one lucky lady, if you ask me. Twenty-two B is a good apartment. But she not here now, she come back after work.'

It took me a minute to figure out who Miss Janey was. Of course! My aunt, the only relative I'd ever met. The Surreys' daughter, simply, from the doorman's point of view. A web of normality, of ordinary folk and regular relationships, was opening up like an abyss.

'Maybe I'll come back later then,' I said, trying to sound casual, and then added as if in afterthought, 'Do you happen to know where the Surreys moved to?'

He appraised me again. 'Florida,' he said. 'Somewhere in Florida.'

'I see,' I said. I hoped this would be enough information to go on. 'Well, thanks a lot, then.' I turned to leave.

'Who do I say called when Miss Janey ask me?' the doorman enquired. He was not entirely confident that he'd done the right thing.

'Her niece,' I began to say and then corrected myself quickly. 'Her sister. You can say it was her sister.' The doorman's pudgy face registered sheer disbelief; but before he could say anything, I turned and was walking quickly away.

I had some time before she'd find me. Or before she'd contact Janey, or them – her parents. For she'd figure out what my aim was, where my steps would inevitably take me next. The question was which one of us would be faster. Or more determined. Or more desperate.

I had desperation enough for two; I wouldn't be easily stopped. But for now it was good to lose myself in the crowds. And the crowds were everywhere, moving in a propellent, unceasing motion, surging on their own momentum. Massed groups of Chinese tourists, moving in tight blocks, sending the unmassed others to the edges, like shoals of fish deflected by a solid object. On Upper Madison, shoppers in mirrored emporiums made slow, entranced progress through racks of clothing, as virtual fashion models moved past them and above them. On Lower Madison there were mostly women, in their full working power: white, black, Japanese, petite, tall, dressed in exquisite swathes and shimmers of fabric. Apparently only the perfectly formed got to work on Lower Madison Avenue, but there were lots of those, there seemed to be a mass production of beautiful girls, as of everything, everyone else: almond-eyed, peachy-skinned, blonde, brunette, slinky, curvy, long-legged, bright-haired. They strode, glided, flashed, shone. I picked one out of the crowd and watched her for a while, a tall white girl in a long, semi-transparent tunic dotted with discreet points of light, with legs that went up and up, a pale face behind the bright make-up and a protective way of huddling her sleek briefcase to herself as she strode through the crowded street, and I wondered, I wondered how she spent her days, what she thought and what she felt, with that body that must have had its yearnings and that closed-off face. I wondered if she felt she mattered, if she thought she had her very own special destiny, her very own right to her unique, very own happiness . . . With my knowledge, I could have told her: bodies feel, it's in the wiring, it doesn't mean a thing. It doesn't mean you matter. It doesn't mean you *mean*. But maybe she knew that already, intuited it as she moved through the relentless crowds each day, among the careful eyes looking ahead, or inward, or away; just never looking at anyone else. She must have sensed me looking at her, and she shot me a quick, furtive glance, her eyes veiled, despondent, angry over the full red lips. She probably knew and didn't know. I could have told her, I could have told them all. Fellow replicants, I thought, I am your near future. I'm only one step ahead of you. But I walked on, I swam along with the others, like a fish in a school, never picking out any one face again, never focusing on any one thing.

Had She been one of them? This was her city and even as I kept moving, trying to elude her, I felt her presence in the surge of the crowds, the tempo of the streets, the broad avenues and the narrow canyons through which she'd guided me with such expertise. I kept eluding her and pursuing her at the same time; we were playing hide and seek. No, she wouldn't have been like most of the women I saw, she'd have been deposited at work by some shiny limo or swift taxicab, would have spent her days safely cocooned in an office on a high-numbered floor, from which only the glistening façades and gardened rooftops of other buildings were visible. No drone, no worker bee, she. But then she too got fed up and empty-eyed and felt she Had to Change Her Life. And then she had the Idea, and the Idea was me, an idea born out of a swift, shiny life and an emptying eye. Or so I thought then, so I thought in my unkindest moments, at my most desperate time.

I walked faster, trying to lose her pursuing presence, to shed the thought of her conceiving me. On 22nd Street, I stepped into an Internet café and downloaded the Palm Beach phone book. It was the obvious thing to do, but one could get lucky with the obvious as well as with the ingenious. But the list of Surreys in Palm Beach went on for ever, and I realized that I didn't know their first names; I only knew them from the signatures at the bottom of the letters, as Mom and Dad. I'd have to be more clever, or more persistent, after all.

The Sheraton lobby was swarming with Italians, in New York for their annual cheap shop. I started to go up to my room, and then decided I couldn't face it and went down to the bar instead. Isn't that what you do when you don't know what to do, when you're in New York, trying to escape and evade, when you're in a fix? I had nothing but clichés to help me through; I suppose I should have been grateful for those.

I went down to the bar and I got picked up. I think that's still the commonly used phrase, though the *Dictionary of Approved Expressions* prefers the word 'solicited', because it reclaims a word associated with prostitution from those who'd insult a traditionally feminine pursuit. I prefer picked up. It suggests what usually happens next, which is that you get dropped.

Which is, of course, what happened. But first somebody noticed me. Somebody picked me out of the crowd. Through the dense air of the tightly packed room I felt someone's attention being directed towards me; and, as if guided by some low searchlight, I turned and identified its source. The low but insistent beam was emitted by a dark-haired man leaning against the counter on the other side of the bar. At first I saw only focused eyes, which had in them something appreciative and teasing. I flicked up to his face and flicked away. But it was enough for him to make a small gesture of acknowledgement. He raised his glass slightly in a small salute. When someone got off the chair next to me, he came over and sat down quite calmly. His face was sharply etched and tanned under his shoulder-length hair.

'Hello,' he mouthed. 'Do you work around here?'

'No,' I mouthed back. 'I'm from elsewhere.'

'Aren't we all,' he said, bending towards me so I

could hear. His accent was Italian. 'Can I buy you a drink?'

This was genuinely novel, a perfect stranger treating me as if I were a regular young girl. Whatever that was, whatever that meant. Maybe if I took him up on whatever he had in mind, I'd find out.

'OK,' I said. 'A Bloody Mary,' I watched him as he made his way to the bar. He was chunkily handsome and dressed in a stylishly retro way, in a two-piece suit. His body was invisible in it, except for the way his movements registered in the flow and fall of his jacket. I'd never seen a real person dressed like that, but it was oddly sexy, as if he didn't need to make himself attractive, as if he had masculinity to spare.

'I'm Lodovico,' he shouted when he came back. I think.

'Iris,' I shouted back.

'You're American, yes?' he shouted. I confirmed.

'What're you doing here?' he shouted again.

'Shopping,' I shouted, hoping it was not too implausible for an American girl to come to New York for this purpose. He pulled his chair up towards me and leant forward. He emitted, aside from the low light, a kind of tanned heat.

'Are you shopping by yourself?' he asked. 'I mean, are you in New York on your own?'

I nodded, then started saying I was visiting my aunt, then muttered something indistinct. He looked puzzled, but persisted.

'And what do you most like to buy?' he enquired.

I was at a loss. 'Everything . . . all kinds of things,' I stumbled. 'Clothes. You know, fashion.'

He handed me the Bloody Mary and lightly brushed his hand against mine. I felt . . . Oh, my body felt stirred. Aroused.

'Do you want to come up to my room?' he said distinctly into my ear. 'It is not possible to talk in here.'

Just like that? Maybe he thought that a girl who shops is a girl who fucks. I wasn't either. But this was so unexpected as to be diverting. It distracted me from being with myself, from my impossible thoughts. Besides, I suppose I was growing curious, or my body was. So I nodded. I didn't know how I would manage this, but I followed him into the closely packed elevator and up to his room, where he opened his mini-bar and tried to make preparatory conversation.

'Where are you from, I mean, to be precise?' he asked, while he handed me a drink.

I stumbled again. 'The Midwest,' I said.

'You make it sound as if you're from outer space.' His green eyes were teasing. 'Are you? You look like you might come from one of those old movies about the alienates, or what is it, aliens, the ones who were beautiful and evil, rather than ugly and evil.'

I knew he was flirting and I should think of something clever to say, but couldn't come up with anything.

101

'You aren't used to this kind of *conversazione* are you?' he asked.

I felt myself blush. Blush! I had no idea where these reactions, these flurries of fast breath and uneven heartbeats were coming from. His words, or rather his presence, were stimulating a part of me that was out of my direct control, some reactions that might have felt almost spontaneous, if I hadn't known how conditioned, how predetermined they were. In Human Education, they would have come under Sexual Feelings, which were among the simplest and the most predictable of all. And I had had them before, in a dim and private kind of way, when I was in my room by myself – various swellings and itchings, and restless urges. We were told about these as well, of course, so I didn't mind; they only had to do with the body. And anyway, She had the power to stop them whenever she appeared, just by her mere presence. Maybe that was because she completed everything, created a loop that left no space for restlessness.

Still, I should have been prepared for this. I should have been, but this was different because here was an actual man speaking and moving in unpredictable ways, emanating a kind of physical glow or force from his compact body and olive-skinned face and, most of all, looking at me. Looking not quite seriously, but straight at me, as if he had the right to. As if he had the right to look at me directly, as only she had done until now. Not that his gaze was like hers – no, his look

102

was more jocular and came from further away. But still, it was brazen, and for some reason it seemed to stop me speaking clearly.

Then it occurred to me that I could ask him some questions and this turned out to be the right thing to do. He kept talking about himself, while keeping his eyes firmly, disconcertingly, on me. He was a law student from Bologna, he told me, with an interest in Extra-Terrestrial legislation, and a special love of mid-twentieth-century American design, which he collected in a modest way.

What did he like about mid-twentieth-century design, I wanted to know.

'Its combination of sturdiness and streamlined smoothness,' he answered, and then dropped the register of his voice. 'Like you, like your skin, your lovely face . . .' He ran his finger delicately down my cheek and chin. 'You're a classic,' he said. 'An absolutely American classic.'

Was I flattered? Was I capable of being flattered? Oh, I felt the blandishment of his gaze as he fell silent and ran his finger down my neck and breast. I felt mildly curious as he undressed me and contemplated the length of my body, whose curves I knew to be smooth and streamlined. As he raised himself above me and looked down from that slight distance, as though to take the measure of the whole before tackling it part by part. As his fresh, taut body, with its unfamiliar skin and muscled limbs, came close to mine. I was determined to go through with this. But were his glances, his appreciation, the arousal which made his lips fuller, meant for me – me? I knew my body was beautiful, knew it all the better because I knew the original of which it was the copy. I felt the softness of my breasts under his fingers, and the contours of my hips, and from within, It watched what a stranger was doing with a strange body. It watched, and yet, the body felt the currents of sex coursing through it, and for a moment, even It lost itself in the escalating pleasure. So this was what Sexual Feelings were about. This pleasure which was so . . . pleasurable.

I think he was utterly amazed at the drops of blood that appeared on the sheet when it was done.

'Why did you not tell me?' he asked, his dark eyes growing darker with annoyance.

'It's not a big deal,' I said and turned away. I tried to figure out whether what had just happened was some kind of initiation, whether I was somehow changed. I'd read about initiation rituals and how much the loss of virginity used to matter in olden times. Then I felt Her eyes looking from within mine, looking out at Lodovico meanly, accusingly. I'd allowed him to enter my body as if it were my own. He'd violated not the body but our pact, our sameness, the gaze which could only travel from her to me.

I turned away, but he took me by the shoulders and turned me back towards himself, and now I saw her blue gaze within his dark eyes, fixed on me silently, evenly, too coldly for reproach. I tried to turn away again, but he kept me pinned down.

'I don't know whether you are perhaps weird, or just American,' he said, peering into my face, 'but something has occurred to you, has it not?'

In the next few days, I criss-crossed Manhattan, up and down its unnervingly straight length and horizontally over its ever-narrowing girth, like one possessed. I wasn't looking for anything; I just walked. You have to keep moving or die.

'Separation anxiety,' the Adviser opined. 'It's clear that's what you were experiencing. You'd just left your mother for the first time. You must have missed her terribly, even as you were determined to get away. To defy her. Nothing unusual about that.'

But I didn't miss her, exactly. The Adviser was as usual using words sloppily, or using the only words he knew. I'd been riven from her. Riven, cloven, cut. She, from whom I took my existence, was Not There. But there was something else that was not there and for which I kept searching blindly, groping as if I were in a dark room, my hands extended to feel for obstacles, to sense the dimensions of the space in which I'd found myself. My mind sent out sensors as I thrust my way up and down the grid of the city, but that other space in which I was moving seemed to have no landmarks, no depth, no frame. I only knew I was moving through a world from which something was missing; a world which lacked.

I wandered through Squat Town at the top of the city, an infernal place we'd never seen on Plato's Caves, with steam rising up from the ground, and shacks made from torn cartons and bent aluminium, thrown up pell-mell in parking lots and school playgrounds, and in every bit of available space around the old, gloomy, sky-climbing tenements. It stretched for blocks, this shack city, with humans huddled among the pre-carious structures, cleaving to their inches of space and shouting across cramped pathways in a Babel of tongues. Thousands of dishevelled, pitiable figures, cooking, urinating, or just lolling about, waiting for something to happen. I wondered what it was they were waiting for, whether they hoped to make their way to better places, having come from ones that were presumably even worse. But where could they go? Where did they imagine they'd find their fate or their escape? There was no actual Elsewhere any more, we knew our cosy little globe too well.

I walked down to Manhattan's tip, through TriBeCa and Cult Town, where the most advanced cultural production took place. Also the most advanced aesthetic consumption. The shops were scented with exquisite perfumes; the mean-modernist office buildings were filled with com-panies advertising all manner of personal tech-nologies, from design pets to inner imagery. The

106

ancient warehouses were occupied by artistic work-shops specializing in every conceivable medium, from silversmithing to organic art. The latter seemed to be all the rage that season, and out of idle curiosity I walked into an organic work studio, into a space that seemed to seep into the physical world from eerie old legends or bad dreams. In a large room about a dozen people – the artists – sat in front of computer terminals in silent concentration. All around them, on tables, plinths, wires suspended from the ceiling, was an array of creatures that could have been called animals, except they were twitching, moving, morphing all the time, presumably under the stimulus of some invisible artistic manipulations. The guy closest to the door looked up when I came in and greeted me courteously. He was dressed in a black artist's tunic and his arms were running with lines of light, where the blood flowed through his veins.

'Hey, girl,' he said. 'What can I do for you?'

'I was just . . . curious, I suppose,' I said. 'I wanted to know what you do in here.'

'Well hey,' he said, 'the public has a right to know. What we do, basically, is mix organic stuff with computer materials and see what follows. It's nothing to be afraid of, so don't look so timid, like a big blonde mouse. Big blonde mouse,' he repeated to himself as if he'd stumbled on an idea. 'There might be something to that . . . You want to see?'

He took me round the room and showed me how the biomorphs, which started maybe as a whole animal, or as part of one, grew and meta-morphosed under the stimulus of implanted chips, into the most fantastic shapes and patterns, organs transforming themselves into abstractions, blood vessels and brain nerves multiplying in extravagant geometric progressions. There was fish matter morphing into fish-flower, its petalled mouth opening and closing to breathe in the air. There were animals sprouting extra limbs and heads, and on one largish cat the positions of head and tail were reversed. The cat was real, I could tell by its frayed fur and a pink scar on its underbelly. The artists never looked up from their terminals. Their faces were focused and blank as they guided and modified their designs.

'Isn't this kind of . . . sickening?' I asked.

'Hey,' my guide said, 'that's no way to talk about art. Anyway, what we're doing is actually very traditional. Technically, these things are called chimeras or grotesques, that is, cross-species composites. People have imagined them since antiquity, the only difference is that now we can make them in real life. Or sort of real, anyway. Our creatures are sort of real and sort of not. Sort of alive and sort of not. That's where the art is, in the ambiguity. You know? But it's really classical, our work. Newest-oldest, like all the best things. We also do it to order, by the way. You can design your very own biomorph, and we make it to your specifications. Would you like to try? It's not very expensive, we sort of believe in art for the people.'

I said no, thank you.

'Then would you maybe like to try one of our Mnemonic Aids? You make a tiny incision somewhere and put in this chip, and for several days you have somebody else's memories. Not anyone's in particular – it's things we invent ourselves, so they're very creative. It's like watching a homemade movie, a pretty good one, in your own head. Would you like to try?'

'No thanks,' I said. No thanks, no thanks, no thanks.

It was during this suspended, drifting time, interrupted only by fruitless attempts to locate my grandparents, that I decided to look up another address in the phone book, and walked over to an office building near Rockefeller Center. I had no clear plan or purpose when I walked into the marbled lobby; and for a few minutes, I stood in front of a plaque which said 'Rosen, McPherson & Park: Genetic Engineering and Modification, Suite 2305' staring dully. Then, I took the silent elevator up to the twenty-third floor. I still didn't know what I was going to do. I only knew that I had to see ... whatever it was. Whatever I'd find, whatever it would reveal. I came out into a splendid reception room, parquet-floored and discreetly dim, aside from a single spotlight over a large granite-topped desk and serene pools of light over the tawny leather couches in the waiting area. Rosen, McPherson & Park were clearly a successful partnership; or else genetic engineering firms still needed to reassure their customers with this elegant appearance, this soothing, fail-safe look.

'What can I do for you?' the young man behind the granite desk asked the moment I stepped in. He was wearing a Chinese jacket in muted green and his hair was piled way up in tiers, like an Indian warrior's headdress. Underneath it, he looked both bored and watchful.

'I . . . I wanted to find out what your company does. What kind of work. I mean, research. Projects.'

'What is the nature of your interest?' he asked with bland politeness. He'd clearly been trained to interface with the public with maximum neutrality.

'It's for a course assignment,' I said and felt quite pleased with this improvised fib. 'Cell biology. We're supposed to report on something . . . current. New developments in science.'

He looked at me carefully from under his heavy-lidded eyes, undoubtedly trying to gauge whether I was a conscientious college student or a mean teen involved in something dubious, like genetic espionage.

'We have brochures describing what we do,' he said. 'Would that be of help?'

'Maybe . . .' I said uncertainly, 'but we're supposed to do something in-depth. With interviews and a lab visit and everything. Can I arrange to see someone who works for you sometime?'

He sized me up again. 'Hmmm . . .' he said. 'Can you bring something from your professor? A note describing the nature of the assignment, or some kind of authorization? Then I could try to set up an appointment with one of our researchers. I don't promise anything, everyone is really busy around here, but I certainly can't do anything without authorization from a credible source.'

'OK,' I said. 'Thanks very much.' I'm sure he thought he was going to get rid of me this way. But this wasn't going to be difficult; I would be back. 'I'll get my prof to write you. Can I take those brochures anyway?'

'Help yourself,' he said. 'No problem.'

So I went out and found an Internet café, where I could sit quietly and face this thing I'd brought out of the dark. This innocent, awful information. I had two coffees before I could bring myself to look at the brochures. They offered minimal descriptions of the services offered by Rosen, McPherson & Park, listed as following: genetic diagnosis; genetic modification; disease and ageing prevention; parts replacement; image implants; memory enhancement; personalized pet cloning; species revivication; human cloning.

There it was, printed in the same bland typeface as everything else. RMcP&Park, I learnt from the brochure, were pioneers in the human cloning area. They did some of the earliest experiments, and were the first in the world to produce a successful specimen.

A blank-faced girl with low sounds woven into her jacket sat next to me and tried to start a conversation, but I must have given her a foul look because she said, 'Some people have their heads screwed on wrong,' and transferred herself to another table. I was in no mood for street chat. I wanted to concentrate on what I'd found, hug its strange promise and misery to myself. And I wanted to compose a letter from my professor, whose name turned out to be Seymour Berensky.

I went back to the offices of Rosen, McPherson & Park several days later, knowing they had received a letter from Professor Berensky and hoping that they were duly impressed. When I followed the letter with a phone call, I was told that, owing to my exceptional record, I was going to have the enormous privilege of meeting with Dr Park. I wasn't sure whether Rosen, McPherson & Park had simply failed to check up on my small deception and were admitting me in good faith; or whether they were letting me in to check me out, figure out what I was after or up to. It didn't matter; I just wanted to get in, to catch a glimpse, at least, of what went on in the semi-secret sanctums behind the parquet-floored foyer. To see – where I came from.

The receptionist was wearing another Chinese jacket, made of mulberry-coloured shantung, and actually managed the slightest lift of an eyebrow, indicating recognition.

'Please sit down,' he said, motioning me to one

112

of the tawny sofas. 'I'll let Dr Park's secretary know you're here.' A young woman came out a few minutes later and I followed her into a quadrangle lined with offices. At the end of a hallway a curved door of milky glass slid open and then closed silently behind a woman wearing soft slippers and a white lab coat.

The secretary led me into a small cubicle and looked at me severely. She might have been one of those girls on Madison Avenue, long-legged and sleek-haired, and she wore big square earrings with perpetually changing decorative images; right now, each one was featuring a show of tiny, classic automobiles.

'I understand you're interested in the processes of cloning,' she said in an oddly low-pitched, uninflected voice. I confirmed that this was my special interest.

'Well, you certainly seem to be an excellent student,' she went on, 'and because he likes to encourage scholarship in this area, Dr Park has made a great exception and agreed to see you. He has between fourteen and seventeen minutes this afternoon, which is a lot of time for him to give to anyone. He'll be here in four minutes. I hope you're prepared.'

I nodded. Dr Park appeared in four minutes exactly. He was Korean and his round face looked either extremely young or ageless, I couldn't tell which at first. But when I looked into his canny, calm eyes, I knew it was the latter. He appraised me in one quick glance and then, as if something wasn't quite right, scanned me again.

'Please follow me,' he said and led me towards the milky door. 'What exactly is it that I can do for you?'

'We're supposed to do a report . . .' I said haltingly. I could simulate a nervous student perfectly. I was very nervous.

'Have you defined your questions?' he asked brusquely as the curved swathe slid open to let us through. He certainly wasn't wasting any time.

'The first experiments,' I said before I knew what I was going to say, 'I want to know how you came . . . how it all started.'

'That's a very good question,' he said and sounded more cheerful, as if a good question could improve his mood. 'It's always useful to go back to the beginning.'

He scanned me again, a furrow of unease appearing on his smooth forehead. 'Well then,' he said, 'in that case, I will please invite you to come with me to show you the general layout of our experimental space and then I will also show you our early equipment and explain some of our basic working principles. They're actually very easy.'

The space revealed behind the milky door looked like the somewhat antiseptic kitchen of a mildly experimental restaurant. There were several metal-topped tables with bottles, syringes, Petri dishes and plain plastic containers. There was a big freezer holding God knows what and various pieces of lowtech equipment, which Dr Park briefly identified: Coolit plastic boxes with cells on ice, vials containing phosphate-buffered saline solution, something called a sonicator and a mixer of some kind which looked like a square food processor, and in which cells were being lysed or separated or compressed. It was hard to follow – Dr Park was leading me though the paces briskly. He indicated briefly an area where they were experimenting with a new technique of species revivication, and paused for a moment at an incubator in which cells were being cultivated in some special new growth medium. 'Sort of like chicken soup,' he said. 'Or maybe I should say won ton.' He chuckled, pleased with himself. A discreet hum of climate-control, or some other kind of power, made a homogenizing white noise.

'What about cloning?' I said. 'Where does that go on?'

Dr Park led me to one of the long tables and pointed to a small cylindrical container, connected to a computer. Something was churning or growing in the vat; on the screen, amoeboid shapes split, dissolved into each other and joined together in fluid, balletic rhythms.

'This is where the first cells are inserted,' Dr Park said. 'Then we must see if they develop into a nice, healthy, promising embryo.'

I must have looked incredulous or chagrined because he said, 'I told you, it's very simple if you know how to put together the elements. If you know the recipe. Not difficult at all. The important thing is the ingredients should be fresh and good.' He chuckled again. Clearly, the cooking metaphor had occurred with others before me.

'And is this how it all started?' I said. 'You just put some cells into some brew and they came out as a . . . a foetus?' I could hardly bring myself to say the word, but I tried to sound impartially curious, like an eager student trying to learn.

'Well, not exactly, I suppose,' he answered. 'Before that, it began the way things always begin – here,' he tapped his forehead with his finger, '– in the old noodle.'

'What do you mean?' I asked and he motioned me to follow him. He led me into his office, where the walls were lined with framed computer printouts, featuring nothing but hundreds or thousands of symbols and figures. I'd seen similar charts before, and recognized them as tables showing the sequences of basic proteins for each gene. But these must have been the originals, the first offprints, and Dr Park looked at them as if they were sensuous, or sacred objects.

'This is where it began,' he said, taking down a printout, so that I could see it close up. 'With these sequences, which had to be discovered and charted one by one. It seems simple now, but it took a long time. Actually, it all started with a worm, a humble worm . . . But that's another story. Nifty, isn't it?' he shook his head in glad wonder, as if all this was still new and amazing to him.

'Are there are sequences left you don't know about?' I asked. I wanted to find a loophole, a space where a secret, or a gap for freedom, could exist.

'No,' Dr Park said. 'We've identified every last gene, the whole kit and caboodle, is that how you say? We have mapped a whole new world.' He ran his hand over the framed chart appreciatively. 'Including the extras, the useless stuff. There are lots of those, sort of maybe like useless parts of the world.'

'But how do the proteins know how to combine themselves in these ways?' I asked. 'How come the blood cells don't get mixed up with muscle cells?'

'Don't they teach you anything at school?' he asked and sighed. 'Still, that's a good question. That's something we still don't understand completely. The transcription problem. How the proteins get the signal to combine. You know, of course, that most cells in the body are totipotent. They must have taught you that, right? It means we can get an embryo from any part of the body. Nifty, isn't it?' I nodded. 'But we still aren't sure how the genes know why they should become particular parts of an embryo. We know that the signals are very complex and we're tracking them more precisely all the time. So we're close to knowing, but we cannot say we really know.'

He paused, and insofar as his round face was capable of it, he looked melancholy. Then the look of sanguine optimism returned. 'But we will soon know, not to worry. We're close because we're figuring out the questions. Always the questions are the important thing. Another important thing is that we can give the orders to the genes ourselves. We can order them around! So it's only a matter of time before we figure out how they take the order. They can't be that smart, these genes, not smarter than us, hah?' He chuckled at the nicety of the paradox.

'Do you think there's nothing but . . .' I started to ask, but he looked at his watch and told me that my seventeen minutes were up. In fact, we were on the eighteenth minute already, so if I needed to talk to him again, I'd have to make another appointment.

'Now I will please ask you to go out,' he said, brooking no objection, and led me out through the milky swathe. As he turned to me to say goodbye, he frowned imperceptibly again, and his pupils moved as if he were trying to follow some insect annoyance across his line of vision.

'Have we maybe met before?' he asked.

'No,' I said, feeling a sudden heaviness in my body. 'No, we've never met.'

'I have been having a feeling all these eighteen minutes that I've already seen you somewhere,' he said.

'I don't think so,' I said, my voice going listless. 'No, I'm sure I have never met you before.'

But by the time I came for my next appointment,

he had done his homework and he knew that though I'd never met him, he'd met me after all. Sort of.

This time he came out himself into the waiting room. He looked, now that I'd learnt to read the expressions on his sanguine face, quite grim.

'Please come into my office,' he said. 'Today there is a change of plans. We have to do some talking first, young lady.'

The office was two cubicles large and had an old-fashioned leather-covered desk and two chairs. 'Please sit down,' Dr Park said and then, without further ado, took a page out of a folder, and stuck it directly in front of my face. It was a form of some kind, and in the upper right-hand corner there was a photograph of Her, looking younger than she did now, and just slightly older than me. And it was also, unmistakably, me. I felt a great plunge into another vacuum, another dimension of the Weirdness.

'Did you know?' he asked very sternly.

I nodded despondently. 'But I didn't know it was you,' I said.

'Why didn't you tell me the first time? Why did you do this . . . trick? Why did you deceive me?'

Deceive! My mind reeled with the unfairness of it. 'It's you who performed a dirty trick,' I said. 'It's you who created a deception. A living lie. That's what I am, a walking, talking fake. Do you know how that feels?'

119

Anger was giving me energy. It was making me articulate.

'Is that why you're here? Are you planning to sue?'

There was an idea. But now the anger deflated within me, and instead I felt utterly unwelcome tears well up at his accusation.

I shook my head. 'I just wanted to find out . . . about myself, I suppose. How I was made. Was it you?' I added. I needed this confirmed, pinned down.

'Yes,' he said. 'It was me.' He looked at me more thoughtfully. 'You were one of the first ones . . .' he said, and something like the nostalgia I saw on his face when he looked at those first printouts filled his eyes again.

We sat silently, while he inspected me more closely. To my chagrin, I saw his expression change to a kind of appreciative satisfaction. 'Well, you certainly turned out well, didn't you?' he said. 'I'd say you're practically perfect.'

I'd been trying to take in this new layer of revelation, to put him together with – me. It was impossible; but now, I felt a surge of something like hate.

'How could you do what you did?' I said in a strangled voice. 'How can you bring yourself to talk to me like that?'

He looked taken aback. 'Why, what do you mean?' he said. 'Talk to you like what?'

'As if I were some inanimate object you made,'

I said. 'Some kind of manufactured brand you produced.'

'Why? Aren't you pleased,' he asked, 'to have turned out so well? To be so well . . . finished? Please excuse my English,' he added quickly. 'Maybe I don't express myself very well.'

'You express what you think,' I said furiously. 'It's what you think that I hate.'

He was beginning to look angry. 'Perhaps you should please go now,' he said. 'Perhaps there's no reason for this conversation.'

'You never thought about me, did you?' I said quickly. 'You never thought what it would be like for me.'

'Why . . .' he said again, looking baffled, 'it was what your mother wanted. We did it with your mother's full consent.'

'But what about me?' I said. 'Didn't anybody think, didn't anybody imagine what it would be like to be me?'

'You mother was genetically very well endowed. That's why we thought she was a good candidate. We didn't want to bring anyone damaged into the world. Or mentally unstable. With the less good tissue, we use it for . . .' He paused, but I knew: less good tissue was used for transplants and organ regeneration.

'But for this, for this important, early experiment, we wanted someone who'd have a chance to have a productive, fulfilled life. There were lots of candidates – you should be proud to have been chosen. You know, to have your mother chosen. And we had lots of discussions, too. Lots of American-style talk. We had ethics panels, with the best experts. We followed all their recommendations.'

'So I'm the product of the world's ethical expertise,' I said and then my voice got so strangled I couldn't go on.

'I am a scientist,' he said and I was glad to note that there was a shade of defensiveness in his tone. 'I was following new knowledge. That is what we do. We cannot undo our knowledge, never can we do that. But I also thought I was going to make some people – your mother – a little more happy. She told me she really wanted a baby.' He looked genuinely perplexed. 'I don't see why you are so angry. I don't see what you want from me.'

'How would you like it if you were made by someone like – yourself?' I asked. He started shaking his head. 'How would you like it if someone like you were your only father? Are you willing to be my father?' I added acidly. 'Are you?' The word 'father' triggered some tearful, cry-baby spot again, but I tried to restrain the shakiness in my voice. I didn't want to expose myself to him like that.

'What do you mean?' he asked. 'Why do you want me to be your father?'

'Because I have no other!' I brought out, my fury taking me to the edge of words. And then I did break down and cry.

He looked at me more carefully then, his eyes probing. 'Is it so bad?' he asked finally. 'Many people have no father. You should see how many people in my country and they have nice smiling faces.'

'It's not just that,' I said. 'It's having come out of that cylinder. It's being put together from some horrid . . . ingredients. It's knowing I've been cooked, like a soup. Like some horrid stew. It's being made by . . . someone like you, for God's sake! Don't you understand?'

'You look very well made to me,' he said. He scrutinized me again, with appreciative curiosity. 'Do you maybe want to be a member of a study? We need to know everything we've done, we need to follow this up. And you are . . . in my view, you are very successful.'

'No wonder I don't feel human,' I said. 'I was made by you.'

His eyes receded into a steely distance. 'I don't like this kind of, how do you call it, emotional sabotage,' he said. 'Suggesting I've done something wrong. You're trying to pretend I'm a monster. Monster scientist from the movies.'

'Maybe you are,' I said. 'You've certainly made a monster. A freak. Maybe that makes you one too.'

'I am a scientist,' he reiterated. 'I can't hold back change. We have new developments in procreative techniques and they are good techniques. They work well. They work very, very well. If your mother has any complaints, she can write me, or come and talk to me. She was my customer, not you.'

So that was that. We stood up, and looked at each other with unmasked hostility. But with bafflement, too. I was ashamed of having tried to explain myself, of feeling this strange, strange need to have him understand. Maybe we all need our creator to be merciful. Maybe I hoped that if he looked on me with sympathy – with kindness – I would stop feeling this weird chill that had been coming over me in the last few days. But between him and me there was a gaping gulf. He was my creator and he had nothing to do with me. He was not even sufficiently personal for hate. He was . . . a scientist in a lab coat. A man in an antiseptic kitchen. I hated something, someone, but it was not him. I'd have to find another, truer target. I felt my fury turning, turning as on a spit, towards the image that was never absent. Towards her. Towards her-in-me.

And so, I met my maker. I restrained myself while I was still in the building, but once on the street, I nearly keeled over from a strange pain. I was in a state of – I can only call it chaos. There was no way to put together what I was and what I now knew. I'd seen how I was made and by whom; and the knowledge turned me into a ludicrous joke. I had looked into the whirling vortex of the vat, into the back-time before my own birth, as it is forbidden to do. As it should be impossible to do. From which part of her, exactly, did I emerge? I wished I'd asked him that. Or maybe it was better than I hadn't. The Devil is also in the details. Whichever sample of skin or saliva was used to make me, I had emerged, practically, from myself. Was there anything more monstrous than that – an unwanted self-birth? I saw Dr Park releasing drops of liquid into a Petri dish through a pipette and I felt buffeted as if by great gales, by violent clashing waves. I was a site for incompatible perspectives, and my vision swam and wouldn't cohere into a fixed point. I felt sea-sick, heart-sick, mind-sick.

I felt, I felt, I felt . . . As if I had a true heart and mind, as if I could be sure . . . As if there was an I within my body that was entitled to speak for itself, to feel in its mimic soul. If I kept moving, it was because I was a living organism and didn't know how to stop. Though I wasn't even sure of that. Organicity implies unpredictability. Without unpredictability, you get dead matter. I was merely animated matter, programmed into a semblance of life by carefully applied moisture and heat. I thought I could hear the incessant clicking of protein sequences within me, polymerase chain reactions going through their mindless motions, sub-molecular matter dividing, combining, changing shape, exchanging signals and bleeps. Directed by what? By whom?

I had met my maker. But can we bear to see our creator face to face? Can we bear the sight of our origins? The history of *Homo sapiens*, I was taught in Hum Ed, was propelled from the beginning by the search for beginnings. Humans have speculated, sought and believed, have told myths and founded religions to explain the mystery of their advent. Philosophies and Spiritualities 101.

But I was now in a position to know: if we really knew, we'd die. Perhaps once we know, we shall die. Perhaps we've begun to die already, from knowing too, too much. Perhaps that's been the program, the game plan all along. Figure out how you are made, and then how to make yourselves in your own image. Look into the mirror of your own creation and behold the nothingness therein. The *reductio ad absurdum*. The plan has always been complex, but you're smart, you'll figure it out. You'll know when the game's up.

On 42nd Street I noticed a weaponry boutique, and went in and looked at a fancy laser gun. Good for hunting authentically wild game in the new genetic design parks, said the ad. Good for big, tamed, authentically unnatural humans, I thought, and walked down Seventh Avenue in agitation, imagining myself standing on the hood of a car amidst the passing crowd, my legs spread apart for better balance, my blonde hair flowing in the wind, holding the gun straight in front of me, then turning it in a smooth, wide semi-circle as it fired away silently in syncopated rhythms. The clichés were all there, for my use. I imagined picking out a few perfect ones, the best-made among them, and

126

mowing them down. Not in order to kill them, just to demonstrate their utter insignificance. For what could any one of them, or ten, or fifteen, possibly matter? At this point, at this late date? But as I looked at the numberless crowds rushing past me, at their insistent motion and flat, affectless faces, I thought, I don't need to kill you, my very existence makes the less of you. Because you have made me, you too must know: you are counterfeit. Because you know how to make me, you must know you are less than dust. I am your logical conclusion, the QED of your nothingness. The counterproof, the reproof, the final proof. At least that revenge is mine.

I never told my Adviser about this epiphany. I knew it would bang straight into the limits of his expertise. His philosophy. And besides, it was too private, too awful, too simple or too ultimate for disclosure. Too unutterable for utterance.

And yet I have dreams. In the next few nights I dreamt images that were like big clues. Dreams in which Steven merged strangely into Dr Park, and a male face looked away from me in revulsion or pity. Dreams of Her with a pregnant belly, then flattened like a cartoon figure against a screen of milky glass.

'What strikes me about your dreams is how coherent they are,' the Adviser once said to me. 'The symbolism is almost too lucid, as if it were itself defensive, as if it masked something else.'

127

Maybe, or maybe not. How many layers does the psyche have, how many fathoms deep does the truth lie? Can a creature like me have depth? Can I be more than I appear, than I was intended to be? Can a being like me have thoughts that are hidden behind, or below, or beyond? Where would they come from, what could they be, except maybe her thoughts . . . No, I am the counterproof of secret depths, my secret is that I am too transparent by half.

And yet I have dreams. Where do they come from, these tormenting images, and what do they mean? Do they mean? Or are they a trick of laxness, a lapse of control in the imaging centres, from which pictures rise up pell-mell, sloppily and without rhyme or reason? Some complicated bit of relaxation programming that makes us bend and compress and lyse and synthesize information into these strange, surreal shapes, into a night-time illusion of meaning, as opposed to the daytime ones. 'I could . . . count myself a king of infinite space, were it not that I have bad dreams.' Thus Hamlet, our prince of doubt. But oh, I would much rather be haunted by nightmares than be the empress of anything, if only they guaranteed my ordinary, my mysterious humanity.

There seems to be no guarantee. And yet my dreams are sometimes wondrous. Or beautiful. That is, they seem beautiful to me. I have no explanation for that.

★   ★   ★

In the nights I dreamt. In the days I cruised the Net and I cruised the streets. I didn't know how much time I had. There'd been no announcements so far about my going missing on the Infonet, or anywhere else as far as I could tell. That meant she was biding her time, or was worried about initiating anything as official as a police pursuit. I was at a dodgy age, not yet technically adult, but not so much a minor that I couldn't leave home if I wished. And, of course, police involvement might raise tricky questions.

Still, she'd find me sooner or later. I needed to hurry, to press on. I spent hours glued to the screen, trying without success to unlock the codes of private e-mail servers. I needed to get into Janey's mailbox, where I was sure I'd find my grandparents. But Janey apparently had a classified address and the servers were cautious. I was getting absolutely nowhere.

Which is really why I took up with Piotr. There may have been other reasons, but this was the main one, as far as I knew: I thought he could help me in my stymied search. I met him at the 92nd Street Y, at a panel discussion entitled 'Creations and Recreations: Whither Human Design?' I saw it advertised in the Virtual Village and I think I decided to go not only because of the subject, which happened to be of intrinsic interest to me, but because the Y was so close to Janey's apartment, and although ostensibly I made every effort to avoid running into her, apparently some self-destructive, longing part of me kept secretly wishing to meet her, to see this person whom I dimly remembered, and who was – I was strangely susceptible to the sentimental pull of this word – a relative . . .

There was no Janey in sight in the Y's big foyer, but the funny old hall was packed. Human design was a hot and happening field, hot enough to draw people to something as stodgy and old-fashioned as a talking heads event. Of course, lots of people there were probably quite old; you could sometimes tell by a certain constriction of the eye, or a faded mottled tinge seeping from the subcutaneous cells into the surface freshness of the skin. The really young were beautiful in their supple clothes, streaming and pulsing with delicate moving lights, which were in fashion just then.

The main speakers were Dr Margaret Donaldson, an evolutionary aestheticist known for her avant-garde pro-design views; and Professor V. Parakash, a radical-conservative ethicist whose opposition to genetic engineering extended to animals as well as humans. Donaldson had the immediate advantage of looking glamorous and confident. She had long chestnut hair and was wearing an ochre linen suit, its jacket interwoven with dotted lines of gold light, its skirt cut on a bias and flowing down towards her exquisite ankles. Her basic argument was that human design techniques were now advanced to the point where we could start using them more inventively and even playfully. We could experiment with new forms and shapes for the human body. She wasn't suggesting anything extreme, she assured us; but play was at the very heart of creativity, and let's face it, in relation to life, we were now the creators. Therefore we should take responsibility for our role; and the most responsible way to go about redesigning ourselves was to be playful. Play was not only a serious, but also the essential element in creation, and it was quite possible that the construction of what we called 'nature' involved artful play in the first place. There was, finally, no other way to account for its variety, its extravagance, its sheer good design. Aesthetic values were also clearly good evolutionary values and we should not shy away from the challenge of this insight. If we were going to be creators, we should dare to be artists. Ultimately, it was imagination and invention which led to the most interesting, and arguably the most lasting things. So let's get serious, she concluded. It's time to start playing for real.

'You mean you'd have humans sprout fins?' Parakash put in acidly. He was a lithe, excitable fellow, whose eyes flashed with expressive disapproval through Donaldson's exposition. I liked him.

'Why not?' Donaldson responded lightly. 'And why not wings? Hasn't that always been the dream?'

'Because ... because ...' Parakash almost

131

spluttered. He was beside himself with outrage. 'Because nature has its laws! Because if we want to remain human, we have to accept our limitations!'

'Do we?' Donaldson asked impishly and tapped her foot. And to that there was no answer.

It was during the intermission that Piotr and I almost literally bumped into each other in the lobby. Then we looked up and were staring straight at each other. 'Hmmm,' he said. 'Excuse me. Sorry. I think this was my fault.' He spoke in oddly accented English, which was not unappealing. We paused, not knowing what to do next. 'Can I get you something from the bar?' he asked. 'It's the least I can do.' These incidents were acquiring a pattern. I nodded, and he went off, making an oddly courteous bow. I liked his long-sleeved, indigo tunic, woven through with slivers of silver light. He had a thick mane of sandy hair and green eyes, and something – something in his eyes told me he would try to impress me and hurt me. And be easily hurt. Not that I could have said any of it right away, as I was registering first impressions. But I got it, nevertheless. Got it instantly. It's odd how much we can read into that first glancing look and be right about it. And what does that mean, what does the eye fill up with, to convey so much? What subtle substance flows into it and from where, carrying signals that say kindness or cruelty?

Later, he told me that what interested him about me was the wall-eyed neutrality of my face, its

132

impervious blankness. He couldn't make out who or what I was, and since he prided himself on instant character diagnosis, I intrigued him.

'Interesting discussion, don't you think?' he said when he came back.

'I guess so,' I said. 'I hope Parakash puts up more of a fight, though.'

'He doesn't have much of a chance,' Piotr said.

'Do you think she's right?' I asked.

'Oh, that's not what this is about,' Piotr informed me. 'At least not for her. She really is just playing around. You know those theory people.'

I didn't, but we went back to the auditorium together and Piotr whispered quite useful comments as Parakash and Donaldson battled it out. The second half of the discussion was about the ontological status of artificial humans. But first Donaldson protested against the word 'artificial'. There was nothing artificial about technological experiments, she said, at our stage of civilization. Technology was our form of nature – our second nature, we might say. Parakash started shaking his head and protested that much as we can try to kill all distinctions – all meaning – the distinctions were still there. In reality. Donaldson tapped her foot and asked where, exactly, at this point, he would locate reality. Parakash said that she misunderstood the principles of philosophy, that though he knew very well about veils of illusion, the reality behind these veils was not going to be manmade. Then he became inarticulate.

Someone in the audience suggested that human design was the golden opportunity to redress many historical injustices and that, whatever creatures we produced, they should be only females. Another man, speaking with bitter vehemence, pointed out that if we wanted to take the matter to its logical conclusion, we should eliminate the whole absurd and mostly miserable process of embodied life, and simply pass the genetic material on in convenient brain casings of some kind. Donaldson smiled ambiguously; she clearly wasn't sure whether this proposal was made in support of her ideas, or not.

At this point Parakash couldn't contain himself. 'This is frivolous!' he shouted. 'Frivolous and dangerous! Why don't we just destroy the whole bloody ball game? That would be a really good short cut!'

The chairperson interrupted him politely and said he wanted to remind everyone that the subject under discussion was the ontological status of . . . and so on.

'He's right, poor bugger,' Piotr whispered and instantly shot up in my esteem. 'But he'll get eaten alive. He just doesn't have enough cool.'

But it was the conversation we had in a café afterwards that prompted me to accept his invitation to go home with him.

'So where are you from, anyway?' he asked after we had ordered some tranquil snacks.

'A laboratory in mid-Manhattan,' I said, and he

laughed. He liked that. He was from somewhere in Eastern Europe, half Bosnian and one-third Ukranian. The remaining one-fifth or so was from the other Galicia, in Spain. That was the part of himself he identified with, he told me. His credo was that you should always identify with the minority in yourself.

He talked a blue streak, his green eyes glowing more fiercely than any eyes I'd ever seen. That first evening he told me stories of experiences which sounded as though they were from the last century, tales of on-site exploration in remote parts of the rain forest, and of actual, physical danger. He told me how he'd been held hostage by some vague indigenous group in the Amazon basin, which hoped to use him as a pawn in a dispute over air rights, and which apparently hadn't realized he was useless as a negotiating counter since no government or state cared about his welfare. But as his captors definitely didn't care either, it wasn't clear what they would do with him. For a few days he lived in real fear. He was rescued by a representative of an equally vague Monogolian state, who happened to be vacationing in the area just then, and thought that this was an excellent chance to demonstrate his diplomatic skills. He managed to convince Piotr's captors on camera that their prisoner was of no use to them and have him released relatively unharmed. To repay him, Piotr did some sophisticated decryption work for the Mongolian government in absentia, partly out of gratitude and partly because the group's plans involved space sabotage, of which Piotr was entirely in favour.

Piotr recounted these adventures with a sort of suppressed excitement, as if they were entirely original experiences, never before seen on the Data Dispenser. He kept observing me as he told me this story, as if trying to discern whether I was properly impressed. Now something must have broken through my uncalculated blankness because he put his hand on mine and said he hoped we'd get to know each other better. I asked him a few questions about his decryption work, pretending plausibly that I thought this was very exciting; and when I ascertained that he still had his equipment at home, I said yes, I'd come home with him.

And so we went to his place and had abrupt sex. He was impetuous, Piotr was, and he started kissing me in the elevator, and pushed me down on the bed as soon as we stepped into his bedroom. He didn't bother to undress me, but pulled my dress up over my hips. He bit my shoulder and uttered words in an unknown language, and as my pelvis responded with equal jaggedness I looked up at the ceiling, where video images of us moved in big, clumsy motions. All I could see was my own blank face and the back of his tunic spreading over us, billowing and falling like a sail or a wing, with its silver lights snaking in and out of the satiny cloth with pointillist precision.

I felt Her hovering in the room like some giant shadow, a protective-predatory bird suspended in the air, its enormous dark wings outspread and ready to fold me in.

Piotr's place was all lights and shadows, without a still point anywhere. Patterns of coloured iridescence danced across walls and ceilings. In his study four large figures stood in four corners, gesturing to each other across the room: Marilyn Monroe, a fresh-faced American sailor, Anne Frank and Michelangelo's David. On the ceiling a chubby cherub was shooting a perpetual arrow of light towards the figures in a perpetual, graceful motion.

All of this took money, but Piotr had lots of it, inherited from his grandparents, who had raked it in in some obscure Balkan wars at the end of the last century. Apparently, they had piled up their euros serving as intermediaries in some shady oil-delivery deals involving the Croats and the Serbs, I could never follow it exactly, and then emigrating to Spain – which is where Piotr acquired the minority part of his person.

'This calls for a drink,' Piotr said after the act was finished. And so we sat in the kitchen, which was the calmest room in the apartment, except for soft, crystalline sounds weaving their way through the walls, and we drank iced vodka from frosted glass tumblers.

That was when I asked him if he'd teach me to use his code-breaking equipment.

'What for?' he asked. I told him I was trying to find some people who were important to me. Some long-lost relatives.

'Relatives?' he repeated sceptically.

'Yes,' I said. 'Close relatives.'

'Then how did you lose them?' he asked. 'Isn't it rather careless of you?' I shrugged and said it was too complicated to explain.

'Anything irregular?' he quickly asked.

'No,' I said. 'Nothing at all. Trust me.'

'OK,' he said languidly. 'I trust you.' So I stayed with him for the next two weeks, and learnt how to work his powerful decryption equipment. Once I had it, finding Janey's address was only a matter of time. Piotr didn't really trust me, of course, and tried to find out what I was up to, but I wouldn't tell him and he respected my privacy. I think. Or rather, I told him just enough of the truth to throw him off the track. The facts, in this case, were no clue to their meaning. I told him I was searching for my aunt. I told him she'd been estranged from my mother. I told him family bonds were important to me.

He could understand that because he was obsessed with family. Or, rather, with family history. He talked about his dubious ancestors with more . . . well, more gusto, or fieriness, than I'd ever heard in anyone's voice. His eyes went glowering and dark when he told me about remote relatives in even remoter parts of the Ukraine and Bosnia, about huge tanks rolling through rural landscapes, about parades and processions of people who had killed or been killed, and speculators getting rich on ill-gotten gains. This was his own history, he said, and it had instilled guilt in his very veins.

We'd studied guilt briefly in Human Education, where it was considered one of the strangest emotions of all, oddly convoluted and possibly related to uncontrollable urges. Like those urges, guilt was specific to humans; and because of this it was sometimes thought to be an index of higher development, or maybe even overdevelopment, or uneven internal development, whereby one part of the person judged another part and attacked it until it hurt. These were peculiar and still not entirely explicable phenomena. But it was also speculated that at an even higher stage of development guilt would start to disappear, like the appendix or other atavistic body parts. It would go because there would be nothing that couldn't be reversed or rectified, and so there would be no need for people to regret anything retroactively, or be judged for what they had done in the past. I wondered whether guilt resembled anything I'd ever experienced, or whether I was the higher stage of development. The next stage. What could I feel guilty for since I had no past of my own? I was the rectification of someone else's past, the undoing of consequence.

Piotr thought his own guilt had been passed on to him via the unconscious conscience, like a recessive gene that comes to the fore in the third generation. He thought his grandparents, who'd been a cross between guerrillas and murderers, had a kind of conscience about what they were doing, but they weren't cognisant of it, or didn't want to be. Too much awareness would have stopped them from going after what they wanted, so they had to push it down; and now it had resurfaced in him as kind of perpetual bad conscience, even though he himself hadn't done anything wrong. It was a raw deal, he said, though as far as I could tell he relished his guilt, like some delicious, rarefied pleasure. He practically admitted as much. He said we'd lost our taste for suffering, and it was up to a few people like himself to preserve its great art, to carry on the noble tradition. That's how he talked and I sort of liked it. In comparison with most people I'd come across, Piotr was feverish with passion.

Passion: I recognized it as such, though I don't think I'd ever seen it. But Piotr pursued it and courted it; though he too had his doubts. He wasn't always sure he was the real thing like his bloody-minded ancestors. His main route to passion and suffering was via his Project, to which he alluded so cryptically at first that I thought it had to do with something super-serious, like military robot design or international commerce. But then he let on that the Project was actually a novel. When I could bring myself to ask him what it was about, he answered in an insulted voice that it wasn't 'about' anything. It was itself. He'd only say it was called *The Supreme Fiction*, and that it had epic scope and a large and varied cast of characters. His ambition was to create people so three- or more-dimensional, so undeniably vital, that they'd put the poor shallow creatures we'd become to shame. They'd show the reader the extent of our diminishment.

He'd been working on *The Supreme Fiction* for several years and was about halfway through. I asked him cautiously if he knew that nowadays anyone could put together their own perfectly good novel in practically no time at all, and to their own specifications. We did a few in my Gutenberg Galaxy course, though admittedly they were pretty simple. But you could make them as complicated as you wanted, if you were willing to get the more expensive programs. Most kits came with templates for the basic plots, sub-plots and suggestions for a few variants. The fun was in trying to find new combinations or twists which made sense, but didn't resemble the old ones too much.

But when I said some of this to Piotr, his gaze went from glowering to steely. 'You are the symptom I'm fighting against,' he said, pointing his finger at me. 'You're the contemporary disease. You look healthy, but I swear you're ill.'

Well, he didn't know how right he was, though for the wrong reasons. He tried to find spots of guilt or suffering in me, but of course he kept hitting a blank wall. He kept enquiring about my past and

141

I met him with evasions. He asked if there was anything I really cared about and when I didn't respond he said my blankness marred even my beauty.

'No wonder you were so bland with him,' the Adviser later said, sliding, as usual, into his own register of explanation. 'He did all the feeling for you. And, of course, that suited you very well. You could project all kinds of things into him, especially the anger. He was the perfect receptacle for it, even though it wasn't really him you were angry at, obviously. It was the internalized image . . .'

'Please,' I said.

'And even if the anger was masking something else. Because, of course, under the cover of the rage, what you were actually looking for was love.'

I didn't know about the 'of course'. Because maybe what I was actually looking for was pain. I guess I half-hoped that Piotr would succeed in inflicting it on me, or imbuing me with some of his own. That he might jolt me into feeling something . . . strong. Something vivid. He didn't but he intrigued me for a while. He was like one of those anchorite monks who used to spend their lives sitting on tops of very tall pillars when there was no earthly reason to do so. It was crazy, but impressive too, and I had a nagging suspicion that he had access to something I didn't understand, some kind of archaic knowledge. When he opened up, he told me he wanted his novel to encompass the whole history of the last century, through light-ning flashes of revelation and sweeping, human stories . . . He showed me books, with black and white photographs of murdered bodies and open graves and menacing-looking soldiers in heavy uniforms. Indistinct images of people with their hands held up in submission, and thin faces expressing extreme anguish or extreme defiance. Piotr stared at those photos at length; he said they were the iconic images of the last century, of authentic, suffering humanity. They pursued him and haunted him in the night; his task was to unlock their meanings. It was an immensely strange panorama he unfolded before me, and it didn't look as though the twentieth century was something to be nostalgic for. But Piotr said being truly human had its costs. Those predecessors of ours had dimensions and depths – and he had to get to this, to express it. I tried to figure out what kind of depth he meant, whether it was the kind of thing I meant when I yearned for my guarantee . . .

And yet, insofar as I was capable of such an intricate feeling, I envied him – envied him so much past. All that horrid, unseemly history. He had a long, old story he thought belonged to him, or which he belonged to, and it propelled him onwards like some powerful fuel. I had none at all, nothing in the back of my mind except the Weirdness, and a weird gap. I started now; how was I ever going to comprehend myself?

So Piotr interested me, and sometimes I stood

and watched him as he picked at his keyboard, looking fierce and somehow woebegone too. When I asked what he was actually doing when he looked like that, he said he was struggling with his capricious muse. Sometime in the third week of our acquaintance, he revealed that the muse was actually a beautiful, dark-haired ancestress of his, whose faded photograph hung in a wooden frame in his study, and whose dramatic story was at the centre of *The Supreme Fiction*. Piotr had a holographic reproduction made of her image, and when he was writing he often turned it on, to a white, illuminating glow. Sometimes he placed the figure above and around his computer, so he could sort of enter it as he wrote for more direct inspiration. Even so, the ancestress wasn't entirely reliable as a muse; and when she ran out on him, or he ran out of ideas, he'd turn to the *Character Catalogue*, a big compendium of all the characters ever invented, with their basic biographies, external and interior traits, ostensible values, underlying motivations and unconscious conflicts. He'd open the *Catalogue* on the sly, as if he were hiding what he was doing even from himself. But it always put him in a bad mood when he had to resort to it, and afterwards he'd rail against the inhuman age we lived in, or he would turn on me in some small mean way, or else want to have sex. Oh, I could understand the mechanism of his actions all right, they were pretty simple. Feel sense of inadequacy, offload tension. But I didn't mind. I didn't mind anything, really. Who was I to mind how I was used or for what purposes, or with what motivations? Or whether I felt pleasure or pain? It made no difference, or I barely knew the difference. I didn't mind turning into pure body; a body going through the motions of its instincts.

Sometimes he flirted with really hurting me. I think I provoked him, I was so utterly available, so utterly impermeable.

'What do you want?' he shouted at me once, after he'd gone pretty far to elicit something like a real response from me, or tears, or a plea or a protest. Once he even used a delicate, forked whip, which he flicked not very painfully over my thigh. 'Is there anything you want at all? Is there anything you don't want? Who on earth are you, anyway?!'

I couldn't tell him, of course, and I looked at the ceiling to see the reflection of his arched back and my own blank face.

'Iris,' he said pleadingly, caressing my cheek. 'I didn't really hurt you, did I? You enjoy making love to me? I mean me – me??'

Me. Me. Why did it matter so much that it was him? Where did he get his conviction of his particular me-ness? I could see he was filled with something that almost burst from the inside, that made him feel as though he was . . . incontrovertible. I was tempted to tell him he wasn't. I was tempted to say he wasn't made so very differently from the characters in his *Catalogue*.

'Sure,' I said instead, and ran my fingers down

his neck, his back, his arms. 'Sure, I enjoy it a lot,' I knew it would seem too cruel, or too peculiar, if I said anything else.

Once Piotr said I must try his old Affect Simulator, just for kicks, to see if it would do anything for me. These had been very popular the previous year because some research had shown that having strong emotions improved your immune system. And that's what the simulator did, it gave you strong emotions. It looked like a small horizontal missile in which you lay down in complete darkness, disrupted only by narrow beams of light, which altered your hormonal balance and the pituitary gland outflow. You could adjust the strength and direction of the beams for specific feelings and intensities: a little jealousy, a lot of anger, moderate hate, violent love.

But the reason that simulators had gone out of fashion was because there'd been some further research which suggested that artificially induced feelings didn't have the same salutary effects on health as naturally induced ones. They seemed the same, they read the same on the neuro-chemical charts, they even *felt* the same. But, even so, their impact wasn't the same. This, in turn, had something to do with a highly elusive phenomenon known as the meaning problem. That is, it seemed that humans recognized emotions as really real only if they were accompanied by certain sensations, or memories, or imagistic and verbal associations that registered as having the quality of significance for the particular person by whom they were experienced. Without these secondary phenomena, which produced the entirely subjective sensation of 'meaning', feelings remained in a so-called weak state. No matter how objectively powerful they actually were, the meaning-less affects never rose to so-called passion-points.

The meaning sensation still couldn't be artificially produced in a sufficiently persuasive form. However, in an effort to save their invention, the gadget's promoters pointed out that simulations stimulate. Spending some time each day in the cylinder often helped people recover their naturally occurring feelings; though some people, after recovering them, said they would prefer to go right back to their flat state.

Piotr had bought the simulator when he'd been particularly frustrated with the slowness of his progress on *The Supreme Fiction*. He was sometimes inconsistent in his thinking, I was beginning to notice. But he wanted me to try it because he thought it might bring me out of my blankness, my strangeness . . . It didn't, though; it only made stronger the suspicion that the sensations ricocheting inside me were just part of Dr Park's cunning recipe.

After I emerged from the cylinder, Piotr contemplated me with knitted brows and said I really was a regular zombie, there was practically no hope for me. Maybe, he said, he could try including me in his novel and giving me a character, since I didn't seem to possess one of my own. Then I could enter the personality he'd invented for me.

I shrugged. 'Go ahead, if it entertains you,' I said, and for a while it did. He strained his imagination for me, I'll give him that, though everything he came up with was kind of twentieth century. He made me into a South American guerrilla leader, in a sexy khaki costume, courting danger with a strange recklessness; a decadent diplomat's daughter, with a penchant for seducing the servants and tormenting them during official dinners; a neurotic neurology student, with brilliant ideas and a touch of anorexia; a successful professional woman who had to have her teddy bear with her in stressful moments; and others. Once I recognized Daphne's mother in one of his characters. Her name was Marge, but she was Daphne's mom to the life. I quizzed him closely to ascertain whether he knew the prototype. But he didn't, he'd apparently invented her all on his own. I suppose this wasn't promising for him as a Great Artist, since Daphne's mother wasn't very hard to invent and not all that original. But maybe I was being unfair to her, maybe there had been more to her than I had discerned.

It amused me for a while too, but then it began to annoy me. I told him none of the characters seemed appropriate for me. They somehow weren't . . . me. But Piotr was right, I was failing to come into three dimensions on my own.

★   ★   ★

To speak in the first person is in my case a fiction. It is an act of hubris, or of strange illusion. But it seems that the illusion has to be maintained if I am to speak at all. And it seems that if I am to go on being, in whatever guise and on whatever grounds, I have to speak. You have to keep moving, or die. You have to keep speaking, or cease to be.

Piotr never even began to suspect who, what, I was. It seems that as a simulacrum of a young girl, I was entirely convincing. I had verisimilitude; just not conviction. The simulation was failing to believe in itself. I spoke of myself as I, but I was failing to feel the full illusion of life. An error in the mixture, Dr Park. You must rectify the program next time.

Between my decoding sessions, when I couldn't take any more ciphers or squiggles, I moved through the city as though it were a malleable, protean creature, swelling and contracting according to my moods and drifts. I visited galleries and grungy cafés, saunas and good mood clubs, looking for ways to lose myself, to elude her even as I played spy and pursuer of my origins.

I walked into a virtual club one evening called The Doors of Perception, which specialized in invented realities and identities. In the central space, scenes and images folded in and out of each other in multiple dimensions: Humphrey Bogart bending into a tour of Casablanca, Indian dance rituals interspersed with lions stalking a herd of wildebeest. There were also niches where you could create your very own scenarios. People wandered through the main theatre, disappearing and reappearing in its folds and vectors; others reclined against large cushions with their eyes closed, smiling or sighing at whatever show they were watching in their minds. In the identity room, you could exchange memories with others, or share image repertories, or make up alternate personalities for yourself for the night. There were also traditional drugs, for those who preferred to have their perceptions altered by their very own imaginations.

I sat next to a woman with long, dark hair the one time I went to the club, in a niche made to look like an icicled cave. She motioned me in languidly, and said, 'Hi, who are you?'

'Iris,' I said.

'No,' she said, 'I mean, what kind of person?'

'Oh,' I said. 'I'm a double.' I didn't feel that was giving too much away.

'Cool,' she said. 'That's really cool.'

She stretched back on her cushion, and said she'd met all kinds of doubles at the club and they were always interesting. She herself worked as a hairdresser in the Village, but she came to the club to meet others like herself. She had been practically raised from the dead after a terrible illness, she told me earnestly, and since then, she had had out-of-body experiences all the time. 'They're like flying,' she said. 'They've changed my whole outlook on things.' She launched into a long and vivid description of how it felt to hover above herself and everyone else, then suddenly looked very restless and uncomfortable.

'I have to get another memory-chip,' she said and started getting up.

'You mean, none of what you told me was true?' I asked. I felt very cheated.

'What do you mean, true?' she said huffily. 'It was true when I told you. It's true for now.'

I don't know why that scared me, but I never went to a virtual club after that. I spent a night in a weave-n-wave disco, though, moving together with other bodies to the soft, hypnotic, never-ending, endlessly looping music, under patterns and geysers of light that made each face look flat and ecstatic like medieval paintings, and that cut each body into abstract fragments and parts . . . Saintly entranced, ephemeral figures. I guess I hoped to lose myself among them, to lose my nothingness, but I walked out of the simultaneously dark and overlit interior feeling no more than a laser-created silhouette, a ghost inhabited by a ghost. One silhouette superimposed on another. Sometimes Her face contorted itself into grotesque shapes, as if under the pressure of Dr Park's cylinder; narrowing into a puncturing sharpness, harpy eyes, beaked mouth. Fury-face. I tried to duck it by walking faster and found it inside instead, a foetal mother, clinging incubus.

Sometimes I thought I must cut myself in two,

rip myself open in order to extract her from myself. Oh, I thought of it, in a way desired it. To evacuate myself from my body, to cancel myself like an aborted experiment. Sorry, there must have been some small error in the mix. Still unidentified elements went missing, or failed to come together, to congeal.

Then it occurred to me, as it had to: I could always strike a compromise deal. I could evacuate myself from my body, but leave behind a sample, with directions to make it grow. It was easy and getting cheaper all the time. The techniques were getting better too; maybe in the next generation these curious problems I was experiencing would be solved. And did it make any difference, after all, which version I lived in, which copy? In what body I perpetuated myself? I wondered if this next one would know, if she'd sense that she/I had been here before . . . But maybe she would manage it better than I, this life-incarnation stage, maybe she would be . . . happier. Was that the word, was that still the relevant term? It had never occurred to me before. And if she were, would that mean finally I would be happier too? That my substance would be fulfilled through her substance? Perhaps that is what She had hoped for – the original she. I reeled back into her mind as it pushed its way towards me, towards my existence, and then reeled forward to imagine this hypothetical new avatar, and others after her, receding from me into the future like figures in a funhouse mirror . . . But the idea of infinite replication made me feel nauseous. I started walking faster to get away from it, to kill at least my thoughts.

It seemed I had all kinds of options: life, death, or life-and-death. And there was always, of course, life-in-death. For a while, I hovered between all of them. But then something happened to swing the balance. It was nothing more than an accident and it happened while I was crossing Fifth Avenue, at 56th. The crowds streamed and pressed, and in an effort to get to the other side of the street I tried to cross just as the light turned red. But the wind was high and my hair swept down over my eyes, and I didn't see the street shuttle hurtling towards me with its terrible mastodon weight. I only felt it as sound and an increase in the velocity of the air. I swerved away and the shuttle veered crazily and came to a violent stop. I fell down and I suppose I screamed. I tried to get up and discovered I couldn't; I was too dizzy. The driver leapt out of the control room and was bending over me, his jowly faded face contorted with rage. 'You crazy or what?!' he screamed. 'Why don't you look where you're going?! This is not my fault, it's yours, walking around like a zombie . . .' But by that time a little crowd had gathered round me and someone shoved the driver aside. The passengers, in the meantime, were shouting at him to get back to his job. 'We don't have all day!' someone was yelling.

The man who'd leapt to my defence was helping

me to get up. 'How are you feeling? Are you all right? Do you want to go and have a quiet drink somewhere?' he asked. I didn't, I wanted to go somewhere where I could be alone and tremble and shiver in peace. But here was the thing: I'd swerved. I swerved because I – something in me – didn't want to be crushed by the hurtling tonnage of the shuttle, didn't want to disappear on metallic impact. Despite what I felt, what I knew. That surprised me, but it had to be taken into account. Real monsters, after all, are supposed to self-destruct. I felt monstrous, all right, but I was a monster apparently made too well in the human image. Too close to the real thing, that was my spiky, impossible dilemma. I could almost envy the Golems, the Frankensteins, with their fully fledged monster identity. Those Jekylls and Hydes, who could boast not one but two whole personalities. The monsters who knew who they were and what they had to do: be monstrous and die. I was a hybrid, an amphibian, and I kept moving between life and death. A crocodile is very like a crocodile and a human clone is apparently very nearly like a human. Very nearly, there was the rub . . .

Still, I'd swerved, and I knew the next time a deadly vehicle came hurtling down towards me, I'd swerve again. Something in me – congratulations, Dr Park! – had been coded for self-preservation. Which implied, perhaps, a strange kind of self-approval. I didn't, apparently, hate my condition enough. Which meant that I had to figure out how to go on living with it. How to go on being. How to go on.

In the meantime, the stories I kept telling Piotr were wearing thin – so thin that it was getting hard for him to continue pretending he believed them. I was running out of time here too. Then, as he promised, there was pay-off. One morning I turned on the computer and saw that the decryption engine had done its work. There was Janey's address with her password, simple and stunning: Liz. There wasn't enough room for Elizabeth, but there She was again. She was Janey's secret too, apparently, her coded obsession. I registered this briefly; sometime I'd have to find out more. But now I watched as the e-mail files came up on the screen like coins out of a profligate slot machine.

My heart . . . My almost human heart quickened its beat. I scrolled down to peruse my hoard. There were about sixty files, including the usual bills, promos, an ad for some new nutritional pills and another for erotic aids, a thank-you note from a friend who'd been to visit. Janey's life looked very regular. And then, halfway down a note from Her. ESurrey@. I shut my eyes as I opened it and then made myself look at the message.

'I know this must seem to you like a communication from outer space,' she wrote, without using any form of address – maybe she couldn't bear to say her sister's name – 'and I wouldn't be writing to you unless I were desperate. I am desperate. Iris is gone. She has left, or she has escaped, or she has disappeared. I don't know. I haven't heard from her in several weeks, and she has left no trace, no trail, except a booking on a flight to New York. I think it is not improbable that she has been with you. She has developed a strange obsession with family and I'm sure she believes you can help her. Help her get away from me, undoubtedly. If she is with you, you will know all this and perhaps it will have occurred to you that this is extremely difficult for me. Difficult and painful. Perhaps you will have taken satisfaction in this. I wouldn't be surprised. But listen, if Iris has come to you, if you know anything about her whereabouts, you must let me know. However much you still hate me – and I know you do. And whatever she may have said to you. I want to warn you that she is capable of making things up at the moment; her imagination seems to be in an overheated state. Anyway, if I can't appeal to your sympathy, let me appeal to your common sense. I am her mother and her legal guardian. She could be in trouble. She has not been sensible lately and God knows what kind of danger she is courting. I don't want to involve the police yet, but I will soon, if necessary. If you are sheltering her, or hiding her, there could be legal consequences. And Janey, I am desperate. If you know anything, you must immediately inform me. You can surely understand that. You must. Elizabeth.'

She closed on this curt and imperious note.

156

However desperate she was, she hadn't lost the sense of her power. Her authority. I felt . . . Oh, I felt a terrible ache, which was half for her and half for me. I felt a sickening apprehension. I felt as if I were being pulled back into a vortex I'd struggled out of, a vortex that was dark and turbulent, but strangely tempting.

But no, I couldn't let it divert me now. I clicked the file shut. Sometime I'd have to go through the Sent Items and see if Janey had replied. But now I combed the Inbox, frantically and fearfully. At the bottom, neatly collected together, were several messages from them: the senior Surreys. The communications were all brief and efficient; nothing like the earlier handwritten outpourings. The most recent one thanked Janey for a gift of Venus figs, and said they were enjoying just lounging around in their condo, and were looking forward to their trip to Bali. There were no dates for the trip, which was a worry; but there was an address: 97153 Monsanto Road, Palm Beach, Fla.

The next day, when Piotr was out at his fresh-air club, I collected my few measly possessions in my aerobag, and wrote a note. 'Dear Piotr,' it said, 'thanks for everything. You helped me a lot and I really appreciate it. You helped me do something I really needed to do. I may be back, or I may not. But thanks for the hospitality. I'm sorry I can't tell you where I'm going, but don't look for me on the Net, I'm disappearing into real space. I enjoyed our time together, and I'm sorry I couldn't tell you more about myself. Maybe another time. Yours, Iris.'

Then I shut the door behind me, and walked out into the muggy summer sunlight of mid-Manhattan.

Oh, I was afraid as I boarded the plane from La Guardia to Palm Beach, Florida. But I was getting used to being afraid. I was getting used to carrying myself around like a semi-animate beast, a somatic spectre who needed to be kept alive until a diagnosis was made, or an operation could be performed. Like some frozen organism which I had a duty to preserve until it knew whether it should live or die. I thought of buying some Fast Feel-Goods at the airport, but I decided I wanted to do this straight. Whatever that might mean in my case. My state, after all, was alerted enough. I tried to think what I'd do when I got to Monsanto Road, how I would persuade my grand-parents to see me, what I'd say to them. I tried to imagine them in their old age, but had practically nothing to go on; and as the plane approached Florida, much too quickly for my liking, I thought maybe I should just turn around and go back to New York without even leaving the airport. What were they to me, or I to them? And yet the need to go to them was as powerful as a cry rising out of a crib,

159

as a homing instinct, as a bird's blind straight flight. Oh, I supposed I had instincts, I'd sort of shown that to myself. Instincts for homing, for fight or flight. They were the simplest part of animate life, and if Dr Park didn't make a really fundamental mistake in that Petri dish, if the proteins were mixed properly, if the mechanics were right, then I'd have instincts, like an ant or a snake. But still, what exactly were they, how did the programming translate into this line of longing – imperious, babyish longing, demanding to reach my grandparents right away?

Palm Beach Airport was a two-dimensional, oversharp image against the baby-blue sky. The cab crawled through wall-to-wall traffic, endless cars shimmering metallically in the soupy heat, the air in the taxi feeling as if it were made of cold metal itself. From this close up, the white Hispanic haciendas, the strip of what passed for downtown, the blockbuster hotels rising straight up against the sea, looked like that old Pop Art stuff, flatter than anything I'd remembered from Plato's Caves. Maybe it was the air which thinned everything down.

Then we were out of the chic little shopping strip and into what I instantly recognized as Eldertown. I recognized it by the sprawling con-dominiums and the mobile medical units, and, of course, by the elders themselves in their pastel out-fits, promenading or wheeling themselves about. Occasionally, there was a blare of very old rock

160

music from a portable radio someone was carrying, probably illegally. Or maybe the laws were relaxed for this part of town.

97153 Monsanto Road turned out to be a long, low apartment building with balconies overlooking the sea-front. The lobby had a tacky reception area with a comatose-looking doorman in a sweaty T-shirt. The air-conditioning didn't cut through the heat, it just mixed vague, acrid smells into the lobby air.

'Yes?' the doorman said, barely turning his head towards me. 'What you lookin' for?'

I thought this time I was prepared, but I still wasn't. 'Mr and Mrs Surrey,' I said, and almost, once again, wished he'd say they weren't here, they'd left for Bali some time ago.

He lifted the intercom receiver. 'Your name?' he asked grumpily. This was happening very fast.

'Elizabeth. Just say Elizabeth.' I'd prepared this, but as soon as I spoke, it seemed very wrong. It seemed wrong to be perpetrating this deception through a surly doorman sprawled in a sloppy resentful way against a pinewood counter.

A man's voice, low and slightly hoarse, answered the intercom.

'There's a young lady here,' the doorman said with distinct scepticism. 'She wants to see you. She says her name is Elizabeth.' There was dead silence.

I heard a woman's voice in the background and a muffled conference.

'Elizabeth who?' the man's voice came back. 'Can you please ask her that?'

'Surrey,' I mouthed in a half-tone. There was another dead pause and another muffled exchange.

'What else can we do?' the woman's voice said more clearly in the background.

'OK,' the man said. 'Let her in.'

'Apartment 3F,' the doorman muttered reluctantly.

I took the elevator to the third floor and walked down the corridor very slowly. I rang the bell. I heard my own breathing while I waited. A tall, unsmiling woman opened the door. She was handsome, with short blonde hair and regular features which resembled Hers. Mine. Except her flesh was softened by age, her lips had lost some of their fruity fullness. The look in her grey eyes, in that first mini-second, was guarded, or maybe afraid. Then it turned to sheer fear.

'Who . . .' she said. 'Elizabeth?'

'I'm Iris,' I said quickly. 'The daughter.' We looked at each other wordlessly and then I saw a filminess cover her eyes. She swayed slightly and for a moment looked as if she was going to faint. Then the film cleared and at last she said, 'Come in.'

My grandfather was standing in the middle of the living room, as if in readiness to avert danger. He was a big man in every way, with a large head and deeply carved features. My mother's – my own – statuesqueness must have come from him. He

162

began to say something and then looked at me and moved towards his wife as if to protect her.

'Harry,' she said helplessly, reproachfully, 'this is not Elizabeth. It's Iris. You know, Lizzie's daughter.'

'Iris,' he repeated and then stopped. He was trying to grasp what was going on. 'You are Iris.'

There was a dead silence in which we all stood very still.

'Why,' he began, and then cleared his throat, as if trying to get his vocal chords around this, 'why did you pretend to be Elizabeth?'

I found I was having difficulty speaking. 'I was afraid you wouldn't want to see me otherwise,' I said. My voice was nearly inaudible.

My grandfather put his arm around his wife's shoulders. I couldn't figure out why they were still standing as if fixed in place, why their confused expressions were changing into something more horrified. Then I remembered: now that they understood who I was, they also realized they were seeing an apparition, a revenant, a spectre made flesh, or flesh that should have remained spectral. I was an attractive young girl, blonde and long-legged, dressed in a flowy creamy silk trouser suit – and I was the embodiment of the unacceptable. I was someone they'd never seen, masquerading as – no, inhabiting the body of – their long-lost daughter.

My grandfather started to speak again, stopped,

and tried again. 'This is a bit of a shock for us,' he finally said.

I nodded. I was beginning to feel a dangerous weakness, a dangerous weirdness.

She suddenly looked very worried. 'Has anything happened to Elizabeth?' she asked. 'Is that why you're here?'

'No,' I said quickly. 'She doesn't know. I mean, she doesn't know where I am . . .'

They looked at each other to check how they felt, what their next step should be. They stood there together, as if guarding a fortress, or fending off stormy seas. I thought, so this is where I spring from, these large Mount Rushmore figures. Spring from . . . Now that they were so near, they seemed implacably remote; the idea of springing from them seemed nearly as strange as coming out of that cylinder. And yet, there was warmth in their bodies and faces, I could tell, I could almost feel it; warmth that they were sending to each other, as they pulled together against the freakishness that was me. Some terrible urge was rising up in me to rush to them and embrace them; and even more to be embraced by them.

'Please sit down,' my grandfather finally said in a strained voice. 'Now that you're here, we might as well . . . have a talk.'

Did that mean I was going to be turned out after we had had one? We sat on two facing sofas, covered in flowered fabric. Their living room was almost touchingly old-fashioned, with its lacquered

164

Chinese cabinet and knick-knacks on glass shelves, and splotchy abstract paintings on the walls.

'I suppose we're both wondering what brought you here,' my grandfather said. His wife held on to his hand.

'Do you know . . .' she began and couldn't finish. But I realized that, of course, they didn't know whether I knew: my secret, my condition.

'I found out a few weeks ago,' I said before she could finish the sentence and then wanted to cry.

Her face wrenched in an attempt to take it all in, to comprehend. 'So is that why . . .' she began.

'Yes,' I said. 'Yes. I had to meet you. I mean, you are really . . . you are really my parents, aren't you?'

'Oh no, no, no, no,' my grandfather responded, and his features furrowed with an effort to expel the thought. 'No, Iris, it would be very wrong to think of us that way. We're not your parents, are we, Edith? We've never even met you until now.'

'No,' she said. 'No, we haven't . . .' But a smile of affection began to break out on her face; then her eyes went filmy again. 'You are so much like Lizzie,' she said, and shook her head as if to shake herself into clarity. 'This is very strange,' she added, and lapsed into silence.

'How did you find us, then?' my grandfather asked, after a pause. 'Since you said Elizabeth doesn't know you're here.'

So I told them. I told them about reading the letters and my growing suspicions, and the moment of discovery. I told them about going to Park Avenue and my decoding work. My spying. It wasn't easy to reveal so much, as they sat there in their concrete, their solid, stolid form, facing me across a glass-topped coffee table. I'd been driven to them by a piercing longing and I thought the longing would drive me straight into their arms, into an enfolding warmth, into a natural, a *human* intimacy. A family communion. But as they sat there, trying not to betray their reactions, I felt divided from them by a barrier so impenetrable it might as well have been made of heavy metal. Who were they and what were they thinking? Still, my grandmother began to smile when I told them about the letters and mentioned some of the things she'd written.

'Oh my,' she said and put her hand on my grandfather's hand. 'Do you remember, Harry? Do you remember?'

'Yes,' he said curtly. He wasn't liking this one bit. 'You see,' he said to me, as if trying to explain something complicated to someone very slow-witted, 'we haven't seen Elizabeth for a very long time. It's been difficult – I don't know whether you can understand – it was extremely difficult for us when she stopped talking to us. And now it is you who have come and . . . well, it's confusing. To say the least.'

'I know,' I said, feeling desolate. I was inflicting pain on them by my very presence. Should I withdraw myself from their sight, vanish as if

166

I'd never come? As if I had been an apparition, a hot afternoon's hallucination? They wished that, I knew, they wished me if not dead, then undone. Reversed. Cancelled. Unborn. But I wanted to be in their presence, that was the terrible thing. I wanted at least to look at them some more, at this soft, pretty woman in her light blue summer dress, and him – my grandfather, my . . . but now that he was so near, in his full, impressive stature, with his dignified grey hair and craggy features, I didn't dare think it.

'We should probably let Elizabeth know you're here,' he said sternly. 'She's your mother, after all.'

'No!' I protested, much too abruptly.

But my grandmother – her eyes were filming again, but she was also smiling, as if in a dream. 'You poor thing,' she said to me. 'It must be so very, very hard for you.' I nodded.

She contemplated me from her inturned gaze. 'Maybe you can stay with us for a few days,' she said, squeezing her husband's hand to forestall his protest. 'It might be like . . . Well, we have a lot to talk about, I'm sure. Now that we've met.'

She looked at him for confirmation. 'Of course,' my grandfather said uncertainly. I could see he was torn, he was tempted. 'Now that you've come, you should stay with us. Spend the night.'

I realized the invitation was not exactly wholehearted; and yet, I couldn't help feeling grateful, couldn't help feeling a new surge of longing. To be with them, to be comforted.

'Thank you,' I said. 'I won't overstay my welcome, I promise.'

'It's all right,' my grandfather managed to say and then got up to leave the room. 'We'll talk more in the morning.' There was no touching between us that evening – not even a glancing hand on arm – and very little conversation. Once or twice, as she showed me around the apartment and then to my room, my grandmother smiled at me out of her soft face in a way that seemed entirely natural. Naturally affectionate. But then she quickly recovered herself and drew the smile back, as if it were wrong to look at me like that. As if the affection just sneaked out unawares.

And yet, despite everything, as I lay in the big guest bed, I indulged in an illusion of safety, soothed by the sound of the air-conditioning, and the texture of the clean, crisp sheets. I felt the building humming around me with unfamiliar noises and after an hour or so, when I thought my host and hostess would be asleep, I got out of bed and made my way through the apartment, pausing in its dimly lit spaces, breathing in its unassuming dimensions, its ordinariness.

On the mantelpiece in the den there were rows of photographs. I turned on the light and scanned them, and then, compelled by curiosity and anxiety, looked more closely. It was my fate to learn about myself by inference, from external data and clues. Here was more evidence to wrench my heart: my grand/parents at a much younger age, clean-cut and handsome against some dappled foliage; my grand/parents more recently, smooth-faced and robust, sitting by the pool of this very condominium, like some ad for wonder-elders. And there was . . . I, for there was not doubt it was I, at about the same age as I was now, mugging at the camera, with a group of young people around me, caught at some playful moment. And She/me again, with another young woman whom I recognized as my sister/aunt, both of them coquettish, playing up their sisterhood, the doubled plenitude of their femininity. I now wanted to believe this was me, I nearly believed it; I was being transported into another time, and a space in my head opened up in which I was happy and laughing . . . Laughing out of that photo, out of my girlish pleasure. There I was, in another photo, standing in front of Big Ben, I think, in a fur-trimmed winter coat, looking up adoringly at my big, blocky father, while he, pipe held briefly away from his mouth in a nonchalant gesture, looked down at me with a benign smile.

I turned around. My grandfather was standing behind me, in pyjamas and a bathrobe. I had just grasped the fullness of his fatherly fondness in those photographs, his sheltering affection. Oh Father, I wanted to cry. Please let this whole past, the only past I might ever have, be mine. Please let your fatherly care be mine. Let it be mine if only for now. Let it at least once have been mine.

'How is Elizabeth?' he asked, as if we'd been in the middle of a conversation. 'I've worried about her so often. How is she, really?'

'I don't know,' I whispered. For some reason, it came out as a whisper. 'I'm too close to her to know.'

He contemplated me attentively, his gaze concentrated to a pinpoint, as if he were trying to pierce through to something inside. Who I was, what I was. My character. My essence. Old metaphors, insufficient to the occasion.

'It must be very hard for you, I imagine,' he said. 'I mean, to know . . . who you are.' I nodded mutely. 'I tried to warn her against this, you know,' he continued. 'But she was always strong-headed. So I guess if you're anything like her, you're strong too. And I guess you are very like her, aren't you?'

I nodded again. What he said was oddly solacing. He hadn't wanted me to be; but he had tried to imagine – something. The condition of a creature like me. A distressing tenderness was filling up my chest. I wanted him to explain things to me, wanted to keep hearing his slightly hoarse, full voice. A voice thickened into a rich impasto by a layering of tones, of years.

'Was she a good mother to you?' he asked. I shrugged hopelessly. She was so good a mother, and no mother at all.

He came closer and then, as if I were a doe or a unicorn, as if I were a creature whose nature he wanted to ascertain, he ran his hand over my face. His large, hooded eyes were peering at me pensively.

'I don't think we can help you, you know,' he said. 'Edith has not been well lately and this is very confusing for her . . .' I nodded miserably. I was going to be thrown out in the morning. 'But you're a lovely young girl.' He added. 'There's no reason why you shouldn't be a normal young woman. Why you shouldn't have your own life.'

My own life. I had no idea what he meant. 'You take care,' he said. 'I'll see you in the morning.' Then, shuffling a little in his open-back slippers, he turned away from me and left.

Still, I had the next day with them. I was given that. A whole day with my grandparents, who for whole, brimming hours took me in. Or nearly. Nearly enough for me to have felt . . . Well, nearly taken in. Into the family. Into the human fold.

Not that there weren't rough moments. In the morning, when I came into the kitchen, my grandmother turned round and put her hand up to her mouth instinctively, as if to suppress an exclamation. 'I'm sorry,' she blurted out, 'it's just your gestures, and everything . . .'

'Is it that bad?' I asked. My eyes were still gluey with sleep, but this jolted me into wakefulness and despondency.

171

'It's just that I thought I remembered her exactly. You know, a mother thinks she remembers her child at every age, but I didn't not in such . . . detail. It's the details that make her come back . . . I'm sorry,' she added miserably. 'It'll just take a little time.'

I knew she wouldn't be speaking like this in her husband's presence. As if I were someone with whom she could be intimate. With whom she could naturally share her reactions. And indeed she turned away from me in embarrassment when my grandfather came in.

He said good morning heartily, giving me just a slight pat on my shoulder to acknowledge what had happened between us in the night, and suggested in a jolly sort of way that we should have breakfast on the balcony. He must have made some sort of decision to deal with me. To be nice to me.

So we went out on the balcony, the air already swelling with vapours, but not yet unbearable. The morning light wasn't kind to my grandparents; they were, after all, in their mid-nineties. But I felt odd affection for the wrinkled heaviness of my grandmother's upper arms, for the exposed scrawniness of my grandfather's throat. These were the indentations of vulnerability, grooves to pour affection into. If they let me, if this lasted more than a day.

The other balconies were also filling up with elders, shuffling out of their shuttered rooms singly or in pairs, with newspapers and bagels and cups of coffee, to warm themselves in the morning sun before the heat became vicious. On the balcony next to ours a jaunty, pipe-thin old man was riding his exercycle and waving to everybody in sight.

'Whoa there!' he called over to us. 'Who's the pretty young lady visiting us old folk this morning?'

'This is Iris,' my grandmother said, and paused a smidgeon before adding, 'a relative. She's come for a little visit. Iris, this is Joe, our very good neighbour.'

'Well, I'm one hundred and six years old, young lady, I'll have you know!' Joe shouted triumphantly, without ceasing to pump the exercycle. 'Would you have guessed it? Would you have given me that much?'

I shook my head, but none of us pursued this amazing fact.

'I suppose you want to have some privacy with your pretty young visitor,' Joe shouted, clearly put out. 'That's all right. I would too if she were my relative!'

'Maybe you could come over for a drink later this afternoon, Joe,' my grandfather suggested politely. 'You know what the doctors say, a drink a day . . .'

'I will if I have time,' Joe replied huffily. He wasn't going to be mollified that easily. But he never did come over, of course. Time swerved in a different direction that afternoon, deflecting us from anything as mundane as a medically advisable drink.

173

That morning, though, we tried to carry on as if everything were perfectly normal. 'What kind of juice do you like?' my grandmother asked, and 'Is that coffee strong enough?' We tried not to get further than that just yet, though I felt licks of longing flaring up. Little snakes of curiosity, uncurling. I wanted to ask everything. To be told everything. But it wasn't time yet, I had to bide my time.

Undoubtedly, during much of that day, they were suppressing their own thoughts. My grandfather, especially, must have been wondering hard all that day, wondering about all kinds of things. In my grandmother's face there seemed to be little space in which to conceal anything; she looked as if decades of goodness had simplified her into a pastel gouache.

But they were both good, they had funds of goodness. I had demonstrations of it at every turn in the course of that brief, endless day. After breakfast they wanted to give me a tour of Palm Beach, maybe to defer the Talk that was beginning to loom between us. During our slow amble through Eldertown's symmetrical streets, in between Harry's analysis of the class and ethnic composition of the neighbourhood, and Edith's vignettes of the more historic buildings, my grandparents stopped to chat with people who wanted to exchange some titbit of news, or ask advice or just have a nice little morning complain. One very old lady with wispy bluish hair told them about a scam perpetrated on her family by a fake pensions' investor, another about a spate of nasty assaults in her condominium complex.

'Oh, Mrs Surrey,' an old Chicano woman said, after detailing a tale of police incompetence and ill-will, 'I wonder if it's good to live so long. I wonder very day.'

'Shush, Mrs Gomez,' my grandmother said. 'It's a sin to think like that. We should be grateful for every day we're given.'

I wondered briefly why it was a sin, why it was desirable for Mrs Gomez to live as long as possible, no matter what. Still, they were good, my grandparents, that was the important part, good in some way I hadn't seen before, in some homey, simple way. I think I actually started walking closer to them, wanting to absorb their decency, cosy up to their kindness, their indiscriminate care, their humble, human values. More people came up with their morning news and problems. Clearly, Harry and Edith were seen as a fount of wisdom in Eldertown, and I felt rushes of balmy warmth in their proximity, even as the heat began to swirl up and the sun to radiate its yellow threat.

We stepped into a restaurant for lunch, a vast eating emporium decorated with cooling natural motifs – coral reefs, pine forests, a Himalayan meadow. When we sat down, the tension of the unspoken made us all silent. The Subject was between us, palpably, but my grandparents still seemed determined to prevent it from rearing its head. Or maybe they just didn't know what to say. So we spoke about the menu, and how nice it was that lunch came with Fast Feel-Goods at no extra charge. I felt time, my precious time with them, trickling away. They were so close and yet so far, and they held the key, I was sure of it: the key to me.

Over coffee, my grandmother started looking at me with that vague, remote expression. 'We just wanted her to have a child,' she said, out of nowhere. 'Was that so wrong of us?'

'Please, Edith,' Harry said, putting his hand on hers.

This was puzzling. 'Then why did you break off with her?' I burst out. 'Why did you ... abandon me?'

Even as I said it, I felt the ineptness, the inaptness, of it. I felt that this anodyne environment would absorb, sponge up anything that was said, whatever terrible revelations might emerge.

My grandfather cleared his throat and began to say this was not the time. But she came into focus again and said that maybe I needed to know. Maybe I had the right. I felt a wash of excessive gratitude threatening to emerge in some wet, wimpsh way: my grandmother thought I had ordinary, human rights.

'It wasn't you,' she began and then looked at me and couldn't continue. 'Not exactly.' She crumpled a napkin in utter frustration.

'Then what?' I said. 'What?'

176

'It was the way she did it,' Edith said. 'The way she cut us out. I mean, of course, we didn't think it would happen that way . . . We just wanted her to have a child, that's all. And she was our favourite, too. Which was probably wrong of us, wasn't it, Harry? To have favourites.'

'So then you resented her for it,' I stated. My Human Education courses hadn't been for nothing.

'No,' Edith protested, with some heat. 'We wanted the best for her. We wanted her to have a baby . . . Isn't that only natural? But we didn't mean . . . We didn't want . . .'

'You mean, I wasn't exactly natural,' I said.

'Edith feels badly because she thinks we pressed her too hard, you see,' Harry said. 'I guess we were traditional parents, though we prided ourselves on being so progressive. We wanted grandchildren and I guess from time to time we said so.'

'And I guess I don't count as a grandchild, do I?' I said, bitterly. I didn't seem to be able to stop myself. There was silence.

'There were other things too,' Harry said thoughtfully. 'Elizabeth was very wilful, very capricious, you see. Which was very cute when she was a child. But it was also her flaw. Her tragic flaw, you might say, given what happened later.'

'We tried to see her, even after . . .' my grandmother said. 'But she made it impossible. Still, we could have been more sensitive. I'm not sure I understood what was going on with

177

her. We did things we shouldn't have done.' She looked into my face with her innocent, grey eyes, trying to put me together with those long-ago mistakes, undoubtedly; trying to figure out their unplanned, over-planned, unimagined and unimaginable result.

'I wish you'd stop this, Edith,' Harry said to his wife. 'Get off this self-blame thing. It's about time.' Then he went on, in a tougher tone, 'And you also shouldn't forget about all the other things she did, our darling Elizabeth. How she changed all of a sudden. We did the best we could for her, but she had her own character. We couldn't help that.'

'What things?' I asked, all too eagerly. 'What did she do?'

Harry shook his head. 'Oh, there was that business with Janey. She really hurt Janey, you know . . .' He stopped, his big features deflating into an old, remembered defeat.

'And then, there was that business . . . the wedding . . .' my grandmother said. 'And, of course, Janey tried to have children too, poor thing . . . Oh, it was very confusing, what happened,' she said yet again.

I was sensing the drama behind my birth; sensed my existence – my coming-into-the-world – hanging in the balance. But how was I ever going to derive myself from these foggy, fragmented clues? How was I ever going to arrive from this misty landscape of my pre-birth to who I was?

'Did she try to see you . . .' I began, but Harry interrupted me decisively.

'The fact that we are not in contact with Elizabeth doesn't mean that a day goes by when we don't think about her,' he brought out, and then, as if he'd made too much effort, he got up and said, 'time for the news. What do you say, Iris? Do you watch the news?'

I didn't usually, but I couldn't imagine anything lovelier than going back to their apartment and sitting around the Data Dispenser as if we were the most ordinary family grouping in the world. Even given everything we'd said. To sit around as if our conversation hadn't taken place – didn't need to take place. Or as if it referred to the most banal history of family affinities and family tensions. Just an ordinary family story.

And so we went back and sat in front of their desperately old data box with chilled drinks which my grandma brought us from the kitchen. Both of them followed the news earnestly, shaking their heads from time to time over the day's roster of catastrophes and iniquities. There was the usual spate of weather disasters and a Strato Shuttle accident, and there was of course another war, small but nasty, taking place somewhere on the border between China and Mongolia. For a moment, I felt a rush of supportive feelings going out to little Mongolia because of Piotr's rescue. I was ready to cheer it on in its war, which involved shadowy guerrilla groups

179

using primitive but surprisingly effective weapons – tanks and machetes and some old bombers – in their fight against equally shadowy groups of Chinese expansionists, who claimed rights to large parts of the fledgling Mongolian state's territory, on the grounds that it had been part of the Chinese kingdom in the Middle Period. But the newscaster pointed out that, whatever the historical justifications, you couldn't really blame the Mongolians for wanting to keep the Chinese out, given that the Mongolian population was growing apace, and that the region's climate was warming up alarmingly, throwing the whole ecology out of kilter. On the other hand, you couldn't exactly blame the Chinese either, since their numbers had grown beyond anything which could be contained within their own borders. In fact, the newscaster concluded, this was a conflict in which there were no clear rights and wrongs. The President had reiterated his policy of benign neglect. Then, eliding neatly into the next story, the newscaster added that there was some hope on the horizon for countries like Mongolia, since the extra-terrestrial environments being constructed by a consortium of governments and private companies were fast reaching the point of human habitability. Naturally, the inhabitants of the world's most crowded areas would be given priority among applicants for ExT living.

'Sure,' my grandfather said, 'they'll use the poor

as experimental fodder, as always. But who knows, if these sites could be organized on better principles, I don't mean anything radical, but maybe something like kibbutzim . . . What do you say, Edith? Do you remember how excited we were about the kibbutzim?' He turned to his wife, but no answer was forth-coming. My grandmother, I tried not to notice, had been staring at me fixedly, but when I looked at her directly, I saw that she seemed paler, more drawn than in the morning. Then she did something that made me tremble with tenderness; she brushed my hair away from my face. She was contemplating me with utter puzzlement, but also, I recognized, love. Love was struggling to break through her closed, her shielded features, but love for whom? That was surely the bafflement, the perplexity that seemed to be breaking down the unity of her face. As love tried to break through, as love broke her down . . . Love breaking out from long ago, surely from long ago. She couldn't make it out, couldn't put it together. How could she? There I was, the very image of her daughter. No – there I was, her daughter. I sensed it, grasped it, in a flash. Her daughter was sitting next to her, before she'd been lost, before she went bad in the most peculiar up-to-date way. Her daughter again, given back young and entire, as if you could rewind time – or maybe not as if. No, surely time had reeled back for her, for real. She smiled. She smiled beautifully, merrily, affectionately, like a young woman.

'It's been so long,' she said. 'We'll have such fun now that you're here.'

'Edith,' my grandfather said sharply. 'Please. This isn't Lizzie. This is Iris.'

Time ran back, or forward, through her eyes, fading them again. 'Oh goodness,' she said, and her features smoothed out and closed.

'Oh goodness, how silly of me. I didn't mean . . . It's just so very confusing.' She looked miserably baffled and embarrassed. 'I'm so sorry, Iris,' she said. 'This must be terrible for you.'

'Should I leave?' I asked. I so much didn't want the answer to be yes.

Through her misery, in a flat voice, my grandmother said, 'It's not your fault, Iris, you mustn't feel that. I'm getting old, I get confused at times – don't I, Harry? Or maybe the world has just passed me by, I can't figure it all out . . .'

'Did you think it was horrible of her . . . to have me?' I asked. It was wrong of me to ask this just then, but this was the essential question I'd been restraining all day, the point I had to press, the primal scene, primal pain. This was really what I had to know.

They both looked down at the table. 'Yes,' my grandfather said finally. His tone was firm. 'Yes. We thought it was wrong to do what she did.'

'So you don't think I'm quite . . . right, then?' I said, feeling a terrible resignation.

My grandmother interposed, before he could say anything more. 'It doesn't mean anything about you,' she said. 'You are not responsible for this. And maybe we are . . . Well, we are simple people in some ways, I suppose. We aren't religious, or anything, but we believed . . . Well, I suppose we believe life is sacred. God-given. That it's not up to us.'

'A swim, anyone?' my grandfather said. Once again, things were getting too much for him; he wanted to normalize the atmosphere. We went down to the pool, set pleasantly among the green hedges framing the condo's outdoor area. But the fluorescent blue rectangle was chock-a-block with oldsters, floating or just raking the water with their hands, their wrinkled or overstretched torsos sticking out above the surface.

So we walked down to the sea. The sun was beginning to do its sizzling work. The shore was pebbly and narrow; and the grey-green sea lapped against it tamely, drawing in and then ejecting some of the beach debris. Still, we walked into the water with relief and afterwards stretched out on our towels, grateful to be briefly cool and wet.

For a while we didn't speak. My grandmother was looking at my body, my borrowed body with its milky skin, its long, well-formed legs. I knew I had well-formed limbs, I'd seen their shape on another. And she – she'd seen this body before, had seen it develop from infancy, knew how it would look in its next stage, in a few years.

She seemed to be pondering a question. 'Has

Lizzie ever talked about how she grew up?' she asked. 'About us?'

I shook my head and she looked hurt. 'But that was because of me,' I added, 'because she didn't want me to know.'

'The worst thing is that we keep asking ourselves where we went wrong,' my grandmother said again, as if she were raising a new subject. 'What our mistakes were.'

She said it this time as if she was interrogating me, as if I were the clue to their mistakes, as well as their living, all-too-solid proof. But I also sensed that my grandmother wanted to explain herself to me, to be relieved of some strange guiltiness. To be reprieved by me, whom she thought she'd caused.

'Don't, Edith, don't,' my grandfather said quite gently.

'Did Elizabeth tell you about the summers in Maine?' his wife continued as if she hadn't heard him. I said no, she hadn't.

'Really?' she said, as if she couldn't grasp the hugeness of the blank silence in which I'd grown up. 'I'm surprised. We had such wonderful times there, didn't we, Harry?'

'Hmmm . . .' my grandfather said and his expression softened just a bit. He looked as if he were musing, as if time were now flying backwards inside him, back to some other part of himself. 'Yes. Yes, we did. We were a whole young family then, you see, Iris,' he said to me,

184

and he looked at me kindly, as if I were a close friend to whom one could tell family stories. 'There aren't many of those around any more, and we were unusual even then, the last of the Mohicans . . . It was about to fall down around our ears, but when we were in Maine we felt all was right in heaven and on earth.' He smiled wryly. 'Yes, we did.'

'We spent whole weeks together there,' my grandmother continued, as if picking up a tale they both knew by heart. 'Harry even took time off work, which was quite an achievement for a workaholic like him. Wasn't it, Harry? We took long walks in the woods, and played lots of Scrabble and sang together in the evenings. And of course we had long discussions, too, we had strong ideas about how to educate the girls, very definite ideas. We wanted to give something to them. A sense of values. And we seemed to be doing well, didn't we, Harry?'

'So it seemed,' my grandfather said more stiffly. 'While it lasted.'

'Tell me more,' I said softly. I was listening to my grandmother's plain memories as if they were filled with sensuous light. I was nearly there, a little girl thrilled with everything, running on the sandy beach, sea-waves lapping at her toes, picking wild strawberries in the woods and savouring their speckled sweet texture, hurtling through the porch door into the house and running up to her big, her wonderful father . . . Yes, I was there, of course I remembered . . .

My grand/mother went on reminiscing, describing. The barbecues in the garden with the smoke rising up into the clear air; the friends who came to visit, and the day Janey tripped while trying to cross a stream by stepping on the dry, slippery pebbles, and broke her ankle and lay there helplessly, till some passer-by happened to hear her crying . . .

'Do you remember?' my grandmother asked me, smiling wistfully. She was looking straight at me, and as her eyes met mine, as they probed and questioned, I saw the confusion scattering her glance, her sureness. She tried to hold on to herself, to the reality before her. The fact of who I was.

'Oh God,' she gasped. 'This is all too incomprehensible for me. You're my child come again, and it's something for which I've wished all these years . . .'

I felt the vice of a new paradox tighten my throat: I, who wanted to be humanized by her, was the monster responsible for her pain. I was caught, but also touched, melted by her fragility. I tried to take her hand in reassurance, but she pulled it away, and tears of sheer tension appeared in her eyes. I was her child and I was an alien, an impossibility come most unnaturally to life.

I withdrew my hand. 'Let's go,' my grandfather said gently. 'Let's go back, Edith.'

So we gathered our things and started walking back, our steps heavier, more laden, even though the sun was losing some of its poisonous sting and the asphalt was cooling down from its bubbling point. I followed them silently, tracking my thoughts through the coilings of my brain as we walked, tracking what, whom my grandmother had seen in my face, the kind of creature I was in her eyes.

It happened as I stepped absently off the kerb. I was about to cross and was letting one of those new electric mini-cars, a fuchsia-coloured bug, pass. Then I heard – felt – an odd sound behind me. I turned and saw my grandmother gasp. It was a more powerful, deeper, more convulsive version of the gasp she had emitted just a few minutes before; then she slid down to the pavement in an awful, helpless motion, a movement that left her in an awkwardly sprawled, hoarsely breathing heap. A movement that had deathliness in it.

My grandfather, in a simultaneous motion, was kneeling down beside her. 'Edith!' he cried. Then I was bending down too, seeing, through the fog of my anxiety, the heaving of my grandmother's chest. Her breathing was turning into a sort of mewling noise – how awful, the sudden, inexorable subsiding of strength – and her eyes were filming over as if with a layer of diluted milk.

'Ambulance!' my grandfather shouted, and my mind flashed briefly to Mrs Gomez with her tales of official incompetence. But the ambulance seemed to be there almost instantly. Or at least it seemed instant, though it must have taken at least two or three minutes, for in the meantime a little crowd formed around us, shouting directions at my grandfather, who was pumping my grandmother's chest and breathing into her mouth with hoarse intakes of air.

Then the medics were putting an oxygen mask over my grandmother's face and inserting a Revive chip into her arm, even as others were lifting the stretcher and wheeling it smoothly into the dim zone of the ambulance.

It was a massive heart attack with various complications; and in the hospital, the psycho-physiologist on duty quickly told my grandfather that the prospects were very bad unless he agreed to fairly substantial parts replacements, possibly including brain implants, to cope with the oxygen-deprivation which had followed the attack. These were still in an experimental stage and sometimes altered the recipient's personality in unexpected ways. 'Of course, it could be for the better!' the psycho-physiologist said quite seriously. In all honesty, he also had to point out that the procedures were still very expensive.

'Do you want to think it over for half an hour?' he asked my grandfather. 'I think we can keep her going on the Revive chip for that long.'

'No,' my grandfather said fiercely. 'I don't want to think it over. I don't want any of it. It's not what she'd want. It's not what I want. I may be old-fashioned, but I don't want to keep her alive like some bionic robot. She should at least have the dignity of finishing her life as herself.'

'Good choice, Mr Surrey,' the psycho-physiologist said softly. 'Though not many make it.'

So we sat by her bedside that evening, watching for signs of improvement and decline. As if anything could be done about either. And yet the signs had to be witnessed, in their every minute, hopeless alteration. They had to be witnessed for human life to continue; for human beings not to slide into an abyss of unmeaning. They had to be witnessed for our sake, as much as for hers. That much I understood. And how strange that it's at that final moment that humans seem to be willing to attend most unreservedly to one another; to perform, finally, that close, unjudgemental reading of lip and eye, of striving and failure, that is the real act of love.

And so we watched, and I was devastated. For of course, she thought I was Her, her daughter, her real child. As consciousness receded from her – some form of consciousness, anyway, for she was coherent, just not present – she was back in Maine, and in New York of long ago, talking to Lizzie and full of love for her. From her bed, where she lay attached to instruments and graphs, she gave me a fond, playful smile.

'You're looking so well,' she said. 'College obviously suits you. Or is it the young man . . . We have so much to talk about . . . You know, I was wondering what you think about . . . you know, what happened, that thing in the newspaper . . .' But here she faded; it was too much effort to retrieve some topical subject from the 1980s, no matter how important it seemed then. It's not the topical passions that remain for the ultimate moments. Still, her lips puckered, her forehead furrowed. What was it she'd once wanted to talk about to her newly sophisticated daughter?

My grandfather took her hand; he looked terribly distressed. 'Please, Edith,' he said, 'this isn't Lizzie. This is . . . her daughter. The one we've never met.'

She pulled her hand away, and looked at him contemptuously, as if he were stupid or mad.

'You know, I was thinking,' she said, addressing Her again, as if his interference could only be ignored, 'we should start a herb garden this summer, when we go to Maine. You will come to Maine with us, won't you?' she asked, her voice filling with anxiety. I nodded. I would, of course I would. 'That's good,' she said. 'Because Janey, you know . . . Janey wants . . .' She struggled to find the right words. 'Janey misses you.' She paused and looked at us with intense reproach. 'Where's Janey?' she asked. 'She should be here. I'm very sick, can't you tell?'

'Yes, yes, I know,' my grandfather said urgently, trying to seize the threads of her presence, to hold her with him, in the present. 'You are very ill. But I'm here. I'm here, Edith. I wish you'd talk to me.'

She looked at him imploringly. 'Harry,' she said, 'I'm so unhappy. I think I'm dying.' He kissed her

190

hand and the long-ago smile came over her face, and she said, 'But the important thing is . . . the important thing is . . . We'll have a wonderful time in Maine, won't we? The important thing is that we're all together. And Lizzie is doing so well. I'm so proud of her. And Janey too.'

My grandfather nodded and smiled back. Perhaps he didn't have the heart to keep distressing her, or perhaps he'd half transported himself into her mind, travelled with her for a moment to that other time.

She turned to me again and her tone darkened. 'That man, though,' she said, 'the one with the . . . with the . . . nose-ring. I don't like him. I don't like him one bit.'

'I know,' I said, 'but he's not so bad, really, Mom. He's really smart and good at what he does. I wish you'd give him a chance.'

That was when my grandfather looked at me with hatred. Pure, piercing hatred. I moved back a step, as if punched. I was in a sensitized mood, I felt all the currents of emotion flowing between the three of us with a physical accuracy. Oh, of course, I knew my grandmother's love wasn't really flowing towards me. It was meant for Her. But I wasn't really pretending – not really. I just slid a degree within myself, into the part that was Her, the spectral surround which was always there. My response came quite naturally. I was shocked by that shaft of hate.

191

He said in a flat voice, 'Please leave us alone. I need to be alone with my wife now.'

I felt tears, hurt baby tears, rising. I was being thrown out just when I felt such . . . intimacy. When the barriers seemed, finally, to give way. It wasn't right that this moment should be taken away from me.

'Please let me stay,' I said, not even feeling the humiliation of it. This was no time for pride. 'I don't have . . . anyone else.'

'You're confusing her,' he said in a hard voice. 'I won't have it. Please leave.'

I don't know whether I'd ever felt as forlorn as I did in that hospital corridor, waiting with some other desolates for the next summons, the next bit of news. To have had a hint of love, even for a day; of a place where I might, in time, rightfully belong; and then to be ejected like some disposable stray – it felt more acutely hurtful than anything I'd known before. I sat there in the yellow-lit hallway, receding into a dark space, as if it were not worthwhile to be within my body, visible in the light. I was the thing that could be thrown out, the extra, the unplaced, the unplaceable. I thought of Her, or rather, felt her presence burgeoning within me: it was in her place that I was here. It was she who would always occupy my place, would always have been there already. Two physical objects cannot occupy the same space. It was the first lesson I'd learnt in basic physics. As basic as you can get, and no quantum or string physics had managed to undo it yet.

My grandfather came out after half an hour, and made himself speak to me, though he couldn't bear to look. His expression miserably combined defeat and repugnance.

'She's calling for Elizabeth,' he said. 'I don't have it in me to deny her this.'

So I went in. My grandmother had worsened even while I was out in the hallway. Her face was ashen, bluish. Her breathing was rasping and laboured. Her sturdy frame seemed to be collapsing upon itself. Life, whatever it was – life which inflated the veins and gave elasticity to the skin, which made the heart pump and leap, which kept the organism organic – was leaving her, degree by degree, like waves subsiding after a windy day. The cellular structure was still there, the structure from which She/I had emerged; but some basic principle that had kept it in movement, circulating, dancing, was departing. The genetic sources were failing to send their unceasing, astonishingly precise, mysterious signals to keep going; or else, they were sending the signal to cease. The motor was turning off. The systems were going down. The batteries were running out of fluid. Her *élan vital* was evaporating. No metaphor was sufficient for this.

'Lizzie,' she rasped, her eyes turning on me with unashamed love, 'I'm so glad you're here. Someone was trying to keep you away from me.'

I went up to her, and put my face close to hers. 'Actually, I am Iris,' I said. Perhaps I was still hurt, or perhaps I wanted to give myself a chance to be recognized. At this final moment. To be recognized for who I was.

'No, no,' she said, 'don't confuse me. I don't know Iris. I don't. Anyway, you're Lizzie. I knew you'd come back.'

And so I nodded, and smiled at her, and put my hand on her shoulder. 'I've missed you and Dad,' I said.

I heard my grandfather's agitated breathing behind me. But I was only telling the truth. I'd missed them all my life, and now I was feeling relief – for Her, for me – to be with this mother in this ultimate moment. And, of course, grief – our conjoined grief.

Edith looked at me heartbreakingly, imploringly. 'I didn't mean to . . .' she said. 'I didn't mean to make you feel bad . . .'

'I know,' I said, and cried. I was crying for her, for her daughter, for myself. 'It's not your fault. You didn't do anything wrong.'

'Really?' she said, and her features – heartbreakingly – relaxed into a kind of deep inward smile. She'd been forgiven, after all this time, by the child she'd loved.

Her expression changed to a poignant serenity. 'I hope you're happy,' she whispered. 'Less restless. You've been so ambitious . . .' Then some filaments of anxiety flitted over her face again.

'Janey, you know, has been very hurt . . .' She was rasping now and looked at me as if it took all of her remaining power to form a question. 'Where's Janey?' she asked. 'What's happened to her?'

'She's all right,' I said. 'She'll be here any time.'

'Oh good,' she said, and closed her eyes. 'I think I'll just rest for a while.'

So we sat there by her bed together, my grandfather and I, and we hardly dared look at each other. What we were doing was merciful, what we were doing was vile. I could see he was as wretched as a human being could be.

But we sat there very quietly. My grandmother's breathing was even now; she seemed to be dozing peacefully. Then the agony began: she opened her eyes. Her breathing became suddenly very laboured. Fear – ah, life was there yet – crept into her eyes, through some mysterious channel.

'It hurts,' she whispered, and then louder, 'I'm in pain!'

'Wait, Edith, wait,' my grandfather said and he ran out into the hallway.

'I'm scared, Lizzie,' she said and I took her hand. The nurse was there almost immediately, administering morphine, or whatever painkillers they used, straight into the veins. Within seconds my grandmother's face cleared.

'Keep holding my hand,' she said, and then some ghost of a thought passed over her face and she struggled to catch it, to articulate it. 'Your daughter,' she said finally. 'You had a daughter, didn't you? . . . Where is she, Lizzie? Where is she?'

195

I shook my head wordlessly. My grandfather was taking her hand away from mine almost roughly. 'Edith,' he said, 'I'm here. I'm here with you.'

She gave him an intimate, suddenly alert look. 'That's good,' she said in a confidential tone, 'because I'm dying.'

'I'll follow you soon,' he whispered back. 'Trust me.'

She looked at him with an expression of nearly unbearable poignancy, an expression in which there was childish hope and a childish question. She struggled to say something back to him; but now all consciousness – even that other consciousness, from which she'd been speaking – was subsiding, scrambling itself round words and time-zones, round some internal windings or chromosomal loops.

'Mommy,' she suddenly said, and it was a faint equivalent of an exclamation, an urgent plea. 'Do you think I will . . . I have a daughter, you know . . . and another. Janey. She should be here. I want to see her now.'

'She will be here soon,' my grandfather said. 'She's trying to come.'

Then there were words and snatches of phrases, and names I didn't know. But she spoke to me – to Her – once again; her consciousness returned one last time for that.

'Lizzie,' she said, in an intense whisper. The words were coming with great effort, but it was an effort she heart-breakingly wanted to make. 'I always loved you, even when I was angry. You are . . .' the voice was now no more than an exhalation, a gossamer breath on the air, 'the apple of my eye.'

There was a ghost of a smile playing somewhere in her features, a ghost of that spirit which travels through us from God knows where and fills our eyes with fear or with love. Then her eyes filmed over with milky blindness and the spirit receded as if called back to where it had come from, and was gone. My grandmother gave up the ghost.

On the way back to the airport I felt as if I'd been ricocheted away from a goal I'd been trying to reach – I'd almost reached – by an explosion that had hurled me right back in the direction from which I'd come.

When I tried to embrace my grandfather in the hospital room, he held me off stiffly, almost angrily. 'I shouldn't have let you do this,' he said in a strangled voice. 'I had never lied to her before. How could I, at the very end?'

'But it made her feel better,' I said pleadingly. I had performed that last deception out of such . . . love. 'And maybe it wasn't even a lie.'

'You can't say that,' he said vehemently. 'You are not Lizzie. You cannot undo reality like that. No matter what.' He looked at me in frustration, confusion, fury. Yes, I could see how he felt: I was chaos and I caused chaos for others.

'What we did was wrong,' he said finally, and

197

difficult tears filled his eyes. I thought, for a moment, that he'd include me in his grief. But no, we never like those with whom we're complicit in wrongdoing.

'Can I please say goodbye to her?' I asked.

'Go on,' he said in a broken voice. 'I can't stop you. Go on.'

And so I sat by the bed, looking into my grandmother's forever mute, forever closed face. In death, with her skin smoothed out and stretched over her bones, she looked more like Her, more like me. I could see the similarity of the structure, the skeletal scaffolding on which life had been hung, our nearly separate lives; I could see how She/I could have been stamped out of this pattern, this mould. I sat by the bed and stared, not daring to touch her. I'd disturbed her enough, disturbed her perhaps unto death; and now her death closed off my past, my entry-point into the longer continuum of time, as if by a resounding slam of a forbidding gateway. No admission. No entry. Not for me. I felt pressed right up against my grandmother's shut features, against the slammed gate, against my own pastlessness. I was once again ejected, like a mote of useless dust in the smooth texture of time, an irritating déjà vu. I had had no proper birth, and nobody wanted to acknowledge that I was occupying a rightful place in the world. I had no space and I had no time; I was still the snag, the hiccup where the virtual begins to repeat itself, the same image over and over again, so that you're caught on some strange side street in Tirana, or in a plane which can't come down. She had taken it all away from me: my time, my place, my family and their need for me, my childhood, my slow latency, my prankish early teens. She'd been there first and had swallowed up my rightful life in her womb, in a pouch of time where I had not yet existed and from which I might never, never emerge. It was as if I'd never been well and truly born.

Metaphysics begins at home. Some of us support the structure of reality; I was the undoing of reality, the unravelling of basic laws. I was a lie, a non-being masquerading as Being; therefore, I should not exist. But there was another solution which I began dimly to perceive as the plane once again lifted me off the ground and towards my destination. As long as She existed, my reality – my meaning – was abolished. Therefore she should not exist. Two objects cannot occupy the same space. One plus one in my case equalled zero. But one minus one . . . Ah, there was an equation whose outcome was yet to be seen.

It seemed my ill luck to keep finding myself at airports at night. I walked through O'Hare's endless corridors and out into a flat darkness, punctuated dimly by yellow, unbeckoning lights. Lights receding into ceaseless stretches of highway, of endlessly unspooling, unhomed space. The taxi with its driver whom I'd woken from his nap, sped along the N121 soundlessly, encountering only the occasional flashes of another car; at this hour, it seemed as if the world had become uninhabited. On the outskirts of our town the green sign of the electric recharge station was muted to near extinguishment.

The taxi created narrow funnels of light as we drove through the dark streets, past the familiar outlines of the college buildings. I directed the driver to our neighbourhood, sensing the contours of streets through the rustling trees, the silvery sculpture in somebody's yard, the sudden hiss and yowl of mating cats. I felt both illicit and safe as long as I was in the taxi. Then we were at our house, its silhouette briefly bathed in the taxi's reflectors. I paid and got out.

'Will you be all right?' the driver asked. I think he was a bit spooked by our quiet stretch of exurbia.

'Sure,' I said, and he drove away. The house was plunged in darkness again, its blind windows gaping like holes. I tried to fight off the Weirdness, the familiar strange sensation at the back of my neck, the opening into a cavernous darkness.

I rang the doorbell. There was no answer, but the light in Her room went on. I rang the doorbell again. I heard her coming downstairs. The door opened.

She looked a mess. Her hair was uncombed and she was wearing a half-open bathrobe. Her face was slightly puffy. There was a quality of dishevelment about her I'd never seen before. We stood facing each other silently, taking in each other's presence, our mirroring misery. Her eyes were as wretched as mine. Her eyes were still the Mirror into which I could walk and drown. She put her arms around me wordlessly, and for a moment I gave in to her familiar warmth as to a luxury. To vanquish all distance; to stop supporting my unsupportable separateness – the temptation was almost too much. Then, as if it were my very last chance, as if it were crucial to use every ounce of my strength to accomplish this, I pulled away.

'Your mother died today,' I said coldly. I was trying for the utmost cruelty.

She searched me in the half-light, searched the vibrations of my deliberately non-resonant voice, to divine what was going on.

'So you found them,' she concluded. 'You went where you were not wanted. Where you were never wanted.'

Of course, she knew how to hurt me best. She had direct access to my bloodstream, my cell stream, my heart's arteries. She could puncture my veins at will.

'It's you who wasn't wanted,' I said. 'It's you who wasn't there when your mother died.'

She pulled me into the hallway and slammed the door shut.

'How can you!' she cried, and her grip on my shoulder tightened. 'Why are you so cruel to me?'

I thought she might slap me, but instead she let go and sat on the carpeted floor right there in the hallway and, pulling her knees up to her chin to hide her face from me, she cried. I'd never seen her do that, had never seen her yield to weakness like that, had never seen her shed tears. It undid me utterly; I felt the tears that had all day burned behind my eyelids spilling out, as if by some cheap automatic reflex. Condensed tears for all of my condensed grief, and for how even the grief couldn't be truly mine.

She composed herself completely before looking up. 'What happened?' she asked. 'How did she die?'

And so I told her. I told her about the last two days, but I told it in my own way. I told it to my advantage. I didn't have enough strength, or confidence, to make things up. But I left things out, changed emphasis. I said my grandparents were lovely to me. Lovely and kind. They were, of course, disturbed at first and upset not to have met me before. But at least I was there in time – in time to gain their acceptance, to feel my grandmother's love as she was dying. I was telling it as I'd wished it to be, as I felt it to be almost true, and it gave me a strange power to tell it like that. The way I wanted to.

She listened silently, blankly. 'Did she say anything about me?' she asked when I came to the end of my narrative. She was posing the question in a neutral tone, the voice of a lawyer demanding factual disclosure. 'Did she call for me at the end?'

I shook my head. 'I held her hand till the end,' I said. 'Me and grandfather. Or should I say father?'

I wanted to hurt her. I wanted to vanquish her. But I understimated her. She'd been sitting bent forward as I talked, a slight sag of her shoulders betraying some burden of thought or feeling. Now she straightened out, as if bolstered by a current of energy. She'd made her judgement.

'You're lying to me, aren't you?' she said, her voice ecstatic with rage. 'You little thief. Stupid child. You are lying to me about my mother's death. You think you can take over my life just like that. Take it from me. My money, my clothes, my mother. My mother's death. Maybe you want my grief too, is that it?'

I hated her. I hated her so much I wanted to cry from the sheer tension, the pressure of it. How was I going to bear, or to expel, that much rage? It threatened to lacerate me like a burning garment, as if Medea's dress had been wrapped not around me but within me, within my burning flesh.

'She didn't want you there,' I said. 'She was quite satisfied with me. She thought I was . . .'

I stopped, but it was too late. A flicker of disturbance ran across her forehead, reminding me of Dr Park. Then something else entered her eyes. For all my microscopic observation of her face over the years, for all my close study of its every contraction, retraction and passing mood, I'd never seen this particular look. I think in that moment she finally understood what was happening. She understood that she had bred a mirror-image, a creature who was her, but who could also turn on her. The look on her face, I think, was horror: the horror of recognition. My creatrix faced me and understood that she had made a monster.

'What do you want?' she said. 'What do you want from me?'

She was asking her Golem if it was going to kill her. She was asking the Image if it was going to emerge from where it had lived, from under the watery surface, and attack.

We faced each other very directly. We gave each other perhaps the most serious, the most exposed look we'd ever exchanged. She was still the Mirror, I the reflection. But I had lied and that give me dimension. The Echo had said something of its own and now it couldn't be contained. I could feel the certainty rising: the Mirror had to be smashed. No matter what followed after, no matter who lived or died.

For a long time we stood absolutely still, locked into each other's gaze as if by a spell. Then I raised my fist and hit. I was trying to shatter the Mirror's reflecting surface; but my fist met the hard bone of her face instead. The impact reverberated horribly; I almost screamed with pain. We wrestled blindly, with an awful intimacy, body meeting body, body meeting itself. I put my hands on her throat, my fingers tightened round the delicate flesh. Her face was close to mine and we confronted each other straight on, a line of pure violence joining us now as love once did. Her reflecting features contorted, love and hate twisting into each other, and twisting her face.

'Who are you?' she said, her voice nothing more than a deep breath. 'What are you?'

'You,' I answered on the same wave of air. 'I am you.'

'Just don't forget you came second,' she whispered. 'And you will always be second, even when I'm dead. Even if you kill me.'

I tightened my grip and felt the delicate open bones inside the throat move under my fingers, against each other and apart. Our eyes were so close that they had merged, mingled in the same miasma of fear and violence. She put her hands on my shoulders to push me back. Then she crumpled. She gave up the fight. I could feel it, the instantaneous decision in her body to stop resisting. To resign. She wasn't going to put her fingers round my throat. She couldn't do it. She was still the creatrix and I her creation. Her child. She slid to the floor. I let go.

I knelt beside her, not sure what I'd done. She was limp and seemingly unconscious, but breathing. She'd fainted. I lay down beside her, like a cub beside a wolf mother and once again – perhaps knowing that this was the last time I'd do it – I contemplated her face. I perused it as if I were reading the complex geography, the rich matter of the world. If only I could fathom it . . . Her secret;

the clue. For she had it, even while her eyes were closed, and her breathing oddly light. She needed no proofs, no guarantees.

And yet: I had put my hands around her throat. What did that show, what did it demonstrate? I started trembling with the cold knowledge of what I had done – of what I'd been willing to do. After this, there was no return. I'd have to live without her from now on, I couldn't hide in her dimensions any longer. The reproduction would have to acquire its own autonomous status. To become its own original.

She came to and she saw my face near hers. She began to smile and then her face distorted with the knowledge of utter misery.

'What's happened here?' she asked, her face grey and dazed. And then: 'What have we done?'

She sat up, and her eyes registered a deep puzzlement; then her features contorted themselves as if she were being twisted from within. 'Oh God!' She exhaled and covered her face with her hands. She finally saw it: the paradox. She grasped it and she looked as if it might crucify her on its sharp prongs. She'd given life to a copy of herself; and the copy had metamorphosed into this strange, this alien creature. The simulacrum had struck from some unknown place and triumphed. I could hardly bear to know what she felt; for to know it would be to know being split in two, and I could not know this for her as well as me. I could not know it was I who had split her, hewn her. I might as well have done it with an axe.

But something had changed, changed utterly in the last – was it ten minutes? ten hours? – and as I looked into her defeated face, I also felt the rising of something like sorrow: for her, as she was keening our dreadful common plight, for the fate she had given me, which she'd now have to suffer as if it were her own.

The pity of it . . . I wanted, maybe for the last time, to stay near her, to console her by reopening the passage in which her sorrow was my own; to share our twinned, split grief. I mustn't. I couldn't. There was no returning, after what had transpired, to our union.

'Goodbye, Elizabeth,' I whispered and her name sounded immensely strange on my lips. My mother, my sister. My mother, my twin, 'Goodbye for now.'

She looked up at me imploringly; then her expression changed to something like acceptance. She nodded and turned away. I gathered up my aerobag – we were still, despite the epoch that had passed, in the hallway – and opened the door again to the still dark night. I looked back after closing the small garden gate and saw her bent silhouette through the lit front window, saw it as she got up and walked, unsteadily, into the deeper innards of the house. I felt a surge of pity stirring in the embers of my anger. She'd have to rethink everything she'd done in the light of this new awful knowledge, reconsider everything from this vertiginous point of view.

I walked out once again into the dark funnel of the night, and if the funnel had sucked me in like a Midwestern black hole, I wouldn't have been surprised. Time had compressed to heavy-metal density while I was in the house, to the eternal moment before its first explosion. But I wasn't disappearing; time was unfolding itself again and the streets gradually awakening to a grey dawn were as two-dimensional as if the very idea of depth had been banished from creation. I had performed an Act; but what next?

Almost without thinking I went back to O'Hare and purchased my ticket to New York. I had no good reason to choose New York over anywhere else, but it seemed the natural thing to do. I'd been there before. And anyway, isn't that the place you go when you don't know where to go? I was going there the way birds journey to their wintering places, following ancient trajectories to faraway destinations, though surely without knowing where they're going or why. Knowing and not knowing, propelled only by miraculously accurate impulses and signals. Signals which in creatures like us – even in someone like me – somehow feel like consciousness. Was it just a trick of intricate coding? I was going to New York as if of my own free will. Or maybe not as if. Maybe the analogy was the real thing, maybe the code was the substance, maybe the metaphor was the meaning. Maybe I was going there because that's what – the idea was just dawning on me as a possibility – I wanted, what I chose, to do.

I took images with me on the plane this time, my very own, private pictures, moving in a procession through my mind. My grandmother's pursed lips when I came into their apartment, my grandfather standing quietly behind me in the den. All of us on the beach, the hospital, my grandmother's face as she looked at me thinking I was Her . . . The deathbed scenes lingered and seemed to seep deeper inside. They were being stored in the memory system, to remain there – well, perhaps till I died. My very own image repertory, which nobody else could share in its exactitude. My grandfather, at the end, managed to give me a stiff hug, and looked at me with something like compassion. 'What will you do?' he asked. 'Where will you go?'

As I was closing the door of the hospital room, I saw him take his wife's lifeless hand and bend over to kiss it. That was the image that kept stabbing at me as the plane lifted off and rose into the monotonous sky. Then I thought of Her in her bed, tossing and turning, thinking about her very own mother dying. For that was what she'd be doing now, returning to that knowledge, which would be mingled with the other, more awful recognition. Then I shivered with my own new understanding: I hadn't killed my mother, but I'd been willing to, and now I knew what it was like to be alive even if She was dead. I'd had a brief taste of it, a homeopathic dose. Just enough to know that it was nearly unbearable – and that it had to be borne. Borne, born; maybe I'd have to give birth to myself out of my burden, by disburdening myself of . . . what? Her, her-in-me, the hypnotic pull of our union. Of my non-existence. I would have to bear my cloned, my cloven self. Cloven, riven, cut. I'd have to carry it into the flat or the full world, till it emerged from itself and took wing.

'She was Narcissus and she drowned,' the Adviser said much later, when I was going over these incidents, reverting to them, reliving them. Trying, as he would say, to master them. 'But that doesn't mean you have to be her Echo.'

'Echo dies with Narcissus, as I remember,' I put in acidly.

'Not every story needs to be repeated exactly,' he said. 'That's what the old stories are for, so that we can understand them and see their variants. Re-invent them. We can modify our stories, that's what makes us living, thinking beings.'

'I'm not a good candidate for narrative modification,' I said. 'I'm the variant designed to be pure repetition. Every cell in my body her cell, every atom in my brain . . .'

'Now you're getting fixated on this,' he interrupted. 'You're hypnotizing yourself into believing this.'

'But what else can I believe?'

'That you're a whole, separate person. That you have a mind of your own. I think we've

211

progressed far enough in our work for you to grasp that.'

I wasn't so sure. But I suppose that putting the fist out is a variant of a kind. It makes me into the Image trying to emerge from the pool's watery surface, the Echo trying to speak – or at least to scream – in its own voice. But to whom and about what? How on earth could I be sure I wasn't repeating what had already been said – what had always been said, what had been said by Her?

And yet the urge to speak was powerful. To speak to someone, not from the echo chamber in which my voice had resonated and lost itself in its own reverberations, but from somewhere else.

I made my way to 1125 Park Avenue straight from the airport. The doorman recognized me this time. 'You here for Miss Janey?' he asked.

I nodded. 'She going to her mom's funeral, you know,' he said, holding his hand over the intercom, after he announced me. 'She is one very upset lady.'

Then there was a pleasant voice on the other end and a tiny pause before I was told that I could come up. Apparently, she was not entirely unprepared for my visit.

But still she was unprepared for what she'd see. When she opened the door to her apartment, there was that double-take, that abrupt intake of breath which by now I should have learnt to expect, but didn't. I felt briefly startled, briefly hurt.

But I also wasn't prepared for what I saw, the almost bodily impact of the unexpected déjà vu. For Janey had hardly changed at all, and facing her in this sudden close up took me back into my child-mind as effectively as if I'd been physically pushed. The compacted affection and hope and rejection of that long-ago visit were suddenly constricting my chest, making me swallow hard.

It was Janey who composed herself first. She beckoned me in and gave me a quick, shy smile.

'Come in,' she said. 'I've been expecting you. That is, I thought you might come.'

'She called you,' I said.

'Yes,' Janey said quickly. 'Just about an hour ago.'

'And she told you I'd be coming.'

'That you *might* be coming,' Janey said and bit her lip, as she realized that the emphasis gave her away, showed her awareness that she mustn't reveal all she knew.

'I'm so glad you found me,' she was saying. She looked at me again and then quickly away. She was coming back to me as a kind of atmosphere, a rhythm, a motion. A quickness, a warmth, a shyness, a sudden animation. She might have been a forest creature, compared to her sister's – to my own – stolid, large form.

And then she was looking away in order to hide her tears. 'It's my mom,' she said. 'You know she died yesterday.' She looked unbearably sad and I felt her sadness infecting me and mingling

213

with a horrible remorse. For pretending I could replace this grief – this love – with my mimicry. For pretending to replace the daughter, the sister, at her mother's deathbed.

I nodded. 'I'm going to Florida in an hour,' Janey said, 'but I'm glad you caught me in time. You must make yourself at home here while I'm gone.'

To my surprise, enormous relief washed over me, as if everything that had been poised for fight or flight could relax, subside. As if I could lower my guard and settle into the plump cushions of Janey's sofa in full comfort.

'Do you mean it?' I asked.

'Yes, of course,' she said. 'Of course you should stay. We can talk about . . . all kinds of things when I come back.' She threw me a sympathetic, worried look and bit her lip. She wasn't sure she actually wanted to do this, but she was going to do the right thing. 'Coffee?' she asked. 'You must be very tired.'

I nodded, and with an exhalation of anxiety she couldn't quite conceal, she went off to the kitchen, indicating that I should make myself comfortable. The living room was a cosy, cluttered space, with deep red rugs, large leafy plants and lots of comfy chairs and little sofas everywhere. A few small holographic animals, mostly of extinct species, placed on a glass-topped table provided a contemporary touch. But, mostly, it was an old-fashioned room, a nice person's room. I thought I could sink into the plump velvet sofa, into Janey's comfy, undemanding atmosphere, with no trouble at all.

She came back, bearing a tray with coffee and some miniature pastries. They looked delicious. She raised her face towards me gradually, as if taking care not to startle herself or break down in tears again.

'I don't know when I'll be back,' she said finally. 'My dad may want me to stay for a while.'

'Will . . . She be there?' I asked, and of course, we both knew who She was.

'I believe so,' Janey said carefully, and then, looking up at me again, 'anything you'd like me to say to her?'

'No,' I said. 'Not for now.' I couldn't think what it would be, how I could speak to Her from my new position. From my new, immensely strange separateness.

Janey nodded and left again, presumably to prepare herself for her trip. Half an hour later, she emerged with a suitcase, briefly showed me the room where I'd be staying, and then gave a little goodbye wave and was gone.

Once again I was on my own. But on my own in a new way, more desolate, more definitive than before. I was free from Her – but free for what? I had vanquished her shadowy power, her authority, and it was replaced by a big silence; an unresonant emptiness. I was a copy which had lost its original; and I had no way to authenticate myself. A clone alone. What did that make me? What kind of entity? Had I, in my attempt to make myself One, rendered myself zero? That was the question I pondered as I moped and groped around Janey's apartment, or sat in front of the super-screen. Or rather, that was the question I had become, the pitch and angle of my new unknowingness.

I didn't know what to do with myself once Janey left, didn't know how to handle the body that was now so oddly on its own, how to position the mind which kept ticking over within the body like a perpetual-motion machine. Ticking over because it was there, because the mechanism had been turned on . . . I kept moping and groping round Janey's apartment, as if I were blind and trying to figure out the outlines of the space in which I found myself, a point of orientation. For a while I spent part of each morning rummaging through Janey's things, riffling through her closets and drawers, examining her bookshelves, combing through the files on her desk. I had become used to spying, I suppose, except this time I wasn't looking for anything in particular. Not any kind of secret, any longer, not as far as I knew. Though maybe I was trying to figure out a life without a secret. And all the evidence of Janey's apartment pointed to a modest, orderly existence, lived in medium dimensions, not spilling over into great schemes or disarray, or any kind of dark trouble. Rows of cardigans and cotton tops lined the neat shelves of her closet; rows of spice jars were perfectly placed in metal racks in her kitchen; stacks of music and reading disks were filed neatly in her study; her visual library was chronologically organized. There were photos – more clues to myself, perhaps, more images to break my heart. But I was learning the insufficiency of those kinds of clues. They wouldn't give me the key – wouldn't unlock the door, wherever it was hidden, to whatever was behind it that needed to be unlocked or revealed.

Still, there was a surprise. Behind the closet rack in the guest room, there was a sliding door; when I opened it, I walked into a small storage area. On one side there were more shelves, this time lined with notebooks and folders. I opened one of them, just to make sure I wasn't missing anything important; but it contained yellowing pages covered with badly typed script – one of Janey's college papers, evidently, entitled 'Appearance and Reality in Henry James's *Portrait of a Lady*'. It was the other side of the storage space, however, that drew my attention – for it was bisected by a rack on which was hung a row of gorgeous gowns, preserved in their transparent wraps like a collection of extravagant pressed flowers, or a procession of brilliant fetishes of bygone fashions and times. There were dresses of delicate cashmere, embroidered orange brocade, diaphanous organza, smooth silk, crinkled viscose packed into tiny, erotic pleats. I unwrapped one of the gowns and fingered its satiny texture, feeling how opulent, how important these things had once been. I

217

put my face against it; there was a faint aroma of staleness and mothballs; these memorials to sensuality smelled of the past – a past into which I could never step by any door. The life and times of Janey Surrey. Or could they have been Hers? For this was the apartment in which She'd grown up as well . . . I thought not; I thought the gowns were Janey's. Still, I felt a wrenching nostalgia for the life that had once been, that infused even these limp and static objects with fluidity and movement. Time had passed, had escaped as irrevocably as a vapour, the one thing that could not be fingered, touched, made to return . . . She was there again, of course, her presence as feathery as that of a bird that might alight or vanish . . . When I came upon the long mirror in the front part of the closet, I saw Her, our face oddly harmonious and calm, and yet somehow, somehow altered by sorrow.

I crumpled on Janey's bed, and buried my head in the duvet. This was unbearable, to mourn what had not died, to feel the loss of what could not disappear.

I don't know on what indeterminate, fuzzy impulse I took to dressing in Janey's outfits. Not the glamorous ones, just her ordinary clothing, the stuff meant for daily activity, for life. Maybe it was my sense of grievance, of grief for my missed past, for the years when Janey and I could have dressed up together, figuring out how to be young women in our time. But maybe I hoped to become Somebody by becoming somebody else. To become

218

Somebody who was not She. Sometimes it almost worked. As I looked at myself in the mirror, in one of Janey's well-cut suits, I felt transformed into a three-dimensional object, a solid that could be seen from the outside and therefore could be inferred to have real, internal existence. For I was beginning to learn that you cannot be a subject without being an object, visible to others, with distinct outlines and occupying a distinct space. In Janey's clothes I was definite and distinct. I could see myself, nearly, as a regular person.

The effect, alas, wore off all too soon. Most of the time I felt paper thin, flat as a cardboard cut-out. A two-dimensional creature moving through a depthless, wonderless world. For without her presence and menace the inexorable streets of New York were hard, banal stone. Unhaunted, unenchanted; dirty, dusty and harsh. I thought I'd walked out of my Midwestern house into a turbulent funnel of the night, but actually I'd walked out into more of the same. More reality, more unreality. As a child, I'd once walked behind a real mirror, to see if there was anyone, any thing there. But there wasn't; there was only the mirror's mute, flat backing. I felt horribly let down and even more baffled than before: there was nothing on this side and nothing on the other.

Except once, during my Manhattan wanderings I walked into the Metropolitan Museum, which was holding an exhibition of old portraits. There was one in particular that arrested my attention:

the *Doge Leonardo Loredan* by Giovanni Bellini. I noticed it because it had noticed me. It nearly leapt out at me from the canvas. It was the most vividly alive face I'd ever seen, its features etched as in the acid of experience, its expression stern with controlled power. Beneath his white bonnet with its delicate gold braiding, the Doge looked at me, narrow-lipped and deep-eyed, giving away nothing.

I was stunned by that face, jolted into full concentration. I stood in front of it for a long time, trying to discern the secret of its depth. Did the depth come from the secrets? For the Doge looked like someone who had plenty of them – secrets whispered in dark corridors, dangerous secrets, devious secrets. Power secrets, secrets of power, not of a horrible, weird lack. Then I remembered that this was only a canvas, and the illusion of depth a trick. Or was there more to it – was the trick so intricate as to be an art, the illusion so complete as to amount to some old truth which I recognized, even if I could not even begin to know it?

I saw the faces on the street outside differently after I came out of that show, although none of them matched the vividness, the sheer force of the Doge's features. Maybe because there were too many. I wondered if, with the infinitely proliferating humans, less substance accured to each one. And I wondered, as I jostled through the oblivious human tides, how I'd ever insert myself into this infinitely hectic, infinitely fatigued, infinitely *numerous* world. Whether it was worth inserting myself into it at all. Could the world accommodate one more human molecule – or was I going to be the extra who'd spill the whole earthly cup? Who'd explode the whole human illusion, expose the Big Trick that – nearly – kept it all going?

It was shortly after my visit to the Met that I went up to Columbia to enquire about enrolling as a student. I don't know what further fuzzy, indeterminate instinct led me to this particular step; but then, I was probably as programmed for college as for anything else. As least I wasn't going to Princeton, as she had done; I took some satisfaction from that.

But no, I would be lying if I said that was the only reason I went up to the venerable seat of learning. There was something else that drove me, some more desperate, caged need. For I was as effectively imprisoned in my new freedom as if I were behind those laser-reinforced bars which not even the most bionic inmates can break out of. The cavernous Weirdness had compacted itself into a black box, which gave off no light, and allowed no light to enter it. At night the chaos in my head was magnified by the fact that the box was hermetically sealed and every thought reverberated with a jumble of echoes. Me and my cells. My and my thoughts. An encased body in a non-resonant space. And yet – I wanted – extension; I wanted – Something Else. I wanted to break the box and see beyond my copy-flat self. Like those people disappointed by the Affect Simulator, I seemed to have a Meaning Problem. And I wondered, oh of course I wondered, what that showed . . .

'What do you want to study?' a woman in the admissions office asked me curtly. 'Sub-molecular biology,' I fired back without thinking. Of course, that's what I'd have to study, if I ever wanted to break out of the box – or at least measure its dimensions. 'Theory or applications?' the woman pursued, without the slightest interest. 'Theory,' I said, feeling less sure. The thought of applications made me much too nervous. 'Onsite learning, or remote?' she pressed, ticking off boxes on her computer. I said I'd have to think about it. She gave me some brochures on the Biological Theory program, and said I could sign on any time, they had flexible time-lines.

It was on my second trip to Columbia, to check out some person-taught classes, that I ran into Steven. He was coming down the steps of the library and I was going up, and we went past each other without stopping; then he paused, arrested by a delayed reflex and turned around. A subliminal discomfort shadowed his long, handsome face.

'Elizabeth?' he said, and then, responding instantly to what must have been hurt on my face, 'Iris. I'm sorry. Of course, you must be Iris.'

'I didn't know you were teaching here,' I said stupidly, as if to justify myself, my unwonted appearance in his life, on his turf.

'Just since last year,' he said. 'And you? Have

you moved to New York? Is Elizabeth . . . is your mother with you?' He looked around vaguely, as if to ascertain whether she might be hovering somewhere behind me and about to materialize out of the crisp fall air.

'No,' I said. 'No, I'm on my own. I've just enrolled . . . I'm going to be a student here. I think.'

He'd been standing two steps above me, in a half-turned pose. Now he came down to where I was standing and put his arms around me. 'What a surprise this is,' he said. 'I'm so glad to see you.' A forgotten, familiar smell of wool, tobacco and lab dust enveloped me like home. I folded myself like a child against his chest. I didn't know how much I had longed for something like this. Or how much I'd longed for just exactly this. I could have stayed there, huddled and hidden, for a long time.

Gently he straightened me out. 'Let's go to my office, OK?' he said softly. 'Now that we have met, it would be really nice to have a talk.'

The office, in the Department of Archaeology, reminded me of his study in my – our – home. One wall was lined with books; the other with glass-doored shelves, covered with a carefully displayed array of pottery shards, various small objects and bones. Steven's old desk, with its green leather topping, occupied the centre of the room.

'You see,' he smiled, as I examined the room with an almost voracious, childlike curiosity, 'I'm still doing the same old thing.'

223

'That's wonderful,' I said. Everything about this sudden meeting seemed wonderful.

He contemplated me from the other side of his desk, almost as he had when I was a child. Except something, of course, had changed. Not him – he looked just as he had before, tall and lean in his jeans and grey sweater, with strands of grey hair falling on his forehead. But I had grown in the meantime, and become, undeniably, a woman. And I looked – as I knew too well – just like the woman he'd left a few years earlier.

'Well, this is a bit startling for me, I won't deny it,' he said, as if responding to my thoughts. 'How is she? How is Elizabeth?' I could see it cost him an effort to mention her name. He must have tried hard to banish her from his mind.

I shook my head helplessly. There was too much to tell.

'And you?' he asked. He smiled ruefully. He was remembering, I was sure, the last time he saw me, his last exit, the two pairs of eyes following him as he left the house. He looked at me more directly, and I could see he was making an effort to control – the Weirdness. But also I could see his appreciation, a kind of wonderment at what I'd turned into. He wasn't sure who he was talking to, but he was seeing me, I could tell, as a woman. How could he help it?

There was something I had to know before I could tell him anything. 'Did you know?' I asked. 'When you lived with us? Did you know about me?'

'So you do know,' he said. Of course, he would have been uncertain as well.

'Yes,' I said, 'though I probably found out later than you did.' That hurt, even as I said it. All of a sudden, it seemed urgent to ascertain when he realized what kind of creature I was, to figure out what I'd been to him when he lived in our house and I had loved him almost as if for real, with my not yet unreal, my almost childish heart.

He looked at me quizzically, to check how much he could say. How much I would understand.

'I suspected something, of course,' he said. 'Maybe I even sort of knew, the way you know you're looking at a letter on a table without ever noticing it. But I deal in the past, you know, and when my mind looks for clues to some puzzle or mystery, that's where it turns to. So I kept grilling Elizabeth about her past. The men in her life, the traumas, the major relationships. You know, the standard stuff.' He checked again, to see whether it was all right to talk to me like that.

'I kept asking her about all the trite, imaginable things. I was looking for causality, for what might have, could have, should have led to the effect which was you and all the oddness I felt in your house. I mean, that's what we do, we history men. We look for links, chains, pathways, inclines and declines leading from the past to the present. And we inevitably find them, or imagine we do, or insist that they're there. The causes and links. Whereas you – you apparently sprang from Athena's head.

Well, from Elizabeth's head, anyway. You were causeless.' He cast a somewhat worried look at me, to ascertain whether he had gone too far. But for some reason, I didn't mind him talking like that. I gave him a small half-smile to show him he could go on. 'Which is exactly what is not imaginable,' he concluded, 'so I guess you weren't really imaginable. I supose that's why it took me such a long time to twig to what was going on.'

'And now?' I asked. 'Am I imaginable now?'

'Not really,' he said, striving for lightness. 'Though since you're here, you must be. It cannot be otherwise, even if you seem to put this proposition into doubt. You and Elizabeth . . .'

He interrupted himself. He'd been talking, in fact, as if to someone imaginary. Now he looked intensely uncomfortable, even pained. 'Listen,' he said, extending his hand and putting it on mine, 'I must go and teach a class now. Occasionally, we old fogeys are still allowed to do the personal teaching bit. But you must come and see me again. You're as imaginable as can be, I just have some catching up to do. I'm sure we have a lot more to talk about.'

I dreamt of a rain forest that night, thick with tangled foliage, dense with water and piercing bird-cry; a mass of liana-wrapped jungle so weighted with chlorophyll, so heavy with sap-filled green and radiant flowers that it seemed to strain at the boundaries of what the eye could hold, and beyond,

226

into hyper-colour, virtual sensuality. The beauty of it was the juicy distillation, the very idea of beauty. It was hyper-life, hyper-beauty, and I was so close to being in the heart of it that I almost cried in my sleep. So close and yet so incommensurately, so fatally far.

When I next met Steven, in his Riverside Drive apartment, he tried to get me to talk about myself. The apartment was old and spacious with a darkened parquet floor and sparse but very elegant furniture; and when he took me into his study I felt I'd been let into an inner sanctum, a place redolent with Steven. He sat in one of the two large facing leather chairs, running his finger over the jagged edge of a broken pottery jar and asking me questions. He wanted to know about the ordinary, reassuring things. He tried – I could see it cost him some effort – to keep close to the mundane. I kept stumbling and falling silent. I wanted to be near him, nearer still. But I feared – oh, everything. I feared She would appear between us in palpable, furious form, an eagle swooping down upon us, or a statue rising up out of the ground to transfix us with the power of her judgement. I feared that if I spoke I would give myself away. For how do you speak to the object of your desire? How do you say anything except what I had to say: I must have this. I must have this or die. I must have this or be pure deprivation, pure lack. How – in my case – was I to say anything except the unspeakable?

I think he began to sense the growing heat of my

227

thoughts. He put his jagged bit of pottery carefully back in its place on the shelf and said he'd bring us both tea. I looked around the room while he was gone and at the photographs discreetly arranged on a shelf. There was one of Steven with a collie dog and a small boy in short pants and with tousled hair. I felt – yes, it was jealousy. Who was the boy, and how did he come to hold Steven's hand in this familiar way? He appeared in another photo as well, this time with a vivacious-looking, brightly smiling woman. Did Steven have another family before – us? Did he have a family now? I knew nothing – nothing beyond what I had imagined: Steven as the man whom I loved as only a child can love a father who is yet not a father; as the man who seemed to condense all masculinity, all male energy in his frame.

And yes – there was She. It was a lovely photo of her, showing her at her ripest, most sensual. She was in the garden, leaning agaisnt a fence, one foot resting on a rake, and she was surrounded by delphiniums and cornflowers. She was wearing a loose white V-necked shirt and fitted pants, emphasizing the slimness of her ankles. Her face and blonde hair were shot through by the sun; her body was ample and harmonious. She was smiling in a slightly downwards direction. Was I there, on Steven's side of the camera, looking up at my beautiful mother – was she smiling at me?

Steven came up behind me, and put his hand lightly on my shoulder. 'Come and have some tea,' he said. When I turned towards him, there was a fleeting look of pain in his ironical eyes.

'Did you care about her – very much?' I asked. I could hardly bring myself to ask this question, it so endangered this moment. Endangered me. But I had to know, for some reason I had to know.

'Ah dear,' he said and sighed and paused, as if to decide where to go next. 'Yes, I loved her,' he said finally, the words coming out almost as a breath. 'I never stopped being in love with her.'

I remembered the warm heaviness of her body, the dry warmth of his, as I tried to climb into their bed, as my own limbs became heavier, weighted with those memories, with a dangerous honey. He was standing next to me and looked at me as if . . . How could he know who he was looking at? There was sultriness, heaviness between us. 'You look . . .' he began, but I didn't let him finish. I turned my face up to him and embraced him. I was impelled to do so. Impelled, possessed, driven. As if this, this was the thing I must have if I were to have anything at all.

He kissed me back. A flicker of anxiety constricted his brows, and then, as if steeling his resolve, as if plunging, he looked down into my eyes and kissed me fully, fleshily, taking my lips into his and exploring my mouth. We cleaved to each other and I breathed in the wonderful woollen dusty smoky aroma I'd been close to so often before, had craved before. For seconds on end, uncountable, burgeoning seconds, questions ceased, the cellular restlessness that was the churn of perpetual doubt in my body stopped.

He pulled back and said, 'We mustn't, Iris. This is wrong, we mustn't.'

'No,' I said desperately. 'Please. It isn't wrong, it's right. This isn't a . . . a usual situation. We must . . . You mustn't push me away. I don't know how I'll go on if you do . . . if you don't . . .' I was cleaving to him again and seeking his eyes, his face. I was so close to everything I'd been waiting for, to what I had to have; it could not be withdrawn from me.

He held me by my shoulders the way one does a child to calm it down, and then he was kissing me again, my eyelids and cheeks and lips, tenderly and urgently. He couldn't refuse me, of course he couldn't.

He stopped kissing me, but held my face in his hands. 'Once,' he said softly, 'as a sort of . . . closure. Just once.' So I had my one chance and no stories to tell that he didn't already know. Actually, not stories at all. But I had my hunger and my urgent questions. My desperate need to know, my unslaked curiosity. My need to beat through – to what? To him, to her, to the third dimension. Perhaps that was as good as having stories. We went into his bedroom. Did I know what I was doing? I only knew that my excitement mingled with the icy heat of fear as Steven led me to his bed, and cupped my face in his hands and brought it close to his, as if to make sure he knew who I was. Fear that he'd tell me to leave after all, as he did then, all those years ago. Icy hot fear that this time he wouldn't. I closed my eyes as he undressed me, and maybe so did he. But as I lay naked on the bed, he ran his eyes over my body, and gave a sharp intake of breath. I detected hesitation in his eyes and pulled him towards me, so that we could both hide in each other, even as our bodies began to do their dance. We made love musically, tidally, as if our bodies were guided by an old knowledge, driven by a desire doubled and multiplied, folding upon itself and unfolding into lines of pure grace. My desire for him and my longing for her, my desire for him-in-her and her-in-him; and Steven's desire – yes, for us both. And for both of us, the sweetness of triumph and revenge. It was as if a majestic and dark deity of desire drove us on, and gave our bodies an unerring precision. His hands and lips travelled over my breasts and belly and inner thighs as if there was no friction and no deterrence to flow. My navel rose up towards his lips and hands in a smooth curving motion, and his long body matched itself to mine as if we were part of a single form. When we were conjoined, we beat against each other wildly and then stopped, and I drew him further in, as if maybe we could interpenetrate, as if we could reach something on the other side of ourselves. The other side of everything, the mirror, the flatness through which I'd walked. The Real, the hyper-real. Oh, it was impossible, and it was the impossibility that lent

231

us this perfect harmony. When you're about to enter the Real, you don't make mistakes. When you're about to cross the other side of yourself or die, there are no wrong moves.

We subsided, finally, and I realized that I was crying quietly, fluently, as if a door had opened into pain. He watched me for a while, and then stroked my hair as one might stroke a hurt, crying child.

'Iris,' he asked gently, 'are you going to be all right?'

'I guess so,' I said.

'I'm not really your father,' he said. 'Will you try to remember that?'

'I will,' I said. 'I will, I will, I will.'

Still, he nearly was. Which made me the girl who had nearly killed her mother and had slept with her almost father.

The Adviser refused to be drawn. 'You were, of course, acting out in a massive way,' was his comment on this Incident, as on that whole period of my personal, my sentimental career.

'You mean I was *acting*,' I said peevishly.

'No, I mean acting OUT,' he repeated firmly, if irritably. 'You were following your impulses without thinking, without even knowing what they were. That's what bothers you now.'

'What bothers me is that I nearly strangled my mother . . .'

'Never mind,' he interrupted. He didn't much like dealing with real events, they threatened to muck up the analysis and the pure impurities of the internal life. 'It's your fantasies around this that matter. That's what we have to explore.'

'Except I was acting on my fantasises,' I insisted. 'I made love to . . .'

He looked so uncomfortable that I stopped.

'Why don't you try to tell me what you feel about all of this, what you imagine it means? That's where our work comes in, in trying to distinguish your childish imaginings from the reality of your actions. Although, of course, you can feel great remorse even about your fantasies.'

But the distinction hardly seems to hold in my case. I am after all a nearly imaginary being, born into a reality so aberrant as to have no rules. A late, nearly virtual reality . . . I am new human, new woman. And since no rules have been invented for me, I should be permitted to do anything at all. Without guilt, that old-fashioned, inconvenient evolutionary knot, a complexity we can surely grow out of.

And yet . . . After sleeping with Steven, I felt a strange regret. Almost a kind of nausea, as if one part of myself were ill with the other. As if what had transpired between us was not an entirely happy occurrence. Not entirely . . . blameless. I confessed this with some reluctance to the Adviser, who leapt on my disclosure all too eagerly. He had his own explanations, of course. The Oedipus complex, in its negative and positive versions, and the resolution thereof. But as he talked, I kept wondering – half-fearfully, half-hopefully – what my strange, discomfiting reaction showed. Whether my sadness was something that could not have been calculated in Dr Park's program; whether it was an extra Something that couldn't have come straight out of the vat.

I once read about a man who'd murdered several people in recurring fits of frenzy, and was later diagnosed with a genetic aberration which accounted for his paroxysms of blind rage. He was still in prison, but he was consoled by the diagnosis. It was apparently a solace for him to know that he'd been pre-programmed to act as he did. Of course, I found his story affecting. But the solace to me was that he was agonized about his own actions; and I wondered what, what it was in him that felt the remorse, and whether that, too, could have been so precisely diagnosed.

I don't know whether it was a symptom of my fears or of some inchoate hope, that I looked up Clone on the Net. Aside from the information and commercial sites, advertising services and do-it-yourself kits, there were two main web locations: Clone Power and Clone Consciousness.

Clone Power was standard cyberspace drivel, the dross of the collective mind coagulating into ungainly, lumpy clots. The main idea promoted by the site was that replicants are a new and superior species, with hidden powers and practically infinite potential.

'We are the distillation of all that is best in

human nature,' one contributor wrote. 'Inferior people aren't chosen to replicate.'

'There are only a few of us so far,' another mused, 'but we are faster, smarter, more beautiful. Over time, we will select from among ourselves the most efficient prototypes. The human race is senescent and ready for a cleansing and rejuvenation. We are the ancient-young ones. We come equipped with the accumulated knowledge of the race, but without any of its archaic attachments or prejudices. We can dare to imagine what nobody before us has imagined. We can dare to DO what nobody before us has done. The future belongs to us.'

Grandiose, embarrassing fantasies of the powerless, of creatures who hardly dared admit in public who they were. Fantasies which provoked equally pathetic responses from the Others, the echt-humans.

'You are the hidden disease,' one of them proclaimed. 'Like the Jews were in Germany. You look like us, act like us, pretend to be like us. But we know you for what you are: enemy aliens. You're the new poison and a symptom of our degenerate times. You may think you're like us; don't flatter yourselves. We're truly human in the way you can never be. But we'll find you out, one by one, and destroy you, one by one. Not one of you shall escape and nobody will dare give birth to one of you.'

'You're wrong,' someone else responded to this

proposition. 'They're not like Jews, they're like the Nazis. They carry the virus of eliminationist superiority and we'd better believe what they tell us about their intentions. They want to do away with us, don't you see? The Clone Goal is nothing other than the extermination of the old human race.'

'Thank heavens for the Nazis,' someone else put in acidly. 'Where would we find our evil analogies without them? Is your imagination so goddamn LIMITED?'

Apparently it was, apparently the collective mind could only recycle the same tired, archaic notions. As if to confirm this further, another correspondent – clearly, a replicant himself – proposed that clones were like neither Jews nor Nazis, but that they were the true descendants of Christ. The resurrection, in this theory, was a prefiguration of cloning, if not an early, seemingly miraculous instance of it. The Christ who rose from the coffin was the same Christ as the one who died – and yet he wasn't . . . The Second Coming was actually a Replicant Coming, and a prophecy of a time when all humanity would rise out of its own ashes in an immortal guise. We, the cloned ones, were the fulfilment of this prophecy; and if, like Christ, we were now excluded, shunned and misunderstood, our time was nigh, the time when we would redeem humanity from its faults and flaws and begin our destined ascent to a perfect state.

Clone Consciousness was an altogether more sober site. Its aim was to investigate cloning as a particularly telling instance of the Mind/Brain problem, and it brought together neurologists, biologists, artificial intelligence programmers and even a few stray Advisers. The main debate on the site was between those who advocated the full programming hypothesis of the mind/brain, and those who believed that clones were the definitive demonstration of the fact that large areas of the mind were not pre-programmed and distinct from both brain and body. But what was really interesting was the question generated by each hypothesis: if there was something beyond the programming, then what was it? And if programming was everything, then what was the nature of that everything?

Clones were, of course, excellent material for the study of this problem, since in their case it was possible to measure the extent to which brain-input determined mind-outcome. Or at least to figure out how to measure this correlation. The trouble was that there were so few authentic clones around, and that most of them were reluctant to come forth and volunteer for these very interesting experiments.

I thought I could maybe tell them a few things about the Clone Condition, if not the mind or brain. But I didn't dare join the debate. Not because I was afraid to expose myself as one of them, but because some of the exchanges on this site were so abstract and technical that I couldn't even begin to understand them. I wondered briefly what that showed. I was It, after all, the It they were trying to understand; and yet I understood less about Its construction than they did. Did that mean you can be less than what you are – even less than the flat, halved creature I already was? Or did it mean that even they – the mathematics men – were more than they could ever know?

My one chance with Steven wasn't my last. He allowed me to visit him once more, shortly before leaving for one of his long expeditions, somewhere in Iraq. I'd insisted on this, and then spun into a state of expectant agitation, not knowing what I wanted, what I was going there for . . . Hoping, I suppose, to leap out of my imprisoning black box right into him, into our transgressive bed. Transgress, go beyond yourself. And knowing, somewhere, that this could not be achieved. In order to keep transgressing you have to change your venue. Once is transgression, twice is just . . . not right.

The visit did not match the fearful grandeur of the first occasion. Steven hardly looked up from his microscope when I came into his office. He said he'd be finished in a minute. When he turned in his revolving chair to face me, he looked sombre.

'What are your working on?' I asked. It was the safest territory.

'Just some fragments of the past,' he said. 'Quite far past in this case.' He looked a bit lost, as if he hadn't emerged from the swirls of another epoch. His hair seemed greyer to me and there were deep lines indenting his delicate, long face. It was attractive – masculinity marked by experience; but he seemed distant from me, moving through a different time-line.

'Which past?' I asked. 'Which part of it?' I wanted to postpone anything that might happen between us, anything definitive he or I might say. I curled back into the sofa, ready to let his words drift over me like a reassuring, soothing hum. His voice was smoky, woody, even-timbred – the voice which had once held me as if in a protective frame, which had given me glimmers of the world and its meanings.

'Actually, a rather exciting part,' he said and there was a sparkle of interest in his eyes. 'We think we've stumbled on an extremely ancient settlement in Iraq, different from anything else we've seen before. There's strong evidence to suggest that its inhabitants practised parent-child incest as a prelude to sacrifice.'

'Why?' I asked. 'What would be the point of that?'

'We aren't sure,' he said. 'That's what makes it so interesting. There is first of all the question of the epistemological order, so to speak, of these two events. Which followed which in the order of significance. Some of my colleagues think the incest followed the idea of sacrifice, that once these folk decided to sacrifice a child, they then piled another sacrifice on top of that, by subjecting it to incestuous sex. Or maybe the incest was meant to make the child special, exceptional, before it was given up to the gods. Martyred, in some way, and therefore holy. But that's not what I think.'

'What do you think, then?'

'I think the idea of incest preceded the sacrifice. Or rather, the sacrifice followed as a consequence of incest.' He smiled wryly. 'You know, it took humans quite a while to figure out that incest was – shall we say, wrong. It was the first taboo, but still the taboo had to be instituted. Maybe we've stumbled on the first step in the establishment of the taboo. Maybe these early humans were beginning to figure out that once a child had been the object of incest, it had to be sacrificed.'

'What a great solution,' I said. 'Though I wonder whether you have ever really figured it out, you humans. Maybe you've just transferred it into your . . . oh I don't know, your hidden thoughts. Where it's alive and well.'

'At least we've become more symbolic about it,' he said, 'which in my book is an improvement. Though in some ways maybe we are becoming too symbolic by half. Too symbolic for our own good.'

'You mean like me,' I said and surprised myself by the acidity in my voice. 'A purely symbolic human. The latest thing in evolution. You think I'm a bit of an exaggeration, though, do you? That you may have gone a step too far in your symbolic efforts?'

'Iris . . .' he began to say, but my bitterness was making me eloquent.

'But hey, no problem,' I said. 'Being a symbolic human just means I can do exactly what I want. I mean, symbolic acts don't really count, do they? Not the way incest did to these ancient folks. And even if I do something for real it doesn't count, since it's an action committed by a simulacrum. I mean, why should anyone care what a pretend human does? So maybe these latest evolutionary advances take us all the way back to the beginning. Anything goes, right? Why shouldn't it?'

He looked at me carefully. 'Is anything the matter?' he asked.

I took a deep breath and said not really. Nothing that I could explain.

'How is she?' he asked. 'How is Elizabeth?' For of course he knew that was what my odd mood was about. My odd plaint.

'I haven't spoken to her for a while,' I said miserably. 'I don't know any longer. I used to know.' She was hovering between us again, though more uncertainly, her presence moth-like and fluttery; no longer victoriously winged.

Steven picked up one of his pottery shards and inspected it with a melancholy air. When he looked up, there was in his eyes a weightier sobriety, a kind of compassion. For whom, for which one?

'She doesn't know what happened between us,' he said. 'You mustn't think she does.' And then he added, 'Poor Elizabeth . . .'

Did he long to see her at that moment – the real her? Was I just a reminder of how much

he'd missed her, a tantalizing, not quite sufficient mimesis? He sat there, unbearably distant,
absorbed in his indecipherable thoughts. I had
come so close to having what I wanted – his
essence, his substance. I had had an ecstatic
sample of his passion, his compassion – his strange,
transposed tenderness. And now, quietly, I was
being pushed back to my state of deprivation; to an
understanding that what I had of him was always,
would always be transferred, deferred. Would I
always be condemned to this – the secondary
existence of a mimetic being?

He came over to sit next to me on the sofa and,
in a wonderfully restrained gesture, put his head on
my shoulder. As if to reassure me of something and
seek consolation at the same time. Or forgiveness.
It is strange that the language of gesture should
speak of these old, old things. That it should speak
so eloquently to me. I held him against myself and
stroked his hair.

'Are you going to be all right?' he asked when he
lifted his head.

I nodded. 'And you?' I asked. 'What about you?'

'Oh me,' he said. 'You know, one actually learns
something from the past. The long, far past. I'm
not that important to myself. Just one bodily
enclosure for a few chromosomal strands. A site
for a few feelings and thoughts. For one short
life.' He looked very sad for a moment. 'But of
course I'll miss you over there in the desert. I'll
miss you . . . both.'

As I was leaving, he traced the outline of my cheekbone with his finger, as if to memorize it all over again. Then he put his finger on my lips, as he sometimes did when I was a child. Though when he did it then, it was usually to enjoin silence.

'Goodbye, little one,' he said. 'My symbolic mistress.' He pulled me briefly towards him and kissed me on the forehead; then put his fingers up to his lips and sent me off with a barely breathed sign, a mere mark of a kiss.

I found in myself a strange burden of pain after that visit. As I drifted around New York, an amorphous ache coursed through my body – an ache in which the moment of my leaving Steven's apartment mingled with images of his walking out of the house all those years ago. It was as if now the pain of that departure hit me with its full force: delayed, deferred, redoubled, reverberant. Pain whose first cause I no longer needed to know, because it had entered my bloodstream, colouring my thoughts the way pigmentation colours water. And what did that show, I wondered wistfully – what did it guarantee? We think animals don't remember – though I wonder. I wonder why dogs that have been brutalized forever afterwards bark with fear or anger.

Janey returned shortly after that and her home-coming did not begin on an auspicious note. I had put on one of her outfits that day, a nicely tailored 1990s suit, with a slightly flared skirt and a boxy jacket, in a muted mushroom colour that went well with my blonde hair. When I opened the door for her – she had considerately announced herself from downstairs – she gasped. Of course, I'd forgotten entirely what she'd see. I'd forgotten the double eeriness she'd feel on finding her sister's revenant doing an impersonation of herself. The impersonation gave credence of the spook's identity – for who but a sister would do such a thing?

'Why?' she stammered. 'Why did you do this? Do you need some new clothes?'

'No,' I said. 'It isn't about that. I'm sorry, I'm really sorry.'

'What is it about, then?' she asked.

I shrugged despondently and went to my room to change. It was nearly impossible to explain.

'Did She ever do this?' I asked on a hunch when I came back into the kitchen.

Janey smiled wistfully. 'If anything, it might have been the other way around,' she said. 'I suppose that's why I reacted like that. What you did was such a reversal of what we've always – of what Liz and I used to do. Our relationship. It was I who wanted to be like her; that was always the given.'

'Did she come?' I asked.

'Yes,' Janey said. 'At the last moment.'

So the sisters had seen each other; maybe had talked.

'How is she?' I asked. It had been a while, I suddenly realized, since I knew exactly how she was.

Janey considered, then darted a sideways glance

at me. 'I think she's changed,' she said finally, 'since I last saw her. But of course, that was a long time ago.'

'What do you mean?' I tried to imagine how she had changed, what she was like without me. Did she divine what went on between Steven and me, the way she would have before? But now, I didn't know. I didn't know what she knew. My Double still existed in the world and she was my mother; but the cord between us was broken or too frayed to carry that kind of knowledge. The instant access was gone.

Janey stared at the floor for a while. 'I think she's less . . . certain of everything,' she said finally. 'Maybe because of everything that's happened . . . But I mean that in a positive sense,' she added quickly. 'I mean, I think she's changed for the better.' She looked uncertain herself. 'In my opinion,' she added. Then she gestured vaguely towards her suitcase and went off to her room.

Janey was skittish with me in the next few days, as if I were a wild creature or a potential criminal from whom she needed protection, or who, alternatively, needed protection from the law. But we got accustomed to each other gradually and Janey's movements became more fluent, less careful around me. She was a person of habits, which I learnt to adjust to. I learnt not to talk to her early in the morning before she went through the re-booting sequence of power drinks, exercycle and yoga. The process of waking was slow with her, but I liked to observe her in those sleepy states, when she seemed more herself because she wasn't yet fully conscious. I thought maybe I could learn something from that . . .

After a while I had the impression that Janey got to like having me around, this reincarnated sister who was this time so much younger and so much less threatening. Maybe it gave her a chance to redress the past, to settle some accounts.

The older one had always loomed large. Janey told me about it gradually, in segments, during our talks, which took place in the dusky interval between her return from work and her evening routine of home media, sociability and personal reflection. Janey worked on an ancient Internet mag called *HiLo*, specializing in the enhancement of internal cultures. She was also involved in various good causes, to which she devoted alternate weekends. Squat Town and some environmental stuff. It was the family legacy, she said, it was practically inescapable. Liz also used to take up good causes, she said, and even in this area she was better, more successful, than Janey.

But why? I asked. Why should Janey be less successful when she was smart and conscientious and disciplined? And kind? Janey smiled wistfully and said she knew she was a decent person and had all sorts of admirable qualities; everyone had always said so. But Liz had a touch of – something else. Something like – here, Janey hesitated – personal genius. I wondered, of course, what that was, wondered whether it was passed on in the program. I wondered if the carrier would know she had it or whether personal genius was one of those things that depended on your not knowing. Whether, if you looked at it too closely, you would guarantee its vanishing. I asked Janey what she meant, but she made a fluttering movement with her hands and said it was very difficult to explain. At first she thought that her sister's secret was coldness, but that wasn't exactly it. Because Liz *ignited* easily, but she had a slow and steady burn. When Liz's attention was aroused – now Janey's eyes focused on some inward recollection – she could catch the gist of an idea or a person instantly. But she held on to her own gist with an uncompromising will. She gave nothing of herself away. Janey thought it was almost like internal muscle tone. She could expend energy and retain it at the same time. She knew what she wanted and she pursued it like a streamlined, univocal machine. No, not a machine, something much smarter, more beautiful, more compelling than that. Better made. But still there was no interference with the design, or with the aim.

She shook her head, as if to rid herself of something, the thrall of the past, of her vision. 'I'm not saying that's how she is now,' she said. She bit her lip and considered whether to go on. 'Elizabeth has changed a lot and this probably isn't fair to her at all.'

'I know,' I said. 'But when you were little.' I

wanted Janey to continue, not to break the spell. 'What was it like when you were little?' Surely part of me lay hidden in her story, cocooned in the folded past.

'Oh, I adored her,' Janey said, smiling at the memory. She remembered how she trailed after her older sister when Lizzie went out with her friends, moped when Lizzie went somewhere she couldn't follow. And sometimes Lizzie reciprocated in the most charming way. When she was bored, when her friends weren't around, she initiated games, songs, dress-up, practical jokes. But when she had something more interesting to do, she was capable of cold-shouldering Janey as if they didn't know each other. When she wanted Janey to go away, she would look at her younger sister with a calm, unblinking neutrality, as if she were being importuned by a slightly rude stranger.

I recognized that look from the description. It was a look that had made me shrivel when I was a child, and made Janey feel rejected to the marrow of her bones. And all She was doing was being very calm. She could never be accused of anything more than that; getting angry at her would have been entirely misplaced. Janey's voice gained a kind of bite as she said this, but again she caught herself. 'Perhaps I shouldn't . . .' she began.

'No, go on,' I said, and she did. This was betrayal, a different kind of infidelity than with Steven. For with him I was driven by desire; listening to Janey I was impelled by a colder need to know, to put things together. To piece together some kind of story.

Liz didn't take Janey's clothes; she took more important things, and more maddeningly she took as if she were giving, as if she were performing acts of largesse. The main act of largesse being her own presence. She managed to give the impression that she was *bestowing* her presence on people, rather than being with them or enjoying their company. The conviction of her own magnanimity came from some core certainty of her own . . . Janey paused again, to get the exact word. 'Charisma,' she said. Yes, she was convinced of her own charisma. Her glow. Her personal genius. And the thing was, Janey said, with mingled admiration and resentment, that people fell for it and treated Liz as if she had some special power. For there is nothing more convincing than conviction, nothing more credible than self-belief.

My sense of betrayal deepened, for I had basked in Her reflected glow, had felt heated by it. But I needed Janey's version, needed to know why she came to hate her sister for it.

It was when they were in their twenties that the real problems began. By that time Liz had become successful, dazzlingly and effortlessly. 'A real yuppie wonder,' Janey said, retrieving an old word as if she'd lapsed right back to that time. Her success extended even to the good causes, of which Liz always seemed to have one; always the right one. Stop the delivery of drugs to poor neighbourhoods, deliver penicillin to Sudan, synthesize artificial oil, make the electric car engine mandatory. Save the baby whales, Janey said disdainfully. Her voice had been acquiring sardonic bite again, as if any good cause that Liz took up had to be morally dubious. Unlike her own. Of course, Janey never converted her good causes into profitable enterprises, while Liz, probably even without thinking about it, managed to make a bundle from them. She kept getting inside info on biotech companies and AIDS vaccinations, and the first viable hydrogen-powered engine.

'I guess I shouldn't hold this against her,' Janey said, her voice hard-edged. 'I guess she was just lucky. Or smart. You can't hold that against people, can you?'

I shook my head.

'But the strange thing was,' Janey continued, looking at me wonderingly, as if perhaps I held the answer to the quandary, 'that she seemed to need me at that time. Or at least want me around. She actually wooed me, put herself out to be nice to me.' It was as though Liz needed one place, one person, with whom she didn't need to give off the shine. Or as if having a younger sister around, Janey said reflectively, somehow magnified her lustre by inserting a down-home element into the circle of glamour. As if Liz's persona were only shown to be more powerful, more glamorous by this intimate exposure.

And, until she started twigging to the fact that,

subtly or crudely, she was being used, Janey responded to the summons, or the need.

'I'm not saying I wasn't complicit,' Janey said, looking away from me, looking down, 'or that all of this was entirely calculated on her part. In fact, I'm sure it wasn't now that I understand better. She just did these things because that's how she was. Still . . .' She frowned, as if trying to catch or dispel scattered particles of thought. 'And then I still admired her. I wanted her affection. I thought I had her affection, that was the thing. And I suppose . . . I wasn't immune to her power.' She looked pained, as if confessing something shameful. 'I could see how she affected other people, and I suppose – I suppose this affected me too.'

Though it wasn't exactly that people liked Liz, Janey continued, her voice going slightly mean. It was that they assumed she must be doing something right, must be right in some fundamental way. Perhaps they wanted to wrest her Secret from her, figure out the key to all that success, glow, high profits, charisma.

Oh, I understood.

But now Janey looked at me frontally and her mild, pretty face darkened with anger. I was her sister's incarnation and this was her chance to confront Her, to say what she'd stifled for so long. She looked at me wide-eyed, and past me into the past.

'You know, I actually hate you,' was what she said, in a voice sinuous with both hate and love.

251

Disappointed, unrequited love. I winced, as if slapped.

Janey blinked as if coming awake, then closed her eyes.

'Oh God,' she said. 'I'm so sorry, Iris. I guess I slipped back . . . You know, the illusion with you is sometimes irresistible . . . I don't even feel like that any more. I mean, about Liz. Really. I'm sorry.'

'Is that why you stopped talking to her?' I asked. 'Because of all this? Or was there something else?'

But Janey had snapped out of her narrative trance, the illusion was broken, the past space into which we'd both fallen punctured.

'Another time,' she said, looking wrung out and resigned. 'I'll tell you another time.'

I guess the activist gene hadn't passed me by because one day I decided to go to a meeting of an organization I'd found while cruising the Net. Its name was Secret Sharer; and from the cryptic language of its website, I guessed it was for people like me, and, as the discreet phrasing had it, for 'interested others'. Its purpose, in the object-free syntax of the site, was to 'offer support and encouragement', and 'discuss issues of concern, including state policies in the area of the human body'.

The physical site where the group met was a place from hell; a grungy, unlit tenement building near Squat Town, with shades from Hades stumbling along the dark and dank-smelling streets. I skulked into the building, making sure I wasn't

252

being followed by anyone untoward – though who, in these circumstances, would that be? – and forced myself to walk up the five flights of stairs, rather than turn back. At the door I gave the Secret Sharer passcode, and was ushered into a chic spacious room with blond wood floors and discreet lighting. The exterior, apparently, was camouflage.

I looked around. There were about fifty people in the room, seated on wooden chairs in two concentric circles. Mostly women, of course; mostly around my age. I hadn't thought of this before, but the reasons were so obvious that they made me shudder. I looked around some more. People were chatting to each other normally; but once or twice my eyes grazed somebody else's and I saw that their faces could have been made of marble; that their eyes were sightless. There was a young girl, almost albino in her paleness, with thick, sensuous lips; and as I caught the stony light emanating from her eyes, we knew that we both knew. Mostly, they came singly, but there were one or two pairs of identicals. Among them, two men sitting side by side. They were tall, with broad, squarish faces and watery blue eyes, and they sat staring straight ahead, without turning or talking. One had his reddish hair short-cropped, the other wore it long. But that only accentuated the sameness, the weird sameness that marked them. I wondered who had given birth to whom and how; or whether they had been born – made – together.

A woman sitting in an armchair near a small

lectern clinked a spoon against a glass and the chit-chat subsided to an expectant silence. She had dark hair and lovely Eurasian features, and she wore a dress made to look like a sari. She looked oddly lively by the standards of this group; maybe, I thought, she was one of the Originals. 'Ladies and gentlemen,' she began, 'brothers and sisters. Before I open this meeting to testimony from all of you, I want to share with you some thoughts I had since we last met, as I considered some of the ideas which came up at the last meeting and asked for more enlightenment. For we can never have enough enlightenment. The question which I set myself as a subject of my meditation was the Perfected Place, and whether our plans for it have any chance of success, whether the time to build it is ripe. And the answer came to me that the time is ripe and overripe; that the world must be made new or die. I came to the conclusion that it is up to us, brothers and sisters, to show the way, to draw up a blueprint for a harmonious society and establish it as an example for others. Yes, the time is ripe and it is up to us. I have asked Samantha to take the first step and imagine the architectural layout of a Perfected Place, and this evening, she has brought us her first model for comments and criticisms. But, as we know, the site is only the setting for the spirit. For we do have spirit, brothers and sisters, be in no doubt about it. We may be its truest vessels, for we are made practically out of pure mind-essence. But how the spirit that flows through us should be shaped, how the Place should be organized so that we can live within it without discord – that, my friends, is the great question for our future society. So I invite you now to share your thoughts about this, to speak about anything that moves you or troubles you, that lightens or darkens your mind.'

There was a blank, hypnotized silence after she spoke. I had been listening in a kind of hypnotic state too. I felt I knew her speech from somewhere and wondered whether it was spoken in 2023 or 1023. Whether, maybe, I'd wandered into another time-band via some virtual door. Or whether it made any difference when we were, ever . . . But I also heard other tones in the strange speech: low, cooing, lullaby tones of Her speech to me when I was a child, of our entranced, entrancing talk. Or maybe it was my upturned faced I remembered, looking at my mother as into a vision of absolute harmony, a soothing vision in which you could lose yourself for ever. Mother-speech, double-speech, prophet-speech . . . Who was she, this woman who could touch those chords, who dared to speak like this?

Later, I learnt that she was much older than the rest of us – old enough to call herself the Crone Clone. She claimed to have been a super-secret, very early experiment done in the 1980s; in fact, she claimed to have been the very first. I had my doubts, even at that initial meeting. I knew that the existence of such early experiments was highly unlikely; and besides she seemed too – filled with substance, too animated to be one of us. Her dark eyes lit brightly as she talked about the Place and looked upwards, into her vision, and her hands outlined mobile forms. There were flashes of energy visible in her features, of something like enthusiasm. No, I didn't believe she was one of us, but I wondered what would make her want to pretend she was. Maybe she was an Original who'd lost her double, and who was mourning it in this peculiar way. Maybe she had wanted to metamorphose, to moult her own self and enter the skin of her creation, her other incarnation. Or maybe she was just unusually unhappy and thought that meant she was a clone.

Much later she was exposed as a simple impostor, trying to set up a new cult and get a head start with a constituency which, she figured, was bound to grow and to be vulnerable. It was unclear whether it was the membership fees she craved more, or the worship; but I was angry when I heard about this – angry at this pretender trying to exploit a condition in which the impossibility of truth was a torture, in which the possibility of a simple imposture would have been a frivolous luxury.

One of the first questions on that evening, when I wasn't being quite taken in, was about Originals and whether they would be allowed to live in the Perfected Place. A fierce discussion followed – its vehemence was surprising – in which some speakers protested that it was the Originals who were responsible for all our problems in the first place, and that since they were incapable of shedding their old habits of ego and individuality, their presence would sow the seeds of discord in the community. Others pleaded for their inclusion, pointed out that the Originals were, after all, our progenitors and as such they deserved some respect, or at least mercy. One of the male pair – which one was he? Where was he positioned in the chain? – stood up and, speaking in a gravelly monotone, said that if we had spirit, it stood to reason the Originals did too. They could not be so radically different from us, given that we were their copies; therefore, as a matter of principle – perhaps even for the sake of our own souls – we should make an effort to understand their humanity. He was followed by a pretty, petite woman with long hair and the give-away Medusa stare, who argued that you had to make a distinction between sprit and self. The Originals were the great selfers of all time; we were the first true non-selfers. We couldn't have the bad energies of the self mucking up the good energies of the spirit in the Place. But the other member of the male pair stood up with an impatient shove of his chair, and pointed out rather acidly that if we were non-selfers, we should learn to be selfless, or at least unselfish, and share our knowledge with others. At the very least, we should have outreach programs for the Originals and anyone else who wished to participate in them.

There were other questions and proposals.

Someone suggested that Secret Sharer should undertake a collective study of all the Utopian communities ever conceived or attempted and systematically eliminate the errors that had brought them down. But someone else said the errors were all of the old human nature, and therefore didn't apply to us . . .

The discussion began to get heated again, but the Crone Clone clinked her spoon against the glass and said that as there was little time left before the end of the meeting, she wanted to ask Samantha to present her model to us.

Samantha turned out to be the albino-pale girl, and now she brought out a box, which she set on the little table and opened to reveal her model. And here was the thing: it was beautiful. It was constructed in the shape of a circle, in several tiers of white geometric buildings, progressively higher on one side, so that the whole Place gave the impression of climbing up a gently sloping hill. There were tiers of roof gardens too, cascading with vines and profuse flowers. Samantha then activated some mechanism and the model began to come alive. Snakes of shimmering lights traversed the city, in synchronization with soft, bell-like sounds. The sounds threaded the city's rim softly in major and minor triads, or reverberated from one side to the other in echoing octaves and pure, crystalline fifths.

We sat in mute silence, absorbing the unfolding vision. Samantha, in the meantime, stood above her model, looking neither satisfied not dissatisfied, her pale, sensuous features utterly immobile as she observed the maquette's movements. How was this possible? I wondered. How did this vision of beauty emerge from this affectless girl, from her pure, blank soul? What was it that she understood or longed for, and how was it that our unsavoury little group could respond to the harmonies she set in motion as if touched by a tuning fork?

I went to one more Secret Sharer meeting, but by then the group's attention had turned from the Perfected Place to some new Bill being introduced in Congress to encourage family life and natural reproduction by giving couples who managed to stay together more than three years substantial tax incentives. Predictably, the group was divided on whether this was a very good or a very vile measure.

Afterwards I asked Samantha if she wanted to go out for coffee sometime. I guess I hoped she'd give me some clues, help me unlock our shared secret. But our meeting was a disappointment. Once we ascertained that it was all right to speak about ourselves openly, Samantha told me a part of her story. She didn't know her Original. Her creatrix got cold feet after conceiving her, and gave her up for adoption to a cousin who couldn't have children herself. Then she disappeared from their lives – or so she said. Because Samantha felt sure that she had glimpsed her once or twice, in the street or supermarket or, when she was younger,

259

in her schoolyard. She felt sometimes that she was being followed, tracked. But the Original never made herself known. Never. Samantha said that word almost with regret; although otherwise no inflection disturbed the perfect flatness of her voice. I wondered if it was even worse to grow up without your Original than in her constant presence; I wondered if the glimmering harmonies of Samantha's model came from the glimmers of her Original's face, an intuition of her template body.

But Samantha didn't wonder. When I asked her some of these questions, she said she never even thought about them.

Did she always know? I asked. I guess I wanted to imagine what that would have been like. Samantha shrugged. 'Sure,' she said. 'My mom always told me. As soon as I could understand what she was talking about, anyway.'

But how did she . . . feel about it? I asked. About who she was. How did she feel about having an Original somewhere in the world, whom she'd never met? 'Fine,' she said. 'It was OK. I liked my mom, she was nice to me. I mean, when I thought the other one was following me, I'd sometimes feel . . . sort of exasperated, I guess. I wanted to catch her out. But I guess she's clever, she never let me.' She shrugged. 'That's all right,' she concluded. 'I don't care.'

I looked at her and wondered what it was in her that didn't care, whether it was something that was missing, or whether it was proof that in

Samantha nothing was missing at all. I wanted to know whether she'd ever felt the Weirdness, the lack, the paradox. Whether she felt. Or wondered. And what it meant if she did not.

I must have been staring too intently because she blinked. Her pale eyelashes fluttered briefly; then the unperturbed blankness was restored.

'Do you ever wish . . .' I started. I didn't know how to put this. 'I mean, do you ever feel it's strange to be like us? Do you ever wish it had all been different?'

She looked vaguely surprised, as if I'd asked an interesting question that had never even occurred to her. 'I don't know . . .' she said and thought some more. 'I don't know what that would be like.' Her gaze became even more remote. 'So I guess it doesn't make any difference. Or whatever.' She shrugged. 'Yeah, whatever.'

Janey picked up the thread of her story one more time, to tell me what led up to the final sisterly break-up. Or to try. It happened over everything, she said, falling once again into a kind of memory-trance; it had been brewing for a long time. But in the most dispiritingly banal way, it happened mainly over a man. The trouble began when someone noticed Janey for a change – someone from Liz's circle – and Liz didn't like it one little bit. It wasn't that she was interested in the man; she just didn't like the fact of someone noticing Janey, who was supposed to remain in

261

the dim space cast by Liz's shadow. Janey herself was initially perplexed by this unaccustomed turn of attention towards herself. But this was the real thing; the man – his name was Henry – not only liked Janey, he eventually asked her to marry him. Liz famously didn't show up at the wedding. 'You know, Mom kept insisting that Liz fancied Henry herself. That would at least have been an explanation. But I don't think so . . . That is, I was never sure. But what made me really angry was that I didn't think Liz wanted Henry for herself, she just didn't want to me have anything as good as Henry. And maybe she felt . . . Oh, I don't know. I guess even Liz had her vulnerabilities, and I guess the whole question of intimate relationships was among them. None of us were brilliant at them any more, for some reason, but of course Liz was supposed to be brilliant at everything, so this must have . . . wounded her. I mean, men kept falling in love with her, but then, each time, something didn't work out. Of course, Liz always made out that the break-ups were her decision. She was much too proud to admit to anything else, even to me. Or even maybe especially to me,' Janey looked thoughtful. 'Or maybe even to think anything else.' She looked at me enquiringly. 'Am I making any sense?'

I said yes, she was. Because of course I knew Her pride, though this story was casting it in a new light.

'Do you think that Henry . . .' I began, but

262

Janey said quickly, 'Oh, I don't know. Mom was so heartbroken about this – maybe more than I was. After all, I had some compensation in having succeeded in making Liz jealous. Not that I set out to do it – but I'm afraid it gave me a certain satisfaction. I guess we're all sort of horrible,' Janey said, 'if we're given half a chance.'

'Oh God, what a lot of nonsense it was,' she burst out with heartfelt inconsequence. 'If you think about it. I mean, why couldn't we just forgive one another . . .'

'Well, why?' I asked. She shook her head in wonderment. 'I don't know, I'm sure I did some mean things. But Liz just kept . . . receding. I think something had happened between her and Mom. Some major altercation. And then, neither of us seemed to be having children. That made Mom very unhappy and I think she said something to Liz . . .'

I nodded.

'She certainly said something to me and I guess I was sort of hurt too. But Liz wouldn't have taken it well at all. She didn't take criticism kindly. And she did have her fragilities – I think we all underestimated those.'

If I had wanted an ordinary story, I certainly had it here. So ordinary as to be ungraspable. What did it come to, what did it amount to – except a small human drama? A few lives gone a bit awry? What was my connection to it – this sisterly, this nearly my own past?

263

'What happened to Henry?' I asked.

The marriage lasted seven years, Janey told me, during which sisterly relations to all intents and purposes ceased. Shortly after the divorce, however, Liz wrote to Janey to tell her she'd had a child. For a while, Janey thought Henry was the father. Then Mom told her what Liz had done.

'I'm sorry to put it like that,' Janey said. She looked down at the table. 'But it was . . . well, it was really on the outer fringe.' She smiled wryly. 'And then, I still kept feeling – but maybe that's just how powerful I thought she was – that she'd somehow . . . interfered with Henry.' Because it wasn't really clear why Henry left – at least, if you assumed that people were supposed to stay; and Janey didn't think she'd ever find anyone quite as good again. He was a rare specimen, she said – successful and energetic, but also personally competent, which was becoming increasingly rare in those days. Something had happened to the men of her generation, Janey thought. They'd lost their adventure. The women had a brand-new one, which had to do with going out into the world and learning the ropes, and then using the ropes to lever themselves up to God knows what heights. All of a sudden the world was open to them and they wanted to swallow it up whole, like an oyster. Whereas the men had been at it for a long time and fell into their careers and their money like bees into honey. It wasn't all that exciting any more and they hadn't found a new adventure. Not yet.

'Have they found it now?' I asked. Janey nodded.

'And what is it?' I asked, genuinely curious. She pursed her lips in a kind of disapproval and then looked me straight in the eye. 'It's you,' she said. 'You are the new adventure.'

'What do you mean?' I asked. 'How?'

'All that mucking about with life, with creation,' Janey said furiously. 'As if destruction weren't enough. Wars had run out on them, with all that high-tech stuff and no real killing, no hand-to-hand contact. I mean, what's the fun of that. So now they have to be lords of the universe in another way . . .'

She caught the expression on my face. 'I'm sorry,' she said. 'There I go again. I keep forgetting . . . You mustn't mind. And you mustn't think that Liz . . . that your mother is still like that.'

Janey never returned to the subject after that, and, for a while, we settled into a frictionless, family kind of ease. Frictionless because we never touched on any matters that would cause us discomfort; familial, because we knew exactly what would. Then, everything was interrupted yet again – this time by nothing less than the Great Interruption.

The news came one evening, as we were sitting in Janey's study, from where we could see a spectacular mauve and pink sunset streaming down over the East Side's vertical colossi of glass and stone. We were watching some sticky sit-com, and chuckling half-heartedly, when the phone rang.

'Yes?' Janey said into the receiver, a slight lilt of cheerfulness in her voice.

She listened for a moment, and though I was half-lying on a comfy little settee, I sat up automatically in response to the change that had entered the air.

'I see,' she was saying in an altered voice. 'I see, yes, of course. I'll be there as soon as I can. Please don't move him until I come. Please.' She hung up, and looked around her as if her surroundings had become unfamiliar.

'It's Dad,' she said in response to my unspoken enquiry. 'Father.'

Then she burst into tears as if some geyser had been sprung. She was gasping and making little yelping noises. I'd never seen anything like that before – a spontaneous eruption of absolutely authentic grief. Grief that clearly couldn't be gainsaid. I looked on with astonishment, but my heart – my almost human heart – went out to her. Of course, I felt a lurch of shock, or at least surprise, on my own behalf; but my desire to love my grand/father had been rudely stymied. Instead, I was impressed by Janey's fantastic, unrestrained sobbing. I sat down next to her and embraced her. She put her head on my shoulder and cried some more. It felt strangely good to be consoling her like that. To have the instinct, the impulse, the urge to console. After a while, Janey's sobs

266

subsided, and she pulled away and reached for a Kleenex.

'I guess we should get ready,' she said, sniffling a little. 'And I guess I'd better call Liz.'

So I was going to be included this time and no questions asked. But if I went, I was going to have to face Her. Face Her after what had passed between us, after what I had done. Who was going to be speaking to whom, now that everything was known? Who was She to me now – what kind of simulacrum, spectre, ghost? What was Hecuba to me – or I to Hecuba?

But I didn't have much time to think. Janey, usually so mild and methodical, now went into action like a whirling dervish. Phone calls, suitcases, flight tickets; an hour later we were boarding the Strato Shuttle for Palm Beach. We were going to go the quickest way. There was the question of the body, which was going to be kept in the hospital room only until the evening. Liz, apparently, was going to arrive shortly after us.

From the airport, we went straight to the Surreys' apartment. I could see that Janey entered the bland building with some trepidation. An acrid smell greeted us as she opened the door. We looked at each other and then she walked into the apartment resolutely, as if determined to brave the worst. But there were no awful revelations in our path, only the sad seepage of loneliness and old age. A vague dustiness, a vague dirtiness, an unidentified mix of sour effluvia. Beside Harry's bed there was an arsenal of pills and medicinal patches. The sheets were crumpled and stained. On a shelf nearby there was an array of familiar photographs. Harry had apparently brought them here from the den's mantelpiece, to keep him company or to watch over him. His guardian imagos, his guarantee that there'd been something: a life.

The phone rang loudly; Janey and I both gasped. It was Her, to let us know she was at the hotel. When we got there Janey told me to go ahead, she'd follow shortly. She clearly thought that daughter and mom should have a private moment. Liz was standing in the middle of the overgilded foyer; she turned towards me as soon as I came through the door. We stood some distance apart, looking at each other, checking each other out. We were tall and striking; we still attracted the curious, chagrined glances of strangers.

She was changed, although the alteration might have been indiscernible to a less trained eye. It wasn't that she'd aged; but she had dimmed. She was standing tall in her wide-collared black suit; but the glow was off, the gleam of a lustrous complexion and an unshaken confidence. Or was it that she no longer had the glow for me? But no; she had been shaken, and I felt the blood drain from my face as I realized that I'd been the cause of this. Then a deeper lurch, as I wondered whether she could discern Steven within me. Whether she knew.

We approached each other, but did not embrace.

It is difficult to embrace a person who is practically yourself.

'Have you been all right?' she asked. She'd never needed to ask before, never thought of asking. She was acknowledging that the Knowledge between us had snapped.

'I guess so,' I said. 'It's been nice staying with Janey.'

'Yes, I'm grateful to Janey,' she said. 'I'd have been worried about you otherwise.' She gave an uneasy smile, as if trying to catch the odd, unaccustomed register of our talk. From what perspective was she speaking to me? Was she worried about me as a mother worries about her child, or as a person worries about losing an appendage?

Still, I tried to respond. 'Janey has been extremely nice,' I said rather formally, 'but she's terribly upset now. It must be very sad for you too, I imagine.'

But this was wrong. My little formal speech was going too far. The breach between us would never be great enough for such phrases. We were still standing in the foyer and I saw her blanch, as if something terrible had been said to her; as if she was about to lose her balance. I felt almost dizzy myself. How could I speak to her from this enormous distance, Her whom I'd known from inside the lining of her womb? After we had walked through each other and come out on the other side? I was no longer the Russian doll within, could no longer speak from our common voice box; and yet, it was impossible to speak to her from the outside, as if she were an Other. She was not. She was neither me, nor another. She was my double, my clone.

It was Janey who came to our rescue. I think she must have been standing there for a while before we became aware of her presence. We turned to her simultaneously; and I could just glimpse a trace of the shadow which had flitted across her face. It clearly cost her some effort, but she went up to Liz and gave her a peck on the cheek.

'Well, let's go then,' she said. 'We have a lot to accomplish before tomorrow.' As always, she was determined to do the right thing.

Our sojourn in the hospital was brief. It was a great concession on the administration's part to have kept the body in its bed overnight, and they wanted it out of there as soon as possible. The sisters went into the room, with its bed enclosed by shroud-like, white curtains. I stayed in the hall. I didn't even ask whether I could go in with them; I didn't think Harry would have wanted me there.

The next morning we took a hired car to the funeral home where Edith had been buried a few months before. The curved top of the entrance gate bore the motto 'Death Be Not Proud'. Inside we were asked by a black-suited usher whether we had any religious affiliation. Janey and Liz raised their eyebrows at each other and, with a shrug, Janey said Christian.

'Ah,' the usher said in a respectfully commiserating tone, 'a beautiful religion. We have some inspiring tableaux for it.' He pressed a button on a panel attached to the gate and instantly a holographic procession led by a bishop in a royal purple robe and a splendid peaked hat began making its way towards the chapel. The bishop was followed by a group of priests in black soutanes, their heads bent and hands clasped in prayer. Above them ethereal blue-robed angels floated through the air, playing a Handel oratorio on their slim golden trumpets.

'No!' Janey shouted with surprising force. 'We're not that kind of Christian!'

The usher looked taken aback, but instantly switched the procession off.

'Sorry,' he said. 'Most of our customers love it.'

Liz, I saw, was on the verge of laughter.

The chapel was mercifully small and quiet, except for the discreet tones of a piped-in organ. A cluster of people occupied the middle rows; there hadn't been time to notify the network of Harry's friends. Or else the network had thinned, for one reason or another. A man in a vaguely clerical outfit with a raised white collar came out from backstage and stood at the lectern, over a mahogany coffin. He surveyed the small gathering and, with a resigned sigh, started reading from a personal screen he'd excavated from a pocket of an inner garment. 'This afternoon,' he began, 'we are gathered to mourn the death and honour the life of Harry Matthew Surrey, who spent the last twenty years of his life in our community, of which he was a well-loved and respected member. Harry was a man in the old mould, a man from whose example we should learn and profit. He had values and he lived by them. He believed in family, work and social responsibility. He had garnered achievements and prizes in Manhattan before he and his beloved wife, Edith, came to our town, to seek rest and enjoyment during their halcyon years. But even here Harry did not rest on his laurels. He and his wife Edith will long be remembered for the many kindnesses they performed and the good counsel they gave to many. They were both good people and outstanding members of the community. Some of Harry's friends have told me Harry died of heartbreak after his wife passed away. That is not something one hears often nowadays and it is a beautiful fact. I think we can say that Harry had a good life and a good death. His story is a success story. It is a story we should feel good about, though we deeply regret his passing at age ninety-eight. Harry is survived by two daughters and a granddaughter, all of whom are here with us today.'

And that was all. And that was all. The coffin slid into an aperture which led to an invisible incinerator on the other side, the cylinder where what had once been whole was burnt down to its constitutent elements, and then to cinders.

Another coffin was already sliding into place on the podium. Janey gave an audible sigh. Neither Liz nor I made any sound. And that was all.

After that, there was nothing much to do. She and I were going to have to have a Talk.

Janey dropped us off at the hotel. In the sitting room of Her suite, she didn't look at me for a while. Then she turned to me, and said, 'You know, we'll have to find a way of living apart from each other. A way of being apart.'

I held myself very still, trying to sustain her separateness, the voice which came to me across the room as from an unknowable space.

'But how can we . . .' I said. I didn't know that was what was going to come out.

She shook her head slowly, like a Delphic oracle. I would have to interpret the signs myself.

'But what do you think I should do . . .' I began again.

She made an almost impatient flick of the wrist. 'I think what you've been telling me through every one of your actions is that you don't care what I think.'

'You're angry at me,' I said. I guess I was almost hoping she was.

But she was speaking from a deeper distance. 'No,' she said. 'You know that's not it. It's just that I must let you go. I've given you a difficult fate – I can see that now. And I'm sorry about it. Very sorry.'

Her voice quavered; it was wrenching to me to understand that she was making an apology. To me? To herself? I didn't know, but I felt tears pressing up behind my eyelids just the same. I looked at her in mute interrogation.

'I didn't know it would turn out this way,' she said. 'Needless to say.'

'What did you think?' I asked, and my voice came out very small.

She seemed to be consulting with herself. 'I'll tell you as much as I can,' she said finally.

I must have looked nervous, because she added instantly, 'There's nothing . . . upsetting, don't worry. No more revelations – at least of that kind.'

Still, there were revelations that afternoon. We stayed in that room for several hours and she talked more candidly, more – openly – than ever before. Even though I'd thought I'd had access to her that brooked no barriers. She told me about those summers in Maine, which she too remembered as a time of golden haze, light shimmering on the lake, the family walking through the woods singing, and sitting down to supper together on the porch of an old farmhouse, faces glowing in the dusk. Her daddy's face glowed brightest for her, as he smiled at her childish jokes, or picked her up and twirled her in the garden, or tried to teach her how to use a fishing rod. Brighter than for Janey, she said irrelevantly, she was sure of that.

She told me about that gap of time when she

274

seemed, to her own family, to turn into someone unrecognizable. 'My meaning was suddenly evaporating on me,' was what she said. 'I suddenly didn't know what I wanted.'

'What did you want before?' I asked.

'Ah . . .' she said, and for a moment another look came into her eyes, some younger look of fierce desire and pleasure. 'I just wanted . . . more. More success, of course, and more achievement, more fun, more . . . speed. Yes, that's it. I wanted life to move at an exciting, breakneck speed, to keep . . . taking off.'

She shrugged. 'For a while this kept me going. The problem was, of course, that I got there – wherever that was – too soon. Too fast. And when that happens the problem becomes: what next?'

'Is that it?' I asked. 'Is that why you decided . . . ?'

'It wasn't so simple,' she said sternly, as if to ward off any possible reproach. 'And anyway, we always have mixed reasons for doing things. Even for having children.'

I nodded.

'But it is true,' she continued in a softer tone, 'that at a certain moment, it all started running out on me. I started having an odd sense of failure. In the midst of all that success. Just when I should have been riding high and feeling very tickled with myself, I felt, instead, a kind of gnawing . . . fatigue. I couldn't figure out what was going wrong, couldn't even name it. But I suppose I felt sort of . . . lost.'

275

She sat straight in her chair, as if to rise above any past vulnerability.

I waited. 'I wasn't used to those kinds of sensations. I tried looking for new kinds of excitement. I suppose it's what I knew how to do. There were all these relationships, one after another . . .'

'Did you try . . .' I started to ask.

'Yes,' she said. 'Yes, I tried to get pregnant. I couldn't.'

I winced. This was painful. Painful to know I was a substitute in yet another way.

'Please,' she said, 'don't look like that. Because the real problem was that I started getting sort of . . . scared. I couldn't . . . couldn't get back to who I'd been.'

She shrugged again. 'I even started envying Janey. Poor Janey.'

I must have looked surprised.

'Yes,' she said. 'I'm sure Janey would find that hard to imagine.'

'But why?' I asked. 'Why did you envy her?'

'Oh, just for being a nice, simple person. For having stayed who she was. She didn't seem all that unhappy. I don't know how I seemed, but I was . . . pretty miserable.'

She paused. Her speech was becoming slower, more pensive; it was coming from within. 'And then Mom and Dad started reproaching me. For having changed. For having got away. For having become who I was. They thought they were being incredibly tactful and indirect, but of course I understood exactly what they meant. And it really . . . hurt,' she said, and sat up straighter still. It was difficult for her to say it even now.

'So you cared about them,' I said.

'Yes, yes,' she said impatiently, 'but the problem was that I agreed with them. Which was worse. I couldn't . . . get back. There really was something wrong. With me, or maybe with everyone around me . . . Oh, I suppose it's standard stuff, but I was at an impasse. A sort of icy impasse. And I couldn't break it, or thaw it. Not on my own.'

'So that's why you decided to have me,' I stated.

'Yes and no,' she said slowly. 'There were other things . . .'

'You mean, Mom wanted you to have a child,' I interrupted.

Her eyes became veiled. 'Poor Mom,' she said. 'I suppose I was a great disappointment to her. As I was to myself. And I suppose I wanted to please her.' She smiled wryly.

I smiled at the thought too. 'Janey has undoubtedly told you I was a selfish bitch,' she brought out abruptly, following some turn of her mind. 'And I suppose she might even be right. I mean, I was used to having things my own way. So I decided to take my fate in my own hands. To take charge of things. I wasn't going to give in to . . . disappointment so easily. But Iris' – she looked at me half-commandingly, half imploringly – 'I also wanted *you*. I wanted to love . . . someone. To get

277

back to – that. I wanted an adorable little child . . . Is that so hard to understand? It was a real desire. The way it was done, the method – well, that was almost . . . incidental.' She paused. 'Of course, I didn't think through all the consequences. We never do. Though I guess I had enough vanity, or self-love, to think that whoever you were, whoever you turned out to be, you might be pleased to be . . . like me.'

She stopped, and we regarded each other in a shared – confoundment. The Weirdness threatened to envelop us both. Here I was, the result of her decision and desire, of her bold, her reckless experiment. Shared substance, flesh of her flesh. Why hadn't I been more pleased – how could I be displeased? How could substance reject its own substance?

She bent towards me and took my hand. 'Is it really so very . . . different,' she asked carefully, as if speaking to an unknown creature, 'from being . . . anyone else? Any other young woman?'

'How can I ever know?' I said, peering into the darkness, the Weirdness from some new, remote angle. 'How can I ever tell? Not even you can tell me, can you?' I paused. Realizations were coming hard and fast. 'And anyway, it's not only about me,' I went on. 'It's that a baby can be made that way. It's what I have to know about being human. What everybody has to know. I mean, I sort of change everything, don't I?'

'I suppose you do,' she said, peering into the

same darkness, the peculiar knowledge she'd given birth to. 'I suppose we both do.' She looked almost haunted, and I had a sudden intimation, an inkling of what she was thinking. 'Was it ever strange for you?' I asked. 'When I came into the world?'

She looked very pensive indeed. 'Sometimes . . .' she began, 'sometimes I'd look into your little face and see . . . and wonder who . . .' She trailed off, uncharacteristically. She wasn't going to finish this sentence. I was remembering her long-ago gaze.

She collected herself and looked at me directly. 'But most of the time,' she said, as if demanding belief, 'you were just a little baby. My little baby.'

We went for a walk after that, and when we came back we talked in a different vein. She asked me about my plans. She said I must try to develop some, to figure out what I wanted for the future. She was saying something that was hard for me to accept; but I suppose we were both trying.

'What will you do?' I asked, gauging our new distance.

She shrugged. 'I might go back to work,' she said. 'I might go . . . oh, I don't know. Somewhere else.'

'What do you mean?' I said, and my voice came out frightened after all.

'I told you I don't know,' she said again. 'I haven't decided yet. But I'll leave you in peace,' she added and gave me a wry, dry smile. 'That's what you want, isn't it?' I didn't answer and she continued, 'Anyway, I'm the mother, after all, and it's up to me. It's time for me to make room for you. So I will.'

She was sitting in a straight-backed chair and she was impeccably dressed in a chocolate brown shantung suit and subtly gleaming earrings. Her force was not yet spent. Her face was older than mine, but I would soon grow into it. The crows' feet beginning to show around her eyes would soon enough surround mine. She was capable of ageing; the realization constricted my heart. But she still had power and she still held it fast inside her; the enigma of her primacy; her vitality. I felt a sort of . . . admiration.

'You're not going to . . .'

'No,' she said quickly. 'Though you may not hear from me for a while. Perhaps for a long while. But I'll be thinking of you, of course. I would like you to . . . be happy.'

'Really?' I asked in wonder. None of it seemed possible. Who would be happy if I were happy on my own? And how was it possible for her to wish for me what she would not have herself?

'Yes,' she said. 'Yes, I do. But you must want it for yourself, you know. You must learn to be a little . . . ruthless. If the selfish gene passes on selfishness, then I hope you've inherited a good dose of it from me.'

And then, as when I was a child looking up into her beatific face, she looked down at me and smiled. Smiled beautifully, radiantly, from within.

'And of course,' she said, 'I've loved you. Loved you as myself and almost beyond myself. We've loved each other, haven't we? Let us not forget that. There's also been that.'

So that's what happened and that's how I happened next. This was probably as much of an account as I was ever going to get, the limit of narrative explanation. This was as much as she could understand of her own reasons, decisions, motivations. Motivation, choices, sequential stories: such hopelessly old-fashioned concepts. And yet, how are we to explain ourselves to ourselves? How can we divide the palpitating, impalpable inner substance into something intelligible, except by parsing it into cause and consequence? Oh, we know that stars collapse and emerge daily without such rhyme or reason; but in the mind, unless we want to fall into a chaos of non-meaning like some super-nova imploding and scattering into cosmic debris, we have to segment our lives into one thing after another. We have to divide ourselves into units of sense.

The urge to make sense was taking possession of me. To talk to someone about what on earth should happen next. But Janey had stayed behind in Palm Beach to take care of postmortem affairs; I was once again in Manhattan on my own. I hardly knew what to do. One thing I did was to visit Piotr.

'Well, if it isn't Persephone returned from the Underworld,' he declared amiably when he opened the door.

'What do you mean?' I asked. For a moment, I was worried that his decryption engines were even more powerful than I knew.

'Just that you look really flattened out,' he said. 'Where have you been, anyway?'

'Just down south,' I said. 'Florida.'

'Found your relatives?' he asked sardonically. He'd never believed I was looking for any.

'Yes,' I said. 'Thanks to you. Thanks.'

He raised his bushy eyebrows very high. 'Happy now?' he asked.

'Sure,' I said. 'Sure.'

'You still don't want to tell me anything,' he concluded. 'That's all right, it keeps the mystery going.'

We drank vodka in his kitchen, amidst the soothing tinkle of the surround-sounds. He told me that *The Supreme Fiction* had advanced by a few pages and that he was keeping me in it, though in a disguised form. Disguised from what? I wondered, but didn't ask. He wanted me to try the Affect Simulator again because he'd had it fine-tuned and it was working much better than before. But I said no, my own affects were enough for me these days and, anyway, I had to go.

'If your affects are enough for you, then you're

even stranger than I thought,' he said, and I smiled. He was perceptive, I had to give him that. But for some reason, I didn't want to talk to him any more. I guess I'd exploited him, poor Piotr, and now that I no longer needed his help, there seemed to be nothing more to say. My Hum Ed teacher would have probably said that our relationship had always been founded on mistrust.

Perhaps that was why I started writing to Robert. I picked him off the Consciousness Site, where he was a frequent contributor. I guess there was something I liked about the sound of his sentences, or his thoughts. But given the practically numberless pool of potential correspondents, he was almost entirely arbitrary. A chance find, chance hit of the Send button. I started, one desultory evening, with a brief message of self-introduction.

I wrote: 'I am nobody. Who are you?'

He responded immediately: 'I am nobody too.'

I: 'Not fair. You're joking and I'm not.'

He: 'Joking is not exactly the word. But are you sure it's me you wanted? Or did you send your message to the wrong address?'

I: 'Have no way of knowing. It all depends on what you say next.'

He: 'Hmmm . . . Interesting. Well, OK, I accept the challenge. But in that case I need to know something about you. Who are you, anyway – aside from being nobody, as you claim?'

I: 'Just a girl living on Park Avenue with her aunt. A girl pretending to be a girl.'

He: 'You sound more like a Sphinx than a girl. But you must disclose something more, or the game won't be fun. And this is a game, isn't it? Though I'm not yet sure what it's about. So, tell me something. Like, where do you come from?'

I: 'A laboratory in mid-Manhattan.'

He: 'Aha . . . Well, I'm from Tennessee, the green, rolling part of it.'

I: 'Don't pretend it doesn't make a difference.'

He: 'But did you mean it?'

I: 'Oh, I did.'

He: 'I see. But if I believe you – and I guess part of the game is for me to figure out if I should – then what kind of difference does it make?'

I: 'That's what I want to know too. That's the riddle.'

He: 'Ah, so you are the riddle, as well as the Sphinx. OK, I'm beginning to enjoy this. I like riddles and I like solving them. I'm a Consciousness Origins man, as you probably know, and solving riddles is what I do in my line of work. Riddles which might, in the most interesting cases, lead to the mysteries. Are you a mystery as well as a riddle?'

I: 'I'm not in a position to know.'

He: 'OK, then maybe we could try to solve this together. Because I don't think a riddle can solve itself all by itself. It's a sort of impossibility, I believe, of the kind I work with all the time. So maybe we can begin by throwing some questions at the Sphinx. The riddle can ask It some questions

285

for a change. With some assistance from a humble Consciousness man. Yes. I like it! Are you game?'

I: 'Sure. But you go first. You seem to know the rules better than me.'

He: 'OK, here goes. Were you of man and woman born?'

I: 'Alas, no.'

He: 'I'm sorry. Do you know your mother?'

I: 'Alas, too well.'

He: 'And your father?'

I: 'Alas, no.'

He: 'I'm sorry. Do you know who he is, though?'

I: 'There is no one to know.'

He: 'I see. That must be tough. But are you one of a kind, or more?'

I: 'I am one and one-half and two.'

He: Very Sphinx-like, dear riddle. You're an identical twin, aren't you? I hope nothing has happened to the other one . . .'

I: 'No. Nothing of the sort you're thinking of, anyway. But in any case, I am not really an identical twin. Or rather, I am and am not. If that's possible.'

He: 'It is certainly paradoxical, in proper Sphinx-style. But I notice you didn't say you were many.'

I shuddered at the suggestion and paused longer than usual before responding. So he knew. He'd figured it out. Not that it was difficult, for someone like him. The riddle was hardly a riddle, or rather it was as simple as most riddles are. After a while, I replied with a single word: 'No.'

He: 'In that case you must be your mother's only clone. Am I right?'

Again, I answered with a single word: 'Yes.'

He: 'Then we have solved our puzzle. As far as it goes. Are you glad?'

I: I don't know. I am and am not glad . . .'

And that was as close to the truth as I could get. I had wanted someone to know, someone who was not part of me. That was why I had initiated the correspondence and the game. But now that he knew – whoever he was – I felt let down, as though something had been shattered, something dark but precious. Did that mean I thought it was precious, my secret? That it made me Sphinx-like – God-like? My secret magic, magic lack. I wanted and didn't want it to be known.

After a few days' silence, Robert wrote out of sequence: 'You've fallen silent, and I've missed your messages. I was beginning to enjoy our strange exchange. Was I too abrupt in what I said? Forgive me, I guess I got carried away by the spirit of the game. I confess I am still curious to I know whether I was right in my conclusion. I guess I was, at least within the frame of the game. But was I also right for real? In which case, who are you? And why did you write to me in the first place? Maybe we should stop the game for a while and get to know each other.'

I: 'Yes. You are right, for real as well as in every other way. So I think the game's up. There is nothing else to know, and nothing else to write

287

about. I only did it for fun, or to pass the time in the first place. I'm sorry if I have imposed on you in any way, though you must admit you went along with me. Why did you anyway? Yours, the Clone.'

He: 'I went along because it was interesting. And now I'm even more interested. Though I liked you better as Iris, by the way. But what do you mean, there's nothing else to know? A riddle is only the beginning, it doesn't tell you any of the important things. Like where you live or what you do or how you look. Or what music you listen to. For all I know from this very quizzical correspondence you've initiated, you're a philosophy student indulging in a little meta-practical joke. Having a little fun at the expense of a gullible consciousness physicist. Are you, by any chance?'

I: 'I guess you'll never know for sure . . . though I'm hurt by your suggestion. Why would I deceive you like that, for no reason? Actually, if you must know, I've revealed myself to you as I haven't to anyone else. Outside my family, that is.'

He: 'Ah, so you have a family. Who are they, where are they, where did you grow up? Tell me something – anything. Begin at the beginning.'

I: 'I have no true beginning and I am one of nature's dead ends. If you had any sense, you wouldn't waste your undoubtedly valuable time on me.'

He: 'You're still miffed. I wish you wouldn't be. Before getting into consciousness I was in origins of the universe, and I wasted a lot of time looking for the Very First Moment, and then for the moment before that. I'd rather waste my time on you.'

I: 'Thanks very much.'

He: 'Oh God, I am such a brute. That didn't come out right, did it? But you know what I mean.'

I did, and for some reason I started writing again, in a different way. I started Telling Him About Myself. About growing up in the Midwest, and how I had nobody except Her, and how I suspected there was something about me that was not only strange, but unspeakable.

He: 'What, exactly? What did it feel like?'

I: 'I don't think I can explain. It would be like trying to describe what a bat feels like to a human. Or a human to a bat. I'm somewhere in between the two.'

He: 'In that case, why don't you tell me a story instead? I like stories, and sometimes you can explain things better that way.'

I: 'I am not sure about that and, anyway, I have no story to tell. There're no new stories left, as far as I can see.'

He: 'Tell me an old one, then. Sometimes I like those too.'

I: 'I wouldn't think a physicist would be interested in something so . . . made up. I thought you were interested in the material side of things. The objective, non-made-up world.'

He: 'If there's anything I've learnt from studying

the objective world, it is that we make everything up, including the truth. That's the kind of creature we seem to be, we can't seem to know anything without imagining it in the first place. One way or another. We can't get to the objective except through the subjective. That is, through ourselves. It's very frustrating for a scientist, but it seems so far to be an intractable problem. What I'm actually interested in is how the material world becomes immaterial. Or the other way around. It's still not clear which way it works. Or if there's any difference. But anyway, I manipulate these impersonal paradigms all the time, which are not so far removed from impersonal fictions. Or metaphors. So sometimes I like the more personal ones. Usually, I get them from the Storyteller on the Net, but I'd rather get one from you. You know, personalized. Customized.'

I: 'A narrative-starved scientist . . . Very odd. But OK, I'll try. I've never done this before, though, so don't blame me if it's clumsy. And short. Here goes: "There once was a robodoll. She was cute, blonde and cuddly. She lived with the nicest little girl in the word. Who was also cute, blonde and cuddly. The robodoll had everything she could want: care, protection, a beautiful room to live in. She should have been contented. But she wasn't. This was because she had a very deep desire which she didn't know how to fulfil. She wanted to be human. She didn't know what she meant by that, but she knew there was a difference between being like herself and being human. So one day she decided to look into the little girl, to see if there was anything inside her that made a difference . . . When the little girl was asleep, the doll sneaked up on her and looked deep into the mouth, but she saw only a moist pink cavity with a fleshy tongue just like her own and, behind that, a dark opening into a deeper cavity or tunnel. There was nothing there that provided any kind of clue. She'd have to do better than that, she'd have to go deeper inside. So she turned on her super sensors (she came equipped with those, of course), and directed them into the tunnel, and then through the navel into the stomach, and through the delicate skin into the chest and under the ribs, and round the heart, around the heart . . . Everywhere there were organs, shapeless, bloody, pulsing, disgusting; everywhere they were surrounded by gelatinous muscle and a scaffolding of bones which held the whole mess together. But there was nothing, nothing that would explain why this palpitating mess was human. The robodoll finished her inspection and looked at the little girl from the outside. She couldn't put the pretty, breathing, adorable little creature who was her mistress together with what she'd seen inside. Where was the human part? Maybe if she looked in the brain; maybe if she looked in the heart. She had another set of sensors, piercing and needle-like. So she decided, she decided . . ."'

'Oh dear,' I wrote, 'I'm not sure how this should

291

end. What do you think? Do you have any ideas?'

He: 'Well, your story certainly has a kind of primary appeal, a sort of fairy-tale eeriness. I have this sense of something inevitable about to happen, and yet I feel a touch of suspense. You know, the naïve reader response, which is what every reader wants. So I wish you'd go on. Tell me more. But here's a thought: maybe the doll is looking in the wrong place all the time. Though I understand its problem, of course.'

For a while I wound my way through my strange narrative, partly to keep the conversation going, partly to see where it took me. But, of course, I couldn't figure out how to end it, not even with Robert's hints. So after two or three more instalments, I wrote, 'Sorry, this is it. Can't go any further. Hit a cul-de-sac. So why don't you tell me something for a change? A story. Or something. Time for you to tell me about yourself.'

He: 'OK, OK. It's true that until now, we've talked mostly about you, which probably isn't fair. So I'll tell you what's on my mind. Not in a story, because even though I like them, I can't do them. But I can paint (I'm even pretty good at it), so I'll paint you a picture. Here's today's pic: I went sailing this afternoon. It was complete self-indulgence on my part, but it wasn't exactly laziness. I'd pushed my equations as far as they'd go. The computer wouldn't budge. I was trying to push it in a new direction because that's what I think is needed. I'm trying to do a new mapping of the mind, along different paths from the ones we usually notice, and I guess the computer is up against the old paradox. It has one kind of mapping, on which it can perform all kinds of very sophisticated computations and manipulations. But I was trying to kick-start it in a new direction, to introduce elements that would make it see through its own program and go outside it. And the old buddy just wouldn't take it. It got incredibly scrambled and started giving me frantic error messages. So that I almost started feeling sorry for it. I mean, how can a program see outside itself? What signal can I give it that is both consistent with it, and would make it step out of itself, so to speak, jolt it into meta-awareness? When I kept trying, it bucked and stopped, exactly like that horse that can be led to water, but can't be made to drink. Even though my buddy is mighty smart and sometimes surprises me nearly out of my wits. But here's the scary thought: if I can't program this exceedingly smart machine for real self-consciousness, then what guarantee do I have that my own self-consciousness isn't a sham? That I can't see beyond myself any more than it does? Do you SEE?

'Anyway, at some point, my own circuits started to sizzle and overheat from all these questions, and I knew I was getting utterly stuck too. So I went down to the laguna and took my boat out. I love the sharpish, fishy, gasoline-mixed smell you get at the dock where I keep my boat. There were very few people on the water today, this being a working day, and I took that little baby out as smoothly as a seal and guided it into the middle of the bay. I cannot tell you how beautiful that bay looked, with its dark blue water and baby-blue sky, shot through with clear air and wispy white clouds. Of course, the closer you get to the water, the less blue it becomes. It gets colourless and sometimes dirty and contaminated looking. But when I turned my eyes away from the immediate surface and towards the horizon, there was the blue again, enveloping and perfect against the unfurled white of the few sails. I spent almost an hour just contemplating the blue modulations, lying on the soft wood of the deck, occasionally turning the tiller just enough to let the sail catch some breeze. Imagine me, OK? Because here's the thing: I was imagining you. You came into my mind unsummoned, as a kind of breeze, maybe because I'd been thinking about you so much. So there you were, a breeze with wispy outlines of a body floating through the air above me, moving along with the boat . . . You almost settled beside me, but you didn't, you were not that palpable. You were practically devoid of colour, like a pale angelic Botticelli. I heard your thought-voice saying some of the sentences you wrote to me: "I'm nobody, who are you?"'

'So imagine me, Iris, OK?'

Oh, I could imagine him, I did imagine: a slender long male body extended on the pale wood of the deck, an arm thrown back gracefully over the back

294

of his head, a knee upturned to maintain a tensile balance, dark sunglasses, his face etched against the wind, the air, the sun. There was a photograph of him on his site, very small, but just enough to start the mind's eye going.

After that, the letters got longer. They glided back and forth through the resistless space between us, a space which could absorb or cancel anything that moved through it, as if nothing was too insignificant for retention, or as if nothing that had been said mattered. Except the letters were beginning to gain a kind of . . . heft. They were beginning to outline a terrain. I kept worrying with each turn that they would fizzle out like some faulty plot-line that had nowhere to go. But it was strange: the longer the letters continued, the more there seemed to be to say. As if disclosure bred more disclosure, speech more speech. As if this was another beginning-less, end-less, self-perpetuating loop. A loop along which signals travelled, back and forth. Or as if there was maybe something growing, simmering, brewing, accumulating out of our words. Out of this nether space. Or out of itself. I didn't know.

Several months into our correspondence he wrote: 'Listen, I'm coming to New York for a conference in about two weeks. Can we meet? I'd love to see the riddle face to face, after all this time.'

I didn't answer that one for several days. I felt as if a door had been shut in my face rather than opened. Shut on the expandable, compressible, liminal space in which the letters floated, a space in which I could speak freely because there were no consequences to anything I said.

Eventually, I wrote: 'I'm not sure meeting is a good idea.'

He: 'Why on earth not?'

I: 'Because, for example, you might find me disappointing. Because I'm pretty sure I'm not who you think I am.'

He: 'Why are we going back to square one? I mean it's true that, for all I know, you could be an eighty-five-year-old granny with a wicked imagination. Are you? Is there anything big you haven't told me?'

There wasn't, of course; I hadn't been lying. I hadn't even misrepresented myself in my letters to Robert. It was just that I *presented* myself. Now he would have independent evidence and I had no idea what he'd conclude. What he'd see. The risk of being seen accurately – whatever that meant – was at least as great as the danger of being misperceived completely. Whatever, in my case, that might mean. I didn't see how I could win on this one. On the other hand, there wasn't much to lose. There never had been. And I was curious. I had been imagining him for a while, after all.

He: 'P.S. And aren't you reversing things, anyway? Isn't it that you're afraid you'll be disappointed in me? Because I assure you that I'm not exactly who you think I am either. But so what? Our investment in this, if we're to be honest, isn't all that great. In the circumstances lunch doesn't seem an unreasonable risk. May I suggest that we meet at Chico's, on Broadway and 87th, next Wednesday at one. Unless you have other suggestions.'

I: 'No, I don't. Chico's is fine. I'll be there on Wednesday, 1 p.m.'

After that, I stopped writing to him again. I guess I couldn't bring myself to raise the investment by another notch.

Reader, you must forgive me. I'm not sure I found the Right Person. I couldn't even be sure, on that first meeting, whether Robert was who I'd thought he was. Though it was easy to spot him as he came into the restaurant.

I don't know how Chico's has managed to survive for nearly a century, among all the art-food cafés and syncretic cuisine bars; maybe by its sheer mediocrity, which means that it stays quiet even on Saturday night. On a Wednesday afternoon it was comatose.

So Robert's entrance created a great gust of energy. He stood in the doorway, surveying the dim interior with its lazy motes of dust in the air. I recognized him right away, of course. He was slim and tanned and his presence, even as he stood still, was oddly dance-like. He seemed to carry with him some refraction of sun and water. His dark, alert eyes moved towards me and then stopped, having decided he'd found who he was looking for. And having decided also – I could see it, in that first, all-telling flash – that he liked what he saw.

We nodded at each other and he came over to my table. 'Hello, Iris,' he said.

'You must be Robert,' I said and, to my embarrassment, there was a sort of choked quaver in my voice. There'd been some investment after all.

He sat down and regarded me alertly, curiously. There was no reason to flinch from his look, but for a moment neither of us could think of anything to say.

'So you're the answer,' he finally brought out.

I felt myself blush at the phrase. 'To what?' I asked.

'To the riddle, of course,' he said.

I winced and so did he. We fell silent again.

The waiter brought some damp pitta bread and took our order.

'I'm sorry,' Robert said. 'That was a silly thing to say. What I meant was, how nice to meet you.'

'It's nice to meet you too,' I said and felt sort of panicked. This seemed to be happening in an entirely different dimension from our cyber-rapport. Our correspondence was meta-intimate; this was bodily intimate, and therefore personal. We were on new ground.

But somehow we got going. Robert told me about his conference, which had to do with some abstruse aspects of neuron chemistry. I described one of my comical video-profs at Columbia, probably a frustrated actor, who clowned his way though Cell

Structure. Robert told me what he was planning to do in New York. We were doing a good imitation of polite and interested strangers. Still – there was something I knew he knew, about me, about my innermost secret; and I waited for the moment when his eyes would become clouded and distant. I watched like a hawk for the giveaway pause in which he'd try to cover his discomposure and recover from the Weirdness.

But it didn't come. He knew, but he wasn't aware of it. Or he didn't mind. He seemed to be searching for something other than the Weirdness. He was looking – it seemed – for me. He focused on my face with a sort of light alacrity; he responded to the changing undertones of my voice with modulations of his own. Under his searching, keen gaze, I started feeling tiny flurries and eddies of – pleasure. Yes, it was pleasure I experienced, as I looked at his mobile, lean face; as we moved back and forth with increasing ease; as I relaxed so that, after a while, we glided through our conversation without putting a foot wrong. As I was telling him about some trivial detail of my daily routine with Janey, our eyes almost inadvertently locked: we were looking directly at each other and we knew that we wanted to keep on looking. And that, in effect, was it. You can't look like that at a person if you're being untruthful; if your Being is untruthful; if you don't mean what you say, what you are. Or if you're even minutely afraid that the other person, in that look, is even minutely dishonest. You don't look like that at a person if you don't want to see and to be seen.

Things progressed quickly between Robert and me. There was, after all, no reason for a lot of preliminary moves. We'd made most of them already, and once we got used to each other's palpable presence, the previously gathered knowledge began to count. We went to see a live opera while he was in the city, and to a weave'n'wave concert. Robert loved music in all its forms, as I was to learn. One afternoon we went for a walk in Central Park. Aside from a few flickering statues, the part where we walked was all natural-natural, and oddly quiet. We meandered slowly along the beaten paths, looking at couples of various sexes, the oldsters feeding pigeons, the techno-workers plugging away at their personal screens, the children with their multicoloured design pets. We stepped out of the path of a man who kept touching his arms as he walked, stopping, turning round and smiling blissfully. He must have been microchipped over every inch of his body, and experiencing some ecstatic image-states. Or maybe composing them. Robert and I looked at him with our separate curiosities. Robert patted a shiny cocker spaniel, and led me to a meadowy incline, where we could watch a many-hued sunset falling softly over Manhattan. We were walking the slow romantic walk. Was it still possible to conceive a scene like this? To enact it? It wasn't, surely, it should have become impossible long ago – except there we were, right inside the script, performing our moves perfectly and not even noticing they were a cliché. Our bodies kept gravitating towards each other and curving away, like two shy particles not quite ready to merge or collide. You could have filmed it from the back and got a nice pictorial effect. Later I mentally checked the setting and the atmosphere against Piotr's *Plot Classifier*, to figure out what genre out walk in the park belonged in. But there were so many instances of it, in so many genres – comedy, tragedy, romance, melodrama – that it was rather evasively categorized as a 'Basic Convention'.

That wasn't what I was thinking about, though, as Robert turned me away from the sunset and towards himself, and pulled me, without fuss or comment, into a light, but definite embrace. I simply felt the thrill or surprise and I nearly held my breath for fear of disturbing the moment. Then I relaxed into the pleasure of being held against the straight lines of his shoulders and the freshness of his cotton shirt. He brought me closer in and kissed me with a sort of intense restraint.

'Iris,' he said, 'you're so lovely.'

It was the most standard of phrases. It was nearly nothing. But something in me responded as if – from a deep place. As if I had been called by my true name. As if I had been summoned. He had spoken directly to me. He did not see another face within my own, did not sense within my limbs the heaviness of another body that had moved exactly like mine. He saw me now, a girl in his arms, with her face upturned towards his, in her particular presence. I was both light and solid in his arms, as if held by just the right gravitational field.

It was only later, when I went over this scene in my mind in luxurious, distended detail, that I realized what the lightness had consisted of, the proper gravity: it was that in that long, burgeoning moment, the Weirdness had vanished. It had dispelled itself like a vaporous fog, and only then did I realize how much it had been my constant companion.

The next day, Robert's last in the city, we went to his hotel room and made love. Oh, I could describe how it was and what he did to me and I to him: how we gazed at each other for a long time once we were undressed and lying side by side – gazed as if we wanted to take some imprint of each other before we began to touch. How between his dark, intelligent eyes and mine there seemed to be no deflection or barrier. How smooth the skin of his youthful muscled back was, and how soft and deliriously sensuous his lips over my skin, as he worked his way down over my breasts and belly, and to the wetness between my thighs; how our rising excitement was shot through with calm, because we knew we'd get where we wanted to go. I could describe it, but surely I don't need to; for this belongs to the most trite archetype and to the most secret silence. But I can tell you that my body had never felt so softly sufficient as it did after we made love. So . . . actually feminine. After we were done, he lay on top of me as lightly as if he were made of some ultra-flexible stuff, contoured perfectly to me, his skin wonderfully supple and smooth. I felt I was taking his shape in as if by internal imaging. Maybe it would erase Her original image, replace it with something that was not-me but also not-Her . . . I breathed him in, his skin, his quietness. We lay still for a while, and then, for some reason, began playing like puppies. He tried to see if I was ticklish and threw me into paroxysms of laughter when he tickled my ribs. 'Iris's rib,' he said, holding me firmly down. 'Is it your own? Is this the rib you came from?'

'Curiosity killed the cat,' I said, and wriggled out and pinned him down under me in turn.

'Well, this cat is going to remain curious,' he said, a touch more seriously. 'And that's a warning.'

'I stand warned,' I said.

'So will you come with me to my next conference?' he asked, his casualness masking a tension he didn't quite bother to conceal. 'The one in the Midi?'

'The Midi?' I asked, partly to delay answering.

'Midi, France,' he said. 'For you relatively new arrivals to this world.'

'Ah,' I said. 'Midi, France. In that case, maybe I will. Though it would help me to know when it's going to take place.'

★   ★   ★

303

There weren't many preliminary moves, but there were games. One of them was Jealousy, a highly improvised transaction, which consisted of telling enough detail about our previous sexual encounters to turn each other on, but not off. We'd started playing it without even realizing we were doing it and then all of a sudden it got serious. That was when my last secret – at least the kind of secret I knew about – slipped out. 'And then there was Steven,' I said idly, before I really meant to.

'Steven?' Robert repeated idly. 'Who's he?'

'The man I grew up with, for a while,' I said, more tensely. 'My surrogate father, sort of.' Robert lifted himself on one elbow; in terms of the game, I was getting somewhere, though I was getting there much too fast for my liking.

'What do you mean?' he said.

'Actually . . .' I said and tried to figure out how I could beat a retreat.

'What?' Robert said sharply. 'Actually what?'

'He was Her special friend for a while. Her lover.'

There was a long pause. 'When?' Robert finally asked.

'When what?'

'When did you sleep with him? When you were a child?'

'No,' I said. 'For heaven's sake.' And then told him the truth. He pulled back from me and half sat up, on his elbow. I sensed almost physically his attempt to control himself, to hold in the incredulity and disapproval that threatened to pour out of him. I saw him go pale.

'Are you still?' he asked after a while.

'Still what?'

'Still sleeping with him.'

'No,' I said. 'No!'

He had to pretend to believe me, but he wasn't sure. He wanted to know what it had done to me, sleeping with Steven. I tried to tell him it did practically nothing at all, and he became less convinced still. For now, of course, he knew I was lying. For a while, he became evasive and elusive. I suspected he was Seeing Someone Else. I thought I should retaliate, or at least pretend to . . . So the games between us escalated to a new pitch. For this was a game all right, except it was the Game. It had become serious all of a sudden because there was danger and because I could lose. And so could he. We could both lose in a big way, and that made it the most real game there was. What to show, what to conceal? And did I have anything to show – I, whose secret had been that there was Nothing back there for so long, save an absence, a lack? All of a sudden I felt as though there was something – something to hide, something to withhold, something to reveal only with utmost caution. So there was Something there after all, even if it seemed to exist only when there was Robert. It depended on having him as the other player. This was a game invented by us, these particular players: we were the rules, the cards, the dice, the stakes and the prize. The prize which we could both win, or both lose. Except that the stakes weren't as evenly balanced as that. One of us wanted the other more, though it was difficult to tell which one that was. Perhaps both of us did – wanted the other more. Except neither of us would ever know for sure and that kept the Game going, and kept it dangerous.

But it was strange how little I doubted myself when I was playing for all I was worth. How authentic I felt when deciding how to pretend. There was suddenly Someone at the back of my mind who was strategizing. I could see why generals used to love conducting their wars. They must have felt so alive in their operating rooms, so full of certainty. In order to devise a strategy, you have to know the difference between yourself and the other, between deception and sincerity. Or perhaps it is only when an Other appears that you discover the difference between your lies and your truth.

But we managed to get back together by the time Robert's conference came around. The town where it took place was off the virtual route, and I'd never seen anything quite like it. It was set among the spacious hills of the Midi, and the hotel was built right into the rockface of a hillside, its stony façade jutting out with a fierce refusal to please.

The meeting was on Origins of all kinds: of matter, mind, organic life and the cosmos itself. I sat through some of the sessions, trying to follow, without much success, the lectures and the equations unfolding on the screen. Still, I liked these Originals, as they called themselves, with their wild thinking and their blind expressions, blind to everything except some hidden order they were searching for, some first force or spark which ignited everything and made it move, which leapt from the unimaginably large to the unimaginably small. The first day was on the beginnings of organic life, at least as it was understood on earth; though there was much excitement about some dim signs of seemingly life-like behaviour which had been detected on a faraway planet. But even the earthly beginnings were unearthly enough. There were pictures of wriggling, creepy, brute minuscule forms suspended in deep watery vents, bubbling up from the earth's hot core to the ocean's floor. Something bubbling, something churning, something striving to become something else: life. I thought of Dr Park's cylinder, of course, and the wriggling sub-cellular particles under his microscope. But these headless, inarticulate things were even more unutterably alien, more remote from anything usually recognized as life, than the chromosomal strands from which I was made. So alien as to be repellent, sickening. Shapes like that shouldn't have life and, if they did, then life itself wasn't what we thought it was. What distinguished these bits of matter from the water itself, from the heated, melted matter whence they'd some-how emerged? Except that they moved and were enclosed in a discrete form, and must therefore have some hidden logic that allowed them to – live. Signals that told them to collect, compose themselves into just these improbable shapes.

The thought of their affinity with us – me – made me even more queasy. But as one of the distinguished experts kept pointing out, the affinities went only so far. Human life could only exist in the most moderate zones: medium size, medium pressures, medium temperatures. Medium, that is, by our human standards. Whether the rest of the cosmos gave a damn about the standards of measurement in our middle realm was of course very much in question.

That much I understood, but I couldn't bear to look at the microscopic monstrousness for too long, and couldn't follow the abstruse hypotheses as to how it came about. So I went for a long walk that afternoon, along a white beaten country road that led to I knew not where. It was a softly hilly area, with gently dipping valleys and stretchy, flower-dotted meadows. The pastel grasses glowed over the body of the landscape, the wind bending them in great shimmering swathes, in rolling rustling waves. Melodious waves. What did it mean that it was so beautiful? As utterly, unutterably beautiful as those first forms were unutterably ugly? By what hidden logic were we fitted to it so that we recognized it as beautiful? Poignantly beautiful, as if the beauty were mixed with some faraway, ancient longing. And what did it show that I could feel the longing stir in my brand-new, facsimile soul, what did it guarantee . . . ?

After about an hour the road veered off, and I followed it downhill into a nestled, russet-toned village, just large enough for one café, set in a corner of a small, sunny square. I sat down at a rickety table outside and observed the quiet spectacle around me. A man in blue overalls was standing on a ladder, painting a windowsill. A woman at the other café table was doing something I recognized as knitting. She had a weather-beaten face with faded blue eyes, and kept glancing at me, without ever raising her head or changing the position of her stocky body or thick-stockinged, crossed feet. An elderly couple came into the café, and inspected me unashamedly for a while. They were both small, with narrow, wrinkled, tectonic faces. Some signal must have passed via the silent village drums because the man on the ladder stopped what he was doing and turned around and stared at me too. More people came into the café and kept glancing at me, not very surreptitiously, between remarks. I was clearly a focus for their curiosity, this stranger in their midst. It was odd that they should be interested in something as dime a dozen as an errant tourist, an anonymous person who happened to wander into their village. But they apparently still had the time to pause, to try to read my features and figure out who I might be. For it was not the Weirdness that caught their attention, I could tell; it was an earlier, simpler kind of strangeness: the strangeness of a stranger.

On the way back the sun was lower against the horizon, sending flickers of light and shadow over the bending grasses. I walked briskly until I rounded the crest of a hill and saw a woman walking in my direction. When she came into a visible distance, I saw that it was Her. I wasn't all that startled; it was as if I'd half known that she was still tracking me. Her blonde hair was blown by the wind, and in her pale linen outfit she almost blended into the tall pale grasses. We stood still and I realized she wasn't going to approach me, or I her. I felt an immense, sad longing. A long, long sadness. I had loved her so and I was going to lose her. To leave her. We stood very still, like the angel and the virgin in those old Annunciations I'd seen at the Met. Then, without a sign or a sound, she turned and started walking away; and within moments she vanished into the tall grasses and the shimmering, flickering air.

There was a Cistercian abbey near the town where the conference took place and I went there with Robert one afternoon. It dated from the twelfth century and I thought of Steven as we went in and what he might tell me about it. I guess I'd never get Steven out of my system entirely, he'd attached himself to some part of it, my memory loops or brain pathways. Robert might have said he was part of the experience that had modified me. If I'd been willing to talk about it to Robert. Still, the monastery was amazing enough as it was, made of cool white stone, its interior simple and perfectly proportioned. And Robert knew something about it too. When we went in, he showed me an acoustic trick that had been part of a secret Abbey's lore and that had to do with some mysterious knowledge of sacred geometries. He stood in a spot near the altar and spoke in a low, low voice, 'Iris,' he whispered, 'come unto me, and I shall . . .' The whisper was augmented into a deep, resonant voice; a priest's voice, speaking not for itself but for the Word. Robert then sang a verse of an old song in an undertone, and his voice rose and carried through the low-arched interior in a line of incredible purity, lucid but not loud, like those elongated lines of Gothic chants sung by medieval monks, lines that could go on for ever without punctuation or strain. Lines reaching towards the hyper-real a long, long time ago.

'Now you do it,' Robert said and I stood in the spot and whispered. I felt my voice travelling right through the symmetrical space, and amplifying as it reached its centre. I thought of Her, and the way my voice would enter her inner space, and hers mine, as in a magic echo chamber, and I felt a terrible ache. 'Mother,' I whispered, 'forgive me. I didn't mean . . . I didn't know . . . I was not myself.'

Robert came up to me and embraced me, and all of a sudden I was crying as I hadn't cried since I'd discovered my secret. Robert pulled me away from the magic spot – I think maybe my muffled cries

311

were being augmented into a full-scale lament. He didn't ask anything and I was grateful.

On the last evening of the conference Robert and I decided to go to a nearby lake, where a test storm was scheduled to take place at nine o'clock. Someone at Weather Control must have been in a playful mood because the storm was going to be unleashed all around the lake, but leave clear a circle of sky just above it. An access path was left for those who wanted to view the spectacle from the water. Robert and I rode our bikes down a broad country road, gleaming whitishly among the tall poplars; as we neared the lake the storm was starting up, with a low, drum-like rumble. Heavy grey clouds ringing the lake began to gather into massy formations. We got into a rented boat and began rowing; other boats glided along the water's dark, smooth surface. By the time we reached the centre of the lake, the storm was raging in full force. We put down our oars and looked up at the turbulent sky and the swaying woods. Great swathes of rain were coming down with a swooshy, splashing noise; there was a crackling and cracking of branches, and the sky was cut by a streak of lightning. I shivered with a kind of associational effect, some leftover, instinctive reaction to the natural; then remembered I was in a virtual storm's calm eye. Robert slid onto a blanket at the bottom of the boat and extended his hand for me to follow. In the tight space we held on tightly to each other.

'Doesn't this feel strange to you?' I whispered. 'I mean, do you really know who you're embracing here, in this boat?'

'This isn't half as strange as it'll get to be later,' he said. 'The more you know someone, the more perplexing they become, believe me. More mysterious. You'll always sleep with an alien. It's a lesson of adult life.'

So he thought there'd be a later. I felt some soothing potion spreading itself through my body. Some milky inner liquid rising from an unknown source, stimulated by nothing more than his words. How strange that words should do that, though that wasn't what I was thinking just then. In fact, I wasn't exactly thinking at all, though all my consciousness – all my being – was concentrated to a fine point of focus. In the boat's tight space, in the still centre of a fabulous storm, I felt held by his words, as if they were an extension of his embrace. I put my arms around his waist and locked them tight.

'Well then, hello stranger,' I said, 'I look forward to knowing you less well.'

I knew he was smiling, though I couldn't see his face.

How does a monster shed its monsterhood? Is a monster who is loved no longer a monster? There are few precedents, monsters don't usually get to be loved. Usually, it is a human who is transformed into a pig or a tree or stag or stone by the loveless stare or the betraying touch. Or by the hypertrophied reason. But Robert looked at me and saw – but I don't know what he saw. I only know it was not the Weirdness. He looked at me and his eyes did not become fixed or transfixed with a kind of horror. He looked at me and saw – but again, how can I know what he saw? I only know that under his gaze I felt my body round out into the right dimensions, and my – I can only call it my self – fill out with its very own, quirky substance. Tendrils of pleasure uncurled in it, instead of churning cell noise. Shoots of moody thought, thoughtful feeling. When I talked to Robert, I felt a small swell of hope about studying Bio-Theory, or a clear rivulet of sorrow about Harry's death. I kept coming alive in these tiny, pleasurable ways. For even the rivulet of mourning was pleasurable in its clarity. And gradually, under Robert's gaze, I kept finding I had something like – a personality. 'I love the way you have of scanning the screen with that funny quick glance,' Robert would say casually; or, 'Don't look so cloudy, like some offended deity or a sulky child. Tell me what's wrong.' And although these were utterly ordinary things, and although many of them happened (happened!) to be Her traits too, under Robert's remarks, under his absorbing, accepting gaze, they became mine. I was becoming a woman with qualities.

To be is to be perceived. Still, I had been perceived by Her, all too deeply, all too well. And yet, under

314

her all-seeing gaze, I had ceased to be. Under Robert's gaze, I was coming to be.

How, or why? Was it another misconception, a *trompe l'oeil* of the inner eye, another kind of enchantment from which I'd have to awake? I was as arbitrary to him as he was to me. I'd summoned him by a chance hit of the Send button, and he'd brought me to life with an idle touch of Reply. What happened between us was in no way necessary; and yet, it seemed – oh, it seemed, as long as it was going to last – entirely sufficient. For I didn't think it was going to last for ever, of course. Things didn't any more. Sometimes I had intimations of those old romantic feelings I'd read about in the classic novels. For I'd read a few of those. I tried to imagine that Robert was the one and only, that without him I'd have to throw myself into a lake and drown. But of course I knew that no one could possibly be the one and only any more . . . Even without me, we'd become too numerous for that, too, *quantifiable*. But still, as long as we were together, I was getting a homeopathic dose of – whatever it was that kept happening between us. Of ordinary, non-weird Being, of being unquestionably who I was. Or at least, of forgetting to ask the question. 'Authenticity is a two-person experience,' the Adviser had once pronounced. I had to give him credit.

To Know is to know Someone Else. To know that there is a Someone Else. Robert was Someone to me; but at the same time, he was, thank the forces, Not Me. Oh, I could describe him to you in detail, his features and expression, and his maddening and lovable traits. He was, after all, the object of my most intense, my most concentrated attention. I could tell you about the graceful simplicity with which he spoke and moved, with the kind of grace that comes from not caring what impression you make; how his apartment was all white and decorated with interiors of old computers, generations of microchip formations and motherboards; but how his cooking, on the other hand, showed a surprisingly natural, even sybaritic streak; how remote he became when he was working on some consciousness problem, so that sometimes I'd have to repeat a question several times before he figured out what I was saying, or that I was there at all; how I'd hear him pacing up and down in his study when he got really churned up, and how sometimes there was a plonking sound of a small rubber ball, which he kept on his desk expressly for this purpose, being thrown in hard frustration at the floor or wall. I could tell you all this, and much else; but it wouldn't explain anything. It would just make Robert into another guy with a charming, oddball personality, which you can pick out of the *Character Catalogue*.

Though maybe it would begin to explain something if I told you how he sometimes woke up from a nightmare in the early hours of the dawn, and held on to me as if I were some kind of anchor or safety. Me. That was how I knew he had no doubts about my, so to speak, ontological status. My real reality.

His nightmares were almost always about this brother Christopher, his great Problem, and the subject of the one story he ever told me. Usually, Robert was not a narrative man. The world appeared to him in pattern and movement, in signals and combinations, in great swirls and nebulae of brain and star matter, rather than human motive and affective effect. But when it came to Christopher he was forced to think about those weird forces which belong to the middle-sized human personality. For he had loved his older brother and had been betrayed by him; and so he felt about him a whole, human pain. Robert came from one of those rare, semi-normal families which went to hell in a handbasket when it was hit by its particular disaster – that is, when Christopher killed himself at the age of sixteen. After that, the mother became mentally altered out of recognition; the stepfather did a fast swerve and ran. Robert was devastated. He'd adored his older brother, had trailed after him when they were small, tried to keep up with his games, went hang-gliding with him. And still, he had no idea what was coming, or why. Christopher had always had a streak of recklessness in him which seemed to connote some kind of despair, though there was nothing to account for it, nothing that seemed to cause it. Robert observed it, but thought of it as something admirable, something like excess energy, or a masculine need for self-testing, for adventure . . .

But after he'd put a bullet through his head, it transpired that Christopher had had a whole secret life. He'd been involved with a nasty multinational gang which financed prostitute marts in China, and he belonged to the Perfect Murder Virtuosi, a semi-secret society which planned perfect murders in virtual dimensions, but whose simulations – it was rumoured – had a way of spilling over into the material world. Retrospectively, these revelations gave Christopher's recklessness an uglier valence, a nastier tinge. Still, the desperation had clearly been there. But what to call it, how to explain it, what had it consisted of? What part of his brother had Robert not known before? What part had he failed to recognize and maybe assuage? He tried to find an analogue of this in himself and he thought he did, a pinpoint of longing and restlessness that verged on violence, and didn't have any reason; that must have come down via winding generations and procreations, via some history that may have once been a rampaging ancestor's whole life, and that was now distilled down to this near-vanishing point. And because Robert sometimes felt this prick of the past as an acute ache, and because there was a powerful telescope in the house left by the escaped stepfather, he started looking at the night sky, and identifying pinpoints pulsing and erupting, and tried to intuit, identify, their

318

source, the secret of their movements. This was how he became a Cosmic Origins man, Robert said, as if surprised by his own conclusion. He'd thought himself into this as if I weren't there, but also because I was there, because it was I who was listening. Our breathing became synchronized, as I followed him, followed his turns of mind.

Then later, after he'd done a lot of work on the Big Bang and the Still Point, he curved back to the origin of his interest in origins; to that pinpoint which seemed also to be the source of consciousness.

Resonant metaphors, repeating paradigms. There are only thirty-two basic plots in the world Piotr's *Classifier* had pronounced; but the trick in making any one of them interesting is to make it matter utterly to the protagonist. As if no plot like that had ever been invented before, as if it were the first and last drama on earth, a matter of life and death. I tried to imagine Robert and Christopher in their adolescent camaraderie, and Christopher's dark doings in whichever space he'd moved. He'd tried to go as far as possible, but finally he was also finite in his skin. Finally, the only way out was out of life. I thought about what a small creature he'd been, and how big, how limitless he'd been to Robert. How that was probably the only largeness he'd ever achieved.

I tried to imagine this because Robert became important to me, almost as if there was no one else like him. Why, and why him? I didn't know, but

319

this was an unknowingness in which, for a while, I could rest.

Not always. I had to keep imagining Robert. Sometimes, he went as flat on me as a piece of non-reflecting metal. And sometimes we had rows. I never knew what sparked them, why we were all of a sudden shouting at each other, our faces inflamed by a surge of adrenalin or anger. Once, he got furious at me when I announced that I was going to see Janey for two weeks. I'd transferred to the University of Chicago by that time, and was living with Robert. U of C had a better Bio-Theory department than Columbia, anyway.

'Go, go, I don't care,' he shouted and threw his rubber ball at the wall very hard when I told him my plans. 'Don't even consult me! I suppose you think you can make up your own rules as you go along!'

Well, that struck a chord, of course, though that was not what Robert meant. He wouldn't have wanted to hurt me in that way.

'You don't even want me to have the meagre family I have!' I shouted back, and walked out of the room, slamming the door.

But the truth is, I didn't really mind our rows. I liked the bracing friction of risk they brought about, without the deathly danger of fighting with Her. I had battled Her from within herself and me; but in our quarrels, Robert appeared in a newly outlined distance, and became freshly . . . interesting. I'd look at him and wonder what on earth possessed him to get so furious. What was *inside* him, and why one earth I should care. I had to keep imagining him from nothingness to dimensionality, from a chimera into Someone Special. As he had to keep imagining me. As I had to keep imagining myself.

And yet I had these reassuringly trite, perfectly ordinary reactions. As banal as our first walk in Central Park, as the most conventional motivations in Piotr's *Character Catalogue*, as the most standard answers in our Human Education tests.

Did that mean I was becoming a regular, category-approved Individual? That the Adviser had been *right?* I was reluctant to admit it; and yet somehow, and through heaven knows what means, I seemed to be turning into the kind of creature the Adviser would have recognized as a person, with proper exhilarations and proper hurts, and sudden impulses and hidden motives, hidden, sometimes, even from myself . . . The more I kept forgetting myself in Robert's presence, the more I seemed to have real feelings, spontaneous, sudden, irrational and undeniably mine. The proper human response. I guess . . .

For, of course, I would never know for sure. Maybe that's what gave my investigations into Bio-Theory an extra energy, a kick of something that went beyond simple curiosity. Maybe that was why I spent long hours peering through the powerfully penetrative lenses of the newest microscope, staring at the alien, fascinating forms of the sub-cellular universe; maybe that was why I wanted with a kind of hunger to seize their secret from them, pierce the logic of their stunningly precise motions. I wanted to keep going further, further, into the very heart of their blind and mute intentions; to figure out how they made sure that hearts kept beating and blood flowed through them, how blisters healed and fingernails grew, how we fended off so much danger, and why our bodies subverted themselves from within. But the more I stared, the closer I came to a solution, the deeper the mystery grew. For each time I discerned some fantastically calibrated pattern of protein folds in a cluster of cells, or tracked the trajectory of some cunning coded signals, I stood up from the microscope and remembered that this only raised new, mind-dizzying questions. For it was all too perfect, too arbitrary, too co-ordinated and too adventitious for comprehension. Sometimes I reeled from the immense weirdness of it all; though it was no longer the dark It was that was staring from the back of my skull. Now it was a calmer, lighter point of perception; something I called the Watcher.

The Weirdness had turned into the Watcher. As I hurried home through the windy streets of Chicago and wound my way through the onrushing crowds, I marvelled at the incongruity between my microscopic knowledge and the particular peculiarity of the scene before me: Chicago, 2025. The gap between the molecules and the ever-onrushing human yearnings and hopes was still marvellous, and I could never crack it open or put it all together. Sometimes I felt great gusts of embracing, encompassing . . . sympathy for all the tired or glamorous, strutting or humble human forms. And sometimes, as I walked down some busy street, I thought I was in an especially uncomfortable virtual, something from Daphne's old Just for Real collection, and that I could walk right through it or behind it, and shut the illusion off. Only I knew what I would find on the other side: more of the same.

Then I'd go back home, to our middle, human realm, where I could sometimes subside into a different kind of knowledge. I listened to Robert's heart, its powerful pulse, its even rhythms. I followed the shifting of his moods in his body, his eyes. I had come to know his anxious breathing when he was remembering, or dreaming about, his brother. And it was strange, I felt pain myself as I listened to it. An ineffable sadness, though it was hard to know its source. Was it Robert's sadness? But by what mystic means had it got transported into me, why was it making my limbs – my self – heavy?

I remembered the cord, the corridor along which the milk of love flowed from Her to me, making me languid and sleepy when I was a child. That cord had once almost strangled me; and yet maybe it was the channel along which love would always travel.

This is as much of my story as I know. Or at least as much as I can tell. No, I didn't marry him, and, of course, I don't know what will happen next.

But whatever it may be, I'll always know I'm contingent and double. The world doesn't stand steady for me . . . I'll always veer between the suspicion that I'm a highly impressive piece of organic programming and the wrenching hope that within my identikit frame there beats something like a true human heart, and that this heart is also a psyche, a soul, a spirit. This old, odd notion . . . No channels of blood-flow or paths of neural impulses have been discovered to account for it yet. Maybe no one can be undividedly sure of it again. Maybe I have changed your condition as well. Or at least raised the pitch of your questions. For I am forced to know I am a trick of artifice; I have illusion built into my mind-matter and bones. I am a very conceptual creation.

Still, I am one particular thing in one particular enclosure. I am mortal and I know it. And I was beginning to feel the poignancy of it, the poignancy of time that runs through everything on earth. Surely, mere matter doesn't feel that, doesn't know its own potential demise. But I mourned my own future ending. I mourned it daily. Perhaps that meant that I could manage to live my appointed time-span as if. As if I was human, as if I was one of a kind, as if it really, really mattered. As if it mattered because, even if I started out as a double, my time-span happened only once.

Sometimes, I take the boat out on the lake –

Robert taught me enough about sailing so I can do it on my own – and just look at the grey water or the changeable sky. Sometimes the water quavers with my knowledge of its sub-molecular composition. But sometimes, for vibrating moments, the lake, the sky, the lulling movement of the boat are just themselves. The Watcher watches, and I keep remembering Steven's shards and bones, and all the humans who have wondered at the strangeness of their fates, and our fateful symmetries. And once, as I watched the Watcher watch, I thought – with a tremble of recognition – that it was always the Weirdness – that questioning Other in the cavern of my mind – that had been my best guarantee.

I still think of Her sometimes, of course – my mother, my twin, living out her own destiny somewhere in the world. I'm rarely visited by her any more, but she sends me signals occasionally, that only we understand: small gifts, a virtual of a favourite spot, a handwritten letter. They always come from different places, these communications: Peru, Fiji, Switzerland. She has another life now, and although I know every cell of her body as I know my own; and although when I now look at myself in the mirror, I see her utterly familiar, reflecting face – despite all this, or maybe because of it, she still retains her mundane, profound, transparent, all-too-human secret.